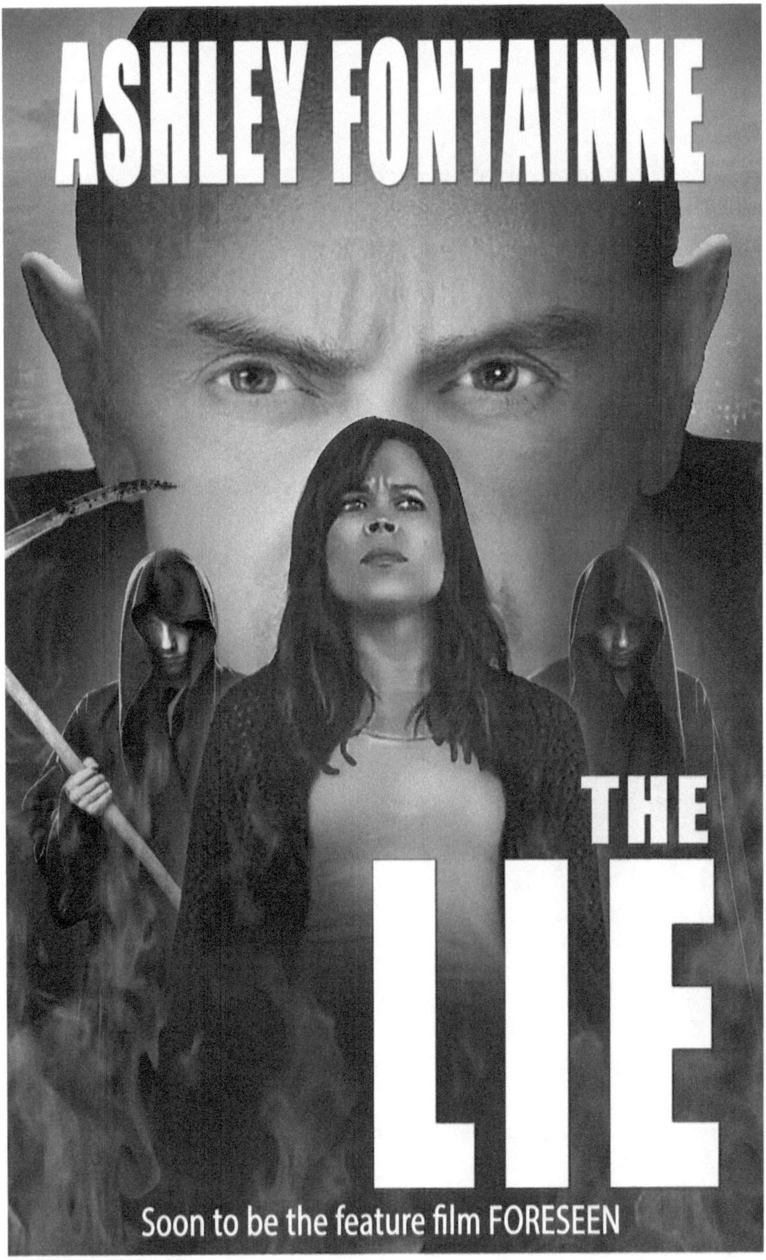
ASHLEY FONTAINNE
THE
LIE
Soon to be the feature film FORESEEN

Cover, interior book design, eBook design,
by One of a Kind Covers

Published by
RMSW Press

ISBN-13: 978-0615882512
ISBN-10: 061588251X

Visit the author at:
Website:
www.ashleyfontainne.com
Blog:
www.ramblingsofamadsouthernwoman.blogspot.com
Facebook:
www.facebook.com/ashleyfontainne
Twitter:
@AshleyFontainne
Goodreads:
www.goodreads.com/author/show/4958072.Ashley_Fontainne

foreword

By Jeff LaFerney

There aren't too many people on the "independent author" journey who do well going it alone. We make connections and help each other by trading what we're strong at for what we're weak at and generally supporting each other along the way. My journey is similar to Ashley's. We both self-published while working full-time jobs; later we found the same publisher and republished; we both later took back ownership of our titles; and we use the same designers at Blue Harvest Creative. And for the last two years, our journeys have included each other as friends. We share an interest in sports, family, and the Lord.

I read Ashley's first book, *Accountable to None*, as a favor. At the same time in my English class at school, we were reading "The Drummer Boy of Shiloh," a short story by Ray Bradbury. I remarked to her that she wrote with the same style. The difference was her story wasn't historical fiction—it was flat out suspense/thriller. The novel was uniquely brilliant and left me wanting more. *Zero Balance* was better and *Adjusting Journal Entries* was better yet. If there was any doubt in my mind that the revenge business is not the business for me, Ashley made me a believer. Inside each book, however, was a kind-hearted,

Christian lady that gave the book some balance, a balance that showed that amongst the evil, violence, greed, and depravity, there are good people in the world who can love, forgive, and live a life of peace.

Once I read Ashley's short story and poetry book, *Ramblings of a Mad Southern Woman*, I began to recognize that Ashley wasn't just a successful writer, driven to succeed in an indie world where success is far from a given. She was a spiritual person who drew strength and purpose from the Lord. Her next novella, *Number Seventy-Five*, was her best work yet, but there was a story gnawing at Ashley, a story I was fortunate to pre-read, and a story you are fortunate to be reading soon—*The Lie*.

Ashley and I have discussed how my novels, whether they be the mystery/suspense titles or the time-travel suspense, all demonstrate my core belief system. They're not preachy, not even aimed at a wholly Christian audience. They're just works of fiction that flow from how I think. *The Lie* is Ashley's work of fiction that takes her core beliefs, her Biblical knowledge, and her crazy-good ability to write suspense/thrillers, expertly combining them all together into a phenomenal book that any and all can enjoy and appreciate. Imagine an evil cult, a fantastical lie perpetuated over more than twenty years, a literary idol, a solitary preacher, and an inspiring political leader ready to advance the world toward the end of times. Imagine one of the best suspense writers of our day pouring out her heart to give you the thrill you've grown to expect while drawing you closer to the Lord she loves. That's what *The Lie* does. Read it, enjoy it, ponder it, and live it. You'll love *The Lie*....That's the truth.

For my son—the light of my life

*Be sober, be vigilant; because your adversary
the devil, as a roaring lion, walketh about,
seeking whom he may devour:*

1 Peter 5:7-8 The Bible, King James Version

prologue

Twenty-Three Years Ago

THE FOREST WAS PITCH BLACK AND SHROUDED underneath the veil of night. The thick tangle of pine, maple and oak trees intertwined overhead, creating a living canopy that blocked the moon's silvery rays. A small group of people made their way through the twisted path in silent unison. Heads bowed, they walked in single file. Their long, gray robes dragged across the damp ground as they navigated the dark, twisted path by senses alone.

The nocturnal cadence of insects and creatures that normally serenaded the lush surroundings was quiet—as if nature itself sensed the power emanating from the invading group. Only the sound of light footfalls could be heard.

Destination reached, the members spread out in a well-practiced move and took their places around the sacred stone altar. Bare feet stepped into well-worn indentations formed by other worshippers throughout the centuries that had beseeched the same powers for guidance. A low, rhythmic chanting began to fill the forest. Each robe-adorned body swayed in harmony, compelled by the intense energy exuding from the blood-stained slab that they encircled. Their vibrating timbre flowed into one collective rumble as the clouds parted and the full moon's tendrils illuminated their faces hidden beneath their hoods.

In a language spoken and heard only by those born into the legacy since the dawn of time, the elder broke the circle and glided to the front of the stone, his arms outstretched to the vibrant moon. His deep baritone voice unleashed the ancient incantations and prayers of supplication, causing the thick slab of hand-carved marble to illuminate from within. Soon, the entire open glen was awash in a sea of red and orange from the pulsating marble that began to resemble solid lava.

When the elder lowered his arms, a man and a woman immediately left their positions in the circle and ceased chanting. They moved toward each other with grace and ease. They clasped hands and nearly floated to the glowing altar, eager to make their offering.

Kneeling together at the elder's feet, brows rested upon the hem of his garment, and the smell of the dank earth filled their nostrils. An almost imperceptible shift of the elder's weight indicated it was time. A tingle of anticipation coursed through the couple. They rose and turned their eager faces to him, mesmerized by his presence and the ethereal pull of the throbbing stone that beckoned with a ferocious intensity.

With a flick of his wrist, the elder produced a dagger from within the folds of his robe. Deftly slicing through the ancient fibers of cloth, the man and the woman soon stood naked before the altar. Their sweaty bodies shimmered in the reddish glow and the bulge of motherhood on the young woman no longer was hidden.

The young man smiled at his wife, the amber red glow of the altar flickered in his dark brown eyes. He mounted the stone and stretched out his body, his torso covering the glowing rock. He reached his hand out and caressed the taut mound of his bride's midsection and nearly groaned in delight.

It was time.

The elder stood next to the young woman and handed her the ancient dagger. Her delicate hand shook with trepidation as she clasped her fingers around the bone-encrusted handle. The elder smiled at her and asked, "Sister, do you make this offering of your own free will and enter into this blood pact with open eyes?"

Her voice resounded throughout the circle. "Yes, Elios, I do."

The response triggered everyone to shed their robes in solidarity. Each of the twelve began to chant once again and the forest floor began to pulse. Naked, Elios resumed his position at the front of the altar and placed his hands atop the man's head, his touch gentle and his voice low as he addressed the sacrifice by his name in their native tongue.

"Yes, Elios, I am ready. Accept my gift of blood and bless my child."

"As you desire, so shall it be," Elios said. He locked eyes with the man's wife.

In quiet obedience, she raised the knife high above the chest of her mate, her voice strong and steady. "So shall it be!" she exclaimed. Ecstasy filled her face as she plunged the knife into the heart of her husband, his crimson life force splashing across her pregnant belly.

Pain and pleasure intermingled across his face. His mouth formed the words that only his wife could hear..."It has begun."

"DADDY, HOW MUCH longer before we get there? I'm hungry."

Jacob Abshire glanced in the rearview mirror at his young daughter, Sarah. Her mass of red curls framed her sweet but impatient face. Mussed from the long car ride, sections of it stood up in clumps, resembling the cloth hair of the Raggedy Ann doll she clutched in her hands. His wife of six years, Deborah, twisted her hand behind her seat and patted Sarah's chubby leg and replied before Jacob had the chance. "Not much longer, sweetheart. Remember, patience is a virtue."

Jacob smiled at Deborah, silently thanking God for the gift He gave him by placing her in his life fifteen years ago. Deborah was the epitome of a pastor's wife: friendly, loving, intelligent and beautiful. Of course, the most important quality she possessed was her love of the Lord. She never missed an opportunity to teach their daughter valuable life lessons that would serve her well into adulthood.

"But Mommy, I'm hungry and have to use the bathroom!" Sarah whined. Her virtuous patience flew out the window, just like her stuffed bear that she accidently let go earlier when the sun was beating down on the car.

Jacob couldn't hold back his laughter and Deborah shot him a look of irritation. He couldn't help it. Sarah had him wrapped around her stubby, little pinky. It seemed that every time Deborah tried to instill a somber life lesson he would find something humorous in the reactions of his only child and render the moment less important when his amusement erupted.

They had been driving for over eight hours and even Jacob was tired of hearing the hum of the tires on the road and the feeling of numbness on his backside. They were asking a lot from a small child to remain content for such an extended period of time, no matter how angelic she normally was. He stole a peek at the dashboard clock. It was near midnight. Jacob decided they could spare fifteen minutes from the steep mountain roads to stretch their legs and find something for Sarah to eat.

Deborah stared at him, her pert lips displaying irritation but her eyes showing a portion of sympathy, too. She sensed Jacob's thoughts and nodded slightly in agreement.

"Sarah, you help us watch for signs for a gas station and restaurant, okay? The first one we see, I promise we will stop and get you something to eat."

Sarah's face lit up in anticipation and she scooted around in the seat to get a better view out of the window, her light blue eyes already searching for the next road sign. "Yeah!" she squealed, bouncing her doll in her lap, both sets of red curls flopping up and down.

The mild skirmish over, Jacob focused his eyes back onto the road and his thoughts turned to their destination. He hoped his daughter would acclimate to their new surroundings as quickly as she changed moods. Uprooting his family and moving across the country was the major sticking point he had when offered the lead pastor position at Forest Hills Baptist Church. Not to mention it was located in the hills of Martin, Kentucky which he had never heard of before. But, as usual, Deborah was his sounding board and they bounced all the pros and cons of moving from their sunny, near the beach house in Pelican Point, Florida to the cold, coal mining town of Martin, Kentucky.

It came down to the fact that this was his calling. Jacob and Deborah devoted their lives to serving God and neither had walked into their roles with blind eyes.

The narrow two lanes of back roads were smothered in pitch blackness. Jacob hadn't passed another vehicle in over two hours. Sharp, staggering mountain peaks engulfed both sides of the winding road that had been carved through the terrain in a haphazard pattern. The only road signs that Jacob had seen in the last several miles warned of falling rock.

"Honey, would you check the map and see how far we are from the nearest town?"

Deborah reached down and picked up the crinkled map from the floorboard and then fumbled around for the flashlight in her purse. Jacob almost laughed at her puzzled expression when she held the floppy paper in her lap and tried to decipher their location, his eyes leaving the road for a split second.

"You know, Jacob, I am not much use in this area. It's like looking at hieroglyphics…"

"Oh, Daddy! Look at the pretty deer!" Sarah squealed.

But not fast enough.

Jacob felt his entire body tense when his eyes averted back to the blacktop. He tried to miss the enormous buck in the middle of the road, frozen in place from the bright headlights of their car. He overcompensated and the small sedan began to spin violently. The back tires of the car slid off the road and hit the slick shale. Jacob jerked the wheel hard to the left, but it was no use. The thick, concrete blocks that served to keep the larger pieces of falling rock off the highway connected with the front passenger side of the car. The jarring impact slammed Jacob's head into the steering wheel. Glass and metal shattered all around him as burning pain engulfed his body. The sounds of his wife and daughter screaming terrified him until he realized only silence hung in the air when the car finally came to a stop.

Jacob was petrified.

The engine sputtered then died. Jacob tried to regain his senses and opened his eyes so he could check on Deborah and Sarah. To his horror, he discovered why he couldn't hear them anymore. His lonely scream of heartbreak reverberated off the twisted wreckage surrounding him.

"Why God, why? Please! Oh please, dear Lord! Take me instead!" he yelled. His screams of anguish silenced as his mind slipped into unconsciousness.

Three Years Ago

KIROLY ADAMIK'S VIBRANT blond locks glistened like spun silk under the lights. He stood behind the podium with casual elegance. His attire was impeccable; not a hair out of place or a bead of sweat on his body. Confidence and maturity exuded from him. His mannerisms and stature were those of a seasoned politician, which the media found captivating. Kiroly was only twenty-seven, a mere pup in the political world compared to the grizzled warriors that came before him.

Today, Kiroly owned the stage as if he had been there before. His luminous eyes scanned the crowd in front of him, briefly stopping on each member's face. A knowing smile graced his masculine features as he silently acknowledged all those present with an almost imperceptible nod of his head. Each member immediately felt a connection with the impeccably dressed man in his black, tailor-made suit. The members of the European Council were all on their feet and cheering wildly in anticipation for Kiroly's speech.

His first speech as President of the European Council.

An electrical current spread throughout the crowd as Kiroly lifted up his hand to silence the commotion. The anticipation of what the charismatic leader would say left the members giddy with excitement.

When Kiroly spoke, the crowd hushed and hung onto every word, mesmerized by his electrifying presence.

Present Day-Tuesday

"KARMEN, WE'RE READY FOR YOU NOW. IF YOU will follow me to your dressing room, our stylist will get you prepped for the show."

My heart was pounding already and it was still an hour before show time. The last ten minutes that my mother and I sat in the waiting area had been pure torture for me. For one, I hated sitting still longer than fifteen seconds and two, my anxiety levels were peaking. The reality settled in that I was about to be interviewed on national television for the very first time. I mentally kicked myself for allowing the pleadings of my mother and my Uncle Cy, who happened to be my editor as well, to sway my opinion and talk me into this living nightmare. Why did they think it was such a grand idea to throw the shy, introverted writer into the limelight?

My mother sensed my apprehension. She gently slid her cool hand into my clammy one, forcing me to follow her lead and stand or risk looking like a dolt glued to the chair. Once on my feet, I tried not to wobble, which was rather difficult considering my knees were literally knocking together.

Realizing that I wasn't going to respond, my mother took control of the situation and answered for me.

"Thank you, Miss…?"

The six-foot Amazon lady in front of us smiled, her perfectly sized teeth gleaming under the fluorescent lights. Her shoulder length hair was too beautiful to be real and not one strand of the flaxen waves was out of place.

"Arianna. Arianna Scarsdale. I'm Renee Jackson's assistant. And you are?" she replied. The phony smile on her lush, red lips never made it past her protruding cheekbones.

"Shasta Moncrille. I'm Karmen's mother and her manager." My mother added the last part with particular emphasis. I guess she wanted to ensure that Amazon Arianna acquiesced to her presence being allowed in my dressing room.

With a slight nod of her head, Arianna turned on her ten inch stilettos (okay, so they weren't really ten inches, but they may as well have been because there was no way I could ever totter around in those toe killers) and sashayed down the hallway. My mother and I exchanged glances and followed, my rotund rump feeling abnormally huge compared to the boney protrusion that I assumed Arianna called her rear. I mentally cursed the heritage that imprinted itself in my DNA with so many curves.

My palms were nearly dripping with nervous perspiration. Arianna was chattering about the sights as we passed each one, pointing out the editing room, the video vault and then the studio set. When I saw the multitude of cameras and an enormous picture of me behind the set, I almost fainted. Thankfully, we stopped in front of what I hoped was the dressing room door.

"Here we are. Have a seat in front of the mirror and Danielle will be right in to do your hair and makeup. Mrs. Moncrille, I'm sure you will find the accommodations suitable. The refrigerator is fully stocked with drinks, and the fruit and muffin basket on the table is our gift to Karmen. Please, help yourselves."

"Thank you, Ms. Scarsdale. Your hospitality is greatly appreciated." My mother guided me through the open door. Before she closed it, she turned back around and addressed the Stiletto Queen once more.

"Ms. Scarsdale, would you mind turning the air conditioner to full blast? I'm afraid Karmen is suffering from a major case of stage fright. Water just isn't going to do the trick to soothe her nerves."

I forced my eyes not to roll in embarrassment at my mother's request and the irritated expression that crossed the face of our usherette. Thankfully, no response was given other than a curt nod of Arianna's head and then she was gone. The *tap, tap, tap* of her dagger-heels faded as she strode down the hallway.

I stopped in front of the swivel chair that was perched before an enormous mirror. The last thing I wanted to do was sit under the hot, blaring fluorescent lights. Strike that, it was the *second* to last thing. The first was the freaking interview. It was too late to back out. Instead I did the next best thing and plopped down unladylike onto the cool leather and glared at my mother.

"Karmen, don't look at me like that. You are acting like a pubescent, hormonal teenager. You agreed to this interview, and you know exactly what it will do for your career." Her voice was steady and calm, just as I recalled from childhood. Not once in all of my twenty-two years could I ever recall her yelling at me.

My mother never raised her voice even during my tumultuous teenage years. Rather, it became a sweet, sticky nectar that oozed forth, cloaking her irritation in sugary words. A person could become an instant diabetic if they listened too long. No wonder I was such an oddity that hated chocolate.

I closed my eyes and took a long, cleansing breath, controlling the air as it left my lungs. Sometimes my deep breathing exercises worked to settle my nerves but not today. What I really needed was to talk to Uncle Cy. Something about him, some undefined aspect of his aura, calmed me in a profound way. He was the complete opposite of my mother, which made sense since they were ten years apart. She was blonde; he had auburn locks. He was tall and wiry, and mom was as curvy as one could be without being considered overweight. She had curves reminiscent of the 1940s that she generously passed along to me. Not that I had any choice in the matter.

I was a strange mixture of both. At only five foot four, I had my mother's body and my uncle's auburn hair, but my face didn't resemble either of them. I was the spitting image of my father, at least as far as I could tell from the old pictures my mother had shown me when I was a child.

The other main difference between my mother and Uncle Cy was that I could actually carry on deep conversations with him about any subject. When my inquisitive questions became too much for my mother she would simply smile and say, "That's a topic for your Uncle Cy, not me." Politics, forensic science, global warming, the economy, literature, religion—you name it and we could converse for hours, completely oblivious to the world around us.

When Uncle Cy spoke, his rhythmic baritone voice pulled me inside a bubble, encapsulating me inside a cocoon of tranquility. When he remained silent and listened to my musings, I sensed deep down in my core that he heard, and understood, what I was saying. It never mattered to me whether he agreed with my opinions or not; I adored the fact that he listened and at least *feigned* interest.

My pining for his calming presence was interrupted by the loud entrance of yet another scrawny, perfectly primped and preened plastic Barbie-humanoid crossover. The woman I assumed was my makeup artist, Danielle. She flounced through the door and quickly made a beeline for the makeup chair. Guess I really looked like I needed a makeover.

"Wow, Karmen Moncrille! I'm so excited to meet you. I'm a huge fan. I've read all your books, which of course were much better than the movies. You know, it's true what they say, the book is always better. I almost fainted when I heard Renee was going to interview you and I would be doing your hair and makeup. What an honor!"

The words gushed out of her full, pink lips almost as fast as her hands dove into the mound of cosmetics on the table. Before I could even respond she began slathering tons of the smelly goo all over my nice, clean face. The woman's rapid fire pace at talking and grooming me was making me dizzy.

"Now Ms. Danielle, not too heavy on the base or concealer. We don't want Karmen looking like a piece of wax, do we?" My mother spoke in her neutral yet commanding voice and to my surprise, Danielle paused in mid-swipe.

"You're right! Look at that complexion. Nice and peachy. The camera will pick up her natural glow quite well. Dabbing at my eyeballs she said, "Let's do a hint of a smoky eye and leave her cheeks and lips nude. It will give her a nice, gothic-esque look and tie in perfectly with the whole 'chic author' thing she has going on with her outfit."

I wanted to roll my eyes but feared Danielle might poke one of them out. Instead, I expressed my irritation with a heavy sigh, a protest at being groomed to conform to what society deemed was beautiful.

My mother and Danielle ignored my obvious discomfort. They chatted about how to best present me to the public like I was a prized show dog. Since they decided to talk about me like I wasn't there, I opted to ignore them and concentrated on my answers to the questions that Ms. Jackson would soon be asking me. Those prepared questions were the one caveat I insisted upon before I agreed to participate in this *farce*. I personally wrote each generic and easy to respond to question and sent them to Ms. Jackson with strict instructions not to veer from them. I was unwilling to entrust anyone else with this responsibility, not even my mom. There was no way I was going to be broadsided with surprise questions, and I was determined *not* to be asked the standard probing one always asked: where do your ideas come from.

If that question was posed, I would come across on national television as a blundering idiot. I wouldn't be able to form a cohesive sentence to answer and that terrified me. People would finally know the truth about me. I didn't want to be remembered as the insane person who talked to the ghosts of dead writers in her dreams.

"Where do my ideas come from? What an interesting question, Ms. Jackson. I have conversations with the dead in my dreams that I only have vague memories of and when I wake up an entire novel is on the computer screen! Isn't that just the neatest?"

Yeah, that response would go over great. I'm sure my mother would have me hauled off in a straightjacket to a padded room at Hotel Hysteria. And my career would go down in a ball of flames.

While I was lost inside the twisted hallways of my mind, Danielle and my mother finally agreed I was ready to face my adoring public. Through a cloud of fine powder and hairspray, I felt my mother's gentle urging from behind to stand up.

"You look incredible, Ms. Karmen! Please, before you head out to the soundstage, may I get your autograph? And a picture? My friends won't believe me unless I have some solid evidence."

Danielle, the Queen of Hairspray, held out her cell phone to my mother then stuck her face next to mine like we were the *bestest* of friends and grinned. I did manage to produce a smile, but only because I recognized the irritation on my mother's face at doing something so menial. My mother preferred being the director. She finished snapping a few pictures and practically threw Danielle's phone back at her.

"Thank you! It has been a pleasure. Come on, it's show time. I'll take you to the stage." Danielle no longer looked our way. She was too busy tapping away on her cell phone and probably sharing her latest custom masterpiece all over every social media outlet she used. I had no interest whatsoever in this trendy pastime. I let my publicist handle my online presence because it held no interest to me. Obviously, Danielle did not feel the same way.

My mother was already at the door raring to get the show on the road. I pretended not to notice and stole one last look in the mirror. My God, I didn't even recognize myself under the layers of product. My curly red hair had been smoothed down into soft waves that delicately framed my face and floated down past the top of my shirt. From a distance, it looked shiny and beautiful except when I reached up to touch it a hurricane wouldn't have been able to lift a strand from place.

I rarely wore more than the sheer minimum of mascara and sometimes lightly colored lip balm. On a night on the town, which *never* happened, I might indulge in a hint of rouge, but that was the extent of my relationship with makeup. I hated the look and feel of the goop on my clean skin. Why women felt the compulsion to masquerade as sideshow clowns escaped me.

Gone was my normal, fresh look that I loved. Now, I had what looked like a pair of hairy caterpillars sitting on top of my eyeballs, matched only in obnoxiousness by the intense colors swooped across my eyelids. Half a tube of ruddy, brownish lipstick was slathered across my lips, which made them look like I had fought and lost a battle with a horde of bees.

If this was Danielle's idea of "nude" I shuddered to think what she considered "colorful." There was enough crap on my face and hair to add ten pounds to my weight. Getting it off later was going to be an interesting experience and would require an entire bottle of shampoo and facial cleanser. Maybe a blowtorch.

I was afraid the scary reflection in the mirror might cross over into my realm and attack me at any moment. Thank goodness my mother brought me back to reality. "Come on, Karmen. You look fine. Quit preening."

The next fifteen minutes were a blur of handshakes, introductions, and a few more cans of hairspray and powder. The lights above seemed like a miniature solar system, making the sweat pool under my arms. Thank heaven I wore a black shirt. Mom said the dark color would set off my fair complexion and complement my red hair. My guess is she knew it would also hide my baseball size pit-stains.

Renee Jackson was pleasant and professional as she walked me through what to expect regarding camera angles, to speak slow and enunciate, and finally, to enjoy the next thirty minutes. Easy for her to say and impossible for me to do. My heart thrummed in my chest and I heard its rhythmic pounding in my ears. Thirty minutes? I wasn't going to last five.

"Good evening. I'm Renee Jackson and this is *Hollywood Moments*. Tonight, our very special guest is the award-winning and reclusive author, Karmen Moncrille. Her novels have received unparalleled acclaim worldwide, and she is the only author to have all thirteen of her works made into movies within five years, three of which received several Oscars. All this has been accomplished by this amazing woman before the age of twenty-three. Never before has she granted any interviews, and it is my pleasure to be the first. Please join me in giving a warm welcome to Karmen Moncrille."

You can do this. Just keep your eyes on Renee. Don't look at the camera. Easy. Breathe.

"Thank you," I managed.

So much for astounding the viewing audience with my sharp wit. Please, please stick to the questions. I don't know how much longer I can do this.

"Well, let's get right down to it, shall we?"

I nodded, my cheeks already sore from the frozen, fake smile plastered on my face.

"You wrote your first full-length novel at the age of sixteen entitled *Shrewsbury*. The high praise for that book, including comparisons to the uncanny similarities to the writing style of William Shakespeare and the modern take of his work, *The Taming of the Shrew*, is legendary. Within three weeks of its release, it hit the New York Times bestseller list and stayed there for an impressive ten months. You were, and still are, so young. What was that experience like?"

Oh man, I have to speak now...

"Well, it was rather overwhelming. Sort of like sitting under these hot lights," I replied with nervous laughter.

"That's an understatement. You have sold over seven hundred million books in sixty languages during the last five years. What an incredible accomplishment. And now your latest book, *Madness*, is being touted as your finest work ever. One critic even said it 'was like Dante Alighieri was resurrected' through your words. I understand that production has already begun for the movie. You are breaking all sorts of records, young lady!"

She is veering from my questions. This isn't going to end well. Where is Uncle Cy when I need him? He promised he would be here. Just focus on the movie. Steer her in that direction.

"I am very excited about the movie. I will be on set as a technical advisor while filming so that will be a first for me."

"How exciting! What is it like knowing that everyone, and I do mean *everyone*, not only reads your work but never has any negative feedback? Every author has at least *someone* that doesn't like their style but not you. To what do you attribute this almost inexplicable connection with your readers and the critics?"

Renee's face was the picture of perfection. Not a hair was out of place. No sweat poured down her face unlike my own. Her bright red lips parted slightly, her white teeth nearly as bright as the stage lights. Her smile made her millions and seemed genuine from a distance. But up close was another matter. Her eyes reflected something dark, sinister and probing. I could almost feel it inside me, like a worm crawling under my skin as she stared.

My chest became tighter and my breath became shallow. The sound of blood pounded in my head followed by the telltale tingling in my feet and hands. Any second now, a full-blown panic attack was going to hit me. Desperate to fight it off, I tried to answer her questions, to focus my thoughts on speaking rather than fainting.

"I really, well, I don't know. I am simply grateful that they do," I muttered.

"Even the harshest critics are saying you are extraordinarily gifted. A child prodigy if you will. Is it true that you never attended public school? That your mother raised you alone and homeschooled you?"

Thank God. She was back to the list of questions again. Okay, Karmen, you can do this.

"Yes, that is true. My mother stuck a book in my hand before I was old enough to hold it. She instilled in me a love for the written word and started my lifelong fascination with reading." I snuck a quick glance at my mother who stood as close to the stage as she was allowed. The ever doting mom watched her baby chick with pride.

"I know the world thanks her since you have graced it with such incredible works. Where do you get your inspiration from? And what is your writing process like?"

No! Not that question.

"Well, um, it's rather hard to explain…" I faltered.

"Don't be shy, Ms. Moncrille. I am sure the viewing audience includes every author alive watching and dying to know your secrets to success. Throw us a bone to nibble on."

My chest froze. No breath could pass between my mouth and lungs. Fire burned in my clenched throat; my words locked behind the budding pyre. The whooshing in my ears grew louder and my vision started to blur. Panic tore through me and exploded out of my chest as my entire body began to tremble.

I tried to lock my eyes with Renee's. If I could just concentrate on them and nothing else, maybe I wouldn't faint. Intense heat pulsed through my legs, past my torso and up toward my neck. I blinked twice and tried to lose myself inside Renee's dark brown eyes. To hold on to consciousness through the sable orbs that looked back at me, unblinking.

Just as quickly as it spiked, the heat began to lessen. I could see Renee's lips moving but couldn't hear her words. I couldn't hear anything for that matter. My head suddenly felt heavy. Fear settled over me when icy fingers gripped me from behind. I wanted to jump and run, but I couldn't move. I tried to turn my head to find my mother except the pressure of the frozen hands pressed harder against my temples, immobilizing me.

The blaring lights around me faded as darkness began to creep in. The walls of my mind compressed as the vise-like grip squeezed tighter. Unable to move or speak, I could do nothing but implore Renee with my eyes for help. The response was lips moving in silence to my deaf ears.

Without warning Renee's face contorted, the once beautiful brown eyes elongating into thin, red slits. Her cheeks and forehead morphed into an unrecognizable mass of flesh while skin pulsated and took on the appearance of things that could simply not be. The woman interviewing me was gone, her face shifting and transforming, changing into the faces of writers long since dead. The same writers I drew inspiration from. The inflated, dried lips began to move and this time I heard the words. They rang past my ears and pierced my very soul.

"It is time, Karmen. Time to fulfill your destiny. We have prepared you well. Go, write it."

The panic attack was miles behind me, the heated flush a distant memory. It was replaced by pure, unadulterated terror as I heard the garbled words spoken in a language impossible for me to know, yet I fully understood. The words weren't simply heard, they were felt throughout me, reverberating inside every cell.

The tight embrace around my head ceased and my body went limp. The faint scream of my mother was the last thing I heard before I succumbed to the enveloping darkness.

2

Tuesday Afternoon

THE FAINT MURMUR OF DISTANT VOICES SUR-
rounded me. Trying to pull me from the murky waters of my
dulled mind back to the present.

"Should we call an ambulance?"

"Good grief, the girl simply fainted. It's not like she had a
heart attack or something."

"I don't know. She's really pale, and her breathing is shallow."

"If you would all kindly move away and let her get some
fresh air, I'm sure she will wake up any minute. A trip to the
hospital is not necessary. I told you earlier that she was nervous.
She just had a massive panic attack. Please, someone get me a
cold cloth and some water. *Now.*"

The sound of my mother's southern lilt did the trick. I was
fully aware that I was stretched out on the hard stage floor.
And that I had fainted on live television after imagining my
interviewer's face morphing into the monstrous faces from my
nightmares. Maybe they would all just go away and leave me
to die of embarrassment. The employees could just cover me
with a sheet and step over me until I rotted into nothing but
a pile of clothes.

"There she is. Hey, baby. Here, sip some water."

My mother's tender voice was full of concern. Her warm fingers caressed my arm while her other hand moved behind my head as she helped me sit up.

So much for slipping away into obscurity.

My parched throat overrode my sense of utter humiliation so I sat up, five pairs of concerned eyes watching my every move.

"See? She's fine. No need to panic. Just a fainting spell, that's all."

"Thank goodness. I do believe that is the first time that has ever happened. Shari, are we still in commercial?" Renee said.

I was relieved her face was back to normal.

"Yes, one more minute left before we're back live."

Renee turned her attention back to me. "Are you going to be able to continue or shall we reschedule?"

Was the woman daft? I just did a massive face plant, live no less, and she expected me to just brush myself off and dive right back in? Maybe in her world that was a possibility, but it certainly wasn't in mine.

"I think we should just reschedule"

I almost choked on my water as I stared at my mother. Apparently she had lost her marbles as well.

"Let's see…I'm booked for the next two weeks. Perhaps next month?"

I had heard enough.

"No and no. I will not be able to continue nor will I reschedule another episode of 'Watch Karmen Crash' on live television. There's enough reality TV out there to feed the eager masses that enjoy that sort of crap." I turned my eyes back to my mother and handed her the empty glass. "I told you from the start this was a horrible idea, and I was right. I prefer the only limelight in my world coming from the soft glow in front of a computer screen."

"Oh come now, Karmen…"

It took a few tries although I managed to stand up. I felt my cheeks flush with blood. I refused to let my embarrassment stop me.

"No. And please don't ask me again. This is not for me. I am going home. *Right now.*"

Before anyone could respond to my outburst, I turned around and headed straight down the hallway toward the dressing room. I heard footsteps and knew that my mother was right behind me. I snatched my bag off the couch and rummaged around for my cell phone and called our driver.

"Kevin, where are you? Good. Stay put. We are coming out the back entrance."

Without another word, I made a beeline to the stage exit. Renee was back in front of the camera yammering away about my sudden illness and promises for another exclusive interview soon.

Yeah, that would happen when Hell froze over.

"Karmen, slow down, darling. You just woke up."

My mother's plea had the opposite effect on me as my pace quickened. I wanted to get out of here and never come back. I reached the door and shoved it open, and gulped in the cool air that greeted my flushed face. The black limo sat sparkling in the afternoon sun, its dark windows giving it that old school Mafioso look. Before I could make it inside and hide, we were assaulted by loud questions and that infernal clicking of cameras from the paparazzi.

"No comments or autographs at this time. Thank you." My mother tried to placate the hungry wolf pack yet they still slobbered after me. Thankfully, two hundred and fifty pounds that rested on a six foot three frame appeared next to me and created a human shield so we could climb into the leather seats.

For such a large man, Kevin moved with the ease of a jungle cat. In less than five seconds, he was back behind the wheel and we were off.

The electricity level in the backseat was high. I knew my mother wanted to talk about what happened. Maybe to offer comfort or her opinions on the situation, but she remained silent. She knew well enough when I was in this kind of mood I was not to be trifled with.

***

I REFUSED TO turn on the television, my cell phone or even my computer. My first foray into the public eye had been a complete and utter disaster, and I knew that the entire debacle would be plastered everywhere. A parody video had probably been made and all ready gone viral. Jesus, my book sales would plummet. Not that I really cared. I had enough money to last two lifetimes, but I worried how Uncle Cy would take the loss of revenue. He was the one that had to answer to the Board of Directors, not me. Of course, had he *been* there, perhaps I wouldn't have lost it and passed out, so if he ended up giving me any grief, I would point that fact out to him.

I sat curled up in the bed of my youth and pulled the frilly, pink comforter under my chin. Furby was snuggled up next to me on the pillow, his purr low while he slept with the contentment that only animals have. At least he wasn't bothered by our current living arrangements. As long as he had a soft, warm spot to sleep on, he was fine and was oblivious to my discomfort. The last four weeks of living with my mother were about to drive me insane. Waiting while my apartment underwent renovations after a fire had gutted my living room and kitchen felt like an eternity.

Then again, I may have already crossed that bridge and took up residence in Crazyville.

I closed my eyes to the sounds of the outside world and tried to think rationally. Most of the time I avoided deep reflections about my life. I forced myself to busy my thoughts with the trivial, mundane everyday experiences of living. Thinking about how things really were inside my head was too damned frightening. But after my earlier fiasco, I knew I needed to.

Over the past six years, I tried to pretend I was just eccentric. That I was just an oddity gifted with the talent of writing prose onto paper. The artistic ability to create something out of nothing, just like a painter that coats a blank canvas or a sculptor that creates beauty from a shapeless lump of clay. I fought daily to convince myself that all artists were a tad quirky. I recalled an article I read when I was eighteen that said the corpus callosum that connects the left and right brain lobes is thicker in individuals who are creative. The theory was the thicker the connection, the more interaction between the left and right hemispheres of the brain, thus a larger capacity for creative thinking.

But I knew my concerns weren't caused by a thickening of my brain tissue. If I were a religious person I might think I was possessed. Thankfully, I didn't believe in all that mumbo-jumbo garbage. So, it wasn't thick brain matter or demon possession, which meant I had to face the fact that something was really wrong with me mentally.

Ghosts of the dead had fed me stories while I slept and made me famous. Then Alexandre Dumas himself appeared out of thin air and began to converse with me at my apartment, in broad daylight no less. When his form came toward me, I hurled the closest thing I could grab at him, a burning candle. Since he was only a figment of my cracked psyche, the candle landed right next to my sheer curtains and created an inferno that gutted half of my apartment.

Now today a complete stranger turned into some weird conductor of faces that used to only haunt my dreams and then proceeded to tell me in some jumbled language, that I actually understood, that it *was time*. My connection to sanity was hanging by a mere thread and after today, I knew it had snapped. I needed to get out of my room, away from New York and go somewhere to escape the madness that threatened to engulf me. The problem was how exactly did one escape the confines of their own mind?

How appropriate that my newest book was entitled *Madness*.

A soft tap at the window interrupted my manic thoughts. Panic frayed my delicate nerves for the second time in less than twenty-four hours. I almost pulled the covers over my head to hide the ethereal vision of my next otherworldly intruder until I realized it was Emily.

I leapt off the bed and sprinted to the window as I had done so many times when I was a teenager. My mother hated Emily and her family. She never gave a detailed reason why when I would pester her about it. Her only response had been, "I don't like their kind." That never made any sense to me since Emily, and her family, were friendly, sweet folks that loved to laugh. My mother, on the other hand, was stoic on a good day.

"Hey, just like old times, huh?" Emily whispered. My best buddy slid her lithe body through the open window like she did when we were kids. She took off her shoes and made her way across the hardwood floors in silence then eased onto my bed. Emily leaned over and rubbed her head against Furby's.

"What's up, old man? Living like a king as usual," she cooed while she stroked his soft fur.

I smiled and joined her on the bed and waited for the questions about my debacle to be asked. Surprisingly, she didn't broach the subject. Her shoulder length black hair was piled high on her head with a bright purple scarf that matched her flamboyant sweats. Emily's skin glowed from the fake rays of a tanning bed and her makeup was flawless as usual. Her eyes sparkled with mischief and concern at the same time. It had been nearly eight months since I saw her and the sudden appearance in my room made the ache for her companionship disappear with one, thousand-watt smile.

"I've been thinking it's high time for you and me to take a little vacation from this dreary city. Your birthday is coming up—the big two-three; we need to celebrate it in style. You know, everyone thinks New York is *the* place to go; however, I prefer the country. Give me wide open spaces, the smell of Virginia pine, and a babbling brook and I'm a happy gal. Oh, and one muscled up farmhand with bulging biceps and not much of a brain who will be more than content with feeding me chocolate-covered strawberries under a shade tree. Naked."

I stifled my giggle with my hand before I let it explode out of me.

"Damn Emily, you sound just like Blanche on the *Golden Girls!* God, remember how much we used to love that show?"

"Why darlin', I recall how yo' Mamma woulda had her a conniption fit if'n she caught you watchin' that *trash*, which is why we loved it so!" Emily's pitch-perfect drawl was spot on.

"Yeah, that's why I had to sneak in through your window at night to watch reruns. What a bad influence you were on me making me watch that tawdry drivel. No wonder I'm crazy."

We dissolved into a pile of muffled giggles and shoved our faces down into the pillows to lessen the noise from our gales of laughter. When we finally got control of ourselves, I reached out and hugged her neck, eagerly inhaling her familiar scent of jasmine and lilacs.

"It's so good to see you. I thought you were still at school? When did you get back?"

Emily straightened up and leaned against the headboard pulling Furby into her lap.

"About twenty minutes ago. My classes are boring this semester, so I decided to come whisk you away to the mountains. Plus, as I mentioned, somebody is having their twenty-third birthday this weekend. It would be a damn shame to spend it here in this childhood prison when handsome, sweaty farm boys await us." Her eyes were playful, their green hue still shimmering from the laughter, but I also saw concern behind them.

"Today, huh? You didn't make that snap decision after watching my performance on *Hollywood Moments* now did you?"

"I plead the fifth, baby. Let's just say the sister bonds felt a little weak. Time to solidify them again with some much needed R&R. I think a visit to your ol' Kentucky home is due, don't you? Seriously, how long has it been since you've been there? From the looks of your complexion, I'd say *years*."

I felt the sting of tears form behind my eyes. There was nothing like having a best friend that knew every inch of your soul almost as well as their own. Emily and I had a special bond that went far beyond the word friendship. She was the yin to my yang, the ivory to my dark ebony. She was the crazy do-stuff-at-the-drop-of-a-hat kind of gal, where I was the brooding, serious one. Since I was homeschooled, I lived my life vicariously through hers while she attended public school. Emily was the track and volleyball star who also was a cheerleader and a homecoming maid her senior year, and even dated the captain of the basketball team. Her personality was vivacious; a smile always lurking in the depths of her bright-green eyes and a laugh never far behind.

When I was younger and immersed in my own studies, I would constantly stare at the clock waiting for her to arrive home from school so she could sneak into my room and fill my day with her exciting exploits. On a few occasions, my mother caught her in my room and made a big production about sending her home. Then she'd bore me with one of her "talks" about responsibility and my studies. Mom considered Emily to be nothing more than a waste, a fine example of what *not* to do with your life.

"Where's she going, Karmen? Nowhere, that's where. The girl flits about wherever the wind blows her, and that's no life. You, on the other hand, are brilliant and grounded. Your life

will be full of wondrous surprises and you will make a difference in the world. A real, everlasting contribution to mankind
through your writing. Your time here won't be just a forget-
table blip on the screen and then over with no lasting value. No
ma'am, not at all."

I respected my mother and loved her unconditionally, but
those moments always made me feel trapped. The normal edg-
iness and angst that teenagers experienced from things like
school, clothes, peer pressure, social acceptance and their place
in the world, was not part of my life. Even though those particular hurdles were not something I had to cross, I did have
my own. Writing was my way of releasing them. When I was
around six I wrote my first poem and by the time I was sixteen
my first novel *Shrewsbury* was completed. The only person I
let read the journal version of the manuscript was Emily since
it dealt with a modern take on being the "shrew" who had no
choice in the matter with her lot in life. The heroine was locked
into a world that she didn't want to be in, so her anger was
exhibited through her nasty, outward nature. I based my mod-
ern-day Katherina on my own life because controlling mine
had never been an option for me.

My mother found the *other* version and read it one day
while cleaning my room when I was in the shower. I figured
she was snooping for evidence that I was occupying my time
with outside interests rather than studying. After a huge argument when I caught her sitting at my desk reading, she insisted
her brother Cy read it for a professional opinion. After all, my
Uncle Cy was the editor-in-chief at Big Hurt Press, one of the
"Big Six" publishing houses, and where Mom worked as his
marketing assistant.

I balked, telling her it was nothing, just the crazed thoughts
of a bored teenager, but she insisted. She said it was a great
story, a fantastic take on classic literature. I told her she was

biased because she was my mother. We ended up agreeing to let Uncle Cy decide.

Six weeks later, Uncle Cy called and informed me that *everyone* at his firm loved it and deemed that it would be a huge success—and that he had submitted the story to them under a different name, thus ensuring a non-biased review of the story. Something changed in me that day when he called. It was one thing for your mother and your uncle to tout your work but others? Complete strangers who were experts in their field? I remember the feelings of fear, satisfaction and pride fought for control of my mind that day. Pride won out and my adventure into the world of being a published author began.

The next six and a half years of my life consisted of being pushed to pen the next book. And another. And another. Sales were off the charts. Then the movie deals began and the money rolled in. Truckloads of cash. I made my first million before my eighteenth birthday. The next million hit my bank account before my twentieth. A month before I turned twenty-one, I bought my own apartment and moved out of my mother's place, hoping that being out from her protective wing would allow me time to breath and work on my anxiety issues. My life up until that point did not allow me to grow emotionally or socially and that led to my almost phobic feelings of terror when dealing with unfamiliar situations. The only constants in my life had been my mother and Emily. Mom was like a shadow that never left my side, pushing, prodding, suggesting, questioning. To say her continual presence had been domineering would be the understatement of the century. Maybe the millennia. Emily, on the other hand, was my only means of mental escape.

For the next two years after my departure from my gilded cage, life had been weird yet grand. I stayed in my apartment a lot and simply let my creative mind expand and fought my fears after Emily left for college. More authors visited my dreams and the books poured out of me. But the more I wrote, the more my books sold, which inevitably led to reporters hiding in hopes of catching me for an impromptu interview.

Their continuous lurking around every corner made me petrified to leave my apartment. Out of sheer anger I refused to ever grant an interview to anyone. My life was my own, not fodder for the snarling journalists with their fake sympathy and compassion. The singer from the eighties nailed it on the head with the song *Dirty Laundry* because that is truly all they wanted. It seemed they lived for the moment when they caught you off guard and aired your unmentionables to the world while they clacked their tongues in disgust at your hidden secrets. Bastards.

While in self-imposed exile, I wrote in numerous genres depending upon the style of the particular ghost who whispered to me in my dreams. I touched upon romance, intrigue, spies, murder mysteries, sci-fi, historical fiction, paranormal and horror, just to name a few. But with each book, I felt myself closing the doors of society out as I barricaded myself inside my own mind. My mental retreat was mostly from the paranoia of the haunting visits. Part of it also stemmed from Emily's enrollment in college and the love of my life, Mitchell, departing for a tour of duty in Iraq. Bitter words were spoken between the two of us the day he left, and I hadn't heard a word from him since.

Sometimes, late at night, I would scour news sites to see if his name was listed as a casualty of war. Every time my phone rang or an email notification dinged, my heart would pound with excitement hoping it was Mitchell. When it became clear the communication wasn't from him, I crashed back to my dim reality. The pain of our breakup was unbearable and I hated myself for letting him leave without telling him my true feelings. Eventually, I had to bury my love for him deep inside of me to keep from going mad.

Emily, however, was my lifeline to the outside world and our bonds were more like sisters than simply neighbors who became friends. I was a sheltered weirdo with no real social skills to speak of and when the lifeline was cut off when she enrolled in college and moved away, I retreated to my mentally created reality. Like a drug addict, I became addicted to the worlds in my head, a new high experienced with each chapter released from the haunting visits of the dead.

One day the words just stopped flowing. No rhyme or reason, simply gone. I remember the feeling of total abandonment washed over me and I had never felt so lost and alone. The junkie was left without her fix. It was like the words just disappeared from my thoughts. My head became an empty bin of nothingness, my body pining for the adrenaline rush. No ideas, no concepts, no "ah-ha!" moments that were followed by hours of pecking away at the computer. It was like someone shut the lights off inside my head and I was lost, wandering around in the drab grayness of my brain.

I became a total recluse. I stopped answering my phone and only went out at night under the cloak of the darkened sky, and prowled the teeming streets hoping inspiration would be around the next block. In my depressed state, I convinced myself that I was just a fluke, an oddity that had a few creative spurts that lasted as long as fireworks splayed across the night sky on the Fourth of July. Bang, flash, then gone in a wisp of smoke.

"Hello, earth to Karmen. That question was directed at you not this little hairball," Emily said. Her long fingers snapped in front of my eyes.

"Sorry. I was visiting my new home in LaLa Land that I recently took up residence in. What did you say?"

"I asked you when was the last time you visited your cabin in Kentucky?"

"Oh yes, right. Well, long enough that I can't really remember. Maybe a year?"

Emily leaned over, her eyes boring into mine. The same fingers that brought me out of my stupor seconds ago now wrapped around my hand and squeezed gently.

"Then it's high time we get you out of this parental hellhole and soak up some fresh air. Don't you agree?"

I felt a lump in my throat as I stared into her green orbs, the compassion and love clearly visible. I returned her squeeze.

"The press will say I ran away to drug rehab or something. 'Author loses mind on live television, disappears soon after. Sources close to the family stated, on condition of anonymity, that Karmen Moncrille'..."

Emily's grip tightened.

"Karmen, who gives a rat's ass where the freaking public thinks you disappeared? People will talk. People will believe whatever is fed to them, whether it is a lie or not. The only thing you need to concern yourself with is what's best for you. And Dr. Emily says that you need a break. And probably some real rest. So, what say you?"

It was next to impossible to say no to Emily when she turned the charm on full blast. And she was right. I wanted nothing more than to get the hell out of Dodge for a while. I had to find a way to wipe the last six months from my memories, especially my humiliating disaster from earlier.

"You're absolutely right. Let's do it!"

Emily jumped up so fast that poor Furby went flying across the expanse of the bed. His look of disgust at his unfriendly removal from her lap was hysterical. Emily started gyrating around the room dancing to her own internal music.

"Oh yeah, hot-n-sweaty hunks coming up. Road trip baby! Paarrtaay!"

A best friend. A gal can't live without one.

3

Wednesday

"THANK YOU FOR UNDERSTANDING, UNCLE CY. Counting on your blessing was never a worry for me, as usual. And whatever you said to mom certainly worked. She barely batted an eye when I told her I was taking some time off and that Emily was going with me. Did you cast a spell on her or something?" I tried not to grunt as I shut one overstuffed suitcase and started to pack the other, balancing the phone against my cheek.

Uncle Cy snorted, the closest thing he could muster to a laugh. Furby stared at me with his enormous, all-seeing eyes and never flinched while I zoomed around the room and grabbed a bit of everything.

"Karmen, you know your mother only wants what's best for you. She knows how hard the last few weeks have been since the fire at your apartment. We all do. What young, energetic and intelligent twenty-something woman wants to be under the eaves of her mother's home again, especially after losing so much of her personal treasures? It's no wonder you are stressed."

"That's an understatement. I wish I was stressed. That would be a welcome break." I cringed at my tart statement. Normally,

I left my snide thoughts on the pages of my books, spoken with the acidic tongues of my characters, or saved my smart retorts for Emily. But since I was unable to type even a single cohesive thought, my mouth was now the portal of releasing my irritation. Uncle Cy didn't deserve to bear the brunt of my mental meltdown. Thankfully, he didn't respond to my rudeness.

"Besides, the weather is perfect in Kentucky for hiking. You can get some spiritual communing with nature while there. Perhaps that will cure your writer's block, get the inspirational juices flowing again. Take whatever time you need, my dear. Your mother and I will man the fort, so to speak."

I held my tongue. I loved my uncle, but I wasn't always fond of him as the role of my editor. I was still irritated at him for missing my one and only live interview. I had yet to broach that subject with him. I was hoping he would bring it up first and apologize without needing a prompt from me.

Uncle Cy cleared his throat, which had always been an indicator that he was about to say something profound or that he thought I would bristle at. The last time he readied his vocal chords was right before he gave me an hour long soliloquy touting the *immense* benefits to my career from doing a television interview.

Yeah, that was a grand idea. Maybe I was going to get an apology.

"Karmen. Please forgive my absence from your interview. It simply couldn't be helped. I was in a taxi and on my way when the downtown traffic screeched to a halt. I was already running late—surprise, surprise—when a dump truck decided to roll over and crushed another taxi a few blocks up. I even tried to make it on time and walked the remaining eight blocks to the studio as quickly as possible for this old man. I arrived just as your limo was pulling out, sweating and completely out of breath, so technically I *was* there."

I flopped back against my ancient comforter, my hands automatically reaching to stroke the calming fur of Furby before I responded. "That does make me feel better. I would hate to think that you simply blew me off and fed me to the wolves, so to speak."

"Karmen! I can't believe you would even think such a thing. Now listen girl, and listen up while I'm talking. This isn't your editor addressing you. This is your Uncle."

I suppressed a child-like giggle. Whenever he was really serious about something his Southern accent slipped out.

"You and your Mom are the only family that I have left. The last of the McMann line—it ends with you. Your Aunt Eleanor may be my wife but she isn't my *kin*. No one, and I mean *no one*, is prouder of you than I am. Oh, your Mom might put up a good argument with me about that statement, but I assure you, I would win. I have watched you blossom into an intelligent, amazing woman. I couldn't be prouder if you were my own daughter. Look what you've accomplished in such a short time! I wanted you to bask in that, to revel in your successes instead of hiding from them. That's why I pushed you so hard. For that, I am sorry. I didn't realize the depth of your fear of public speaking."

Hot tears sprang forth and meandered down my cheeks. There had never been even a brief second of doubt during my lifetime that Uncle Cy loved me. Even though he wasn't the overly affectionate type, I knew it from the first memory of sitting next to him on a bench at the zoo when I was around three. His voice, his mannerisms, the way he gently explained about all the animals, making sure I understood before he started to explain another. Patient. Warm. His rough hand reaching out and gently clasping mine as we waited for a taxi at the end of the day, his face beaming as he listened to me recite what I learned.

The man who was only a phone call away, who had never failed to stand by my side or guide me in the right direction— yep, that was Uncle Cy. During my teenage years I had seriously considered addressing him as "Dad" since that really was the role he played in my life. No father and daughter could have been closer than we were. When I mentioned it to my mother, she promptly dismissed the idea. Although she understood the sentiment, she felt it would dishonor my father's memory.

"Uncle Cy, I need to ask you something. And I want your honest opinion."

"Sure thing, sweetie. You know me. I always speak my mind. What is it?"

I took a deep breath and closed my eyes, forcing back the lump that sat like a heavy stone in my throat. "Do you think I'm crazy? I don't mean the typical author eccentricities. Do you think I could be suffering from a mental disorder?" *There, I had finally said it out loud.*

Uncle Cy actually produced a real laugh. It sounded foreign to my ears, yet the sweet baritone calmed my screeching nerves.

"You really do need a break, don't you sweetie? All the pressures in your life and then my insistence on that interview has really worked you into a frenzy." His voice was the tender and loving tone of my uncle, not the overbearing editor. I felt the sting of tears dance behind my closed eyelids again.

"It has been a bit much. I'm having trouble sleeping, too. I…"

Uncle Cy interrupted me before I crumbled into a weeping mess.

"My dear, let me put some verbal salve on your wounded soul. I can assure you that you are not suffering from mental disease or a defect. It is called stress, my dear. I'm just sorry I didn't see it sooner. After some time away you will come back all fresh and renewed, ready to tackle the obstacles that life has a fun way of throwing at us all. Wipe those thoughts from your mind. Go. Have a great time with Emily and relax. Those are strict orders from your uncle *and* your editor."

Tears showered down my warm cheeks at his response. It didn't matter where they came from. Perhaps voicing my fear about a mental disorder or the fact that the man I trusted more than anyone in the world thought I was sane. Maybe the salty mess spilled from a mixture of both. It was comforting. For the very first time Uncle Cy acknowledged that everyone around me, including himself, was draining me dry.

Of course, he had no clue about my dreams, the apparitions and the full-blown appearance of the dead that replaced Renee Jackson's face two days ago. If I shared those little psychotic tidbits, my much needed vacation would be inside a rubber room.

"Thanks, Uncle Cy. For everything. You're right, I have been under a tremendous amount of stress. I need some girlfriend time and to reflect on things. Maybe sow some wild oats and relive my teenage years since I missed them the first time around. Cause havoc and chaos, maybe break a few laws and get arrested. That should fix me right up and give me plenty of inspiration for the next book. You know, expand my horizons through depravity."

Had I spoke those words to my mother she wouldn't have known I was joking. She never understood my wry sense of humor. On the occasions I did let it fly, I was subjected to endless stories of not wasting the gifts that were bestowed upon me, negative behavior being reported in the press that might ruin my reputation—*blah, blah, blah.*

Uncle Cy recognized my tongue-in-cheek response and roared with laughter. I nearly dropped the phone in shock. Laughter was a rarity, but I had never heard him literally cackle with delight. Maybe my madness had seeped through the phone lines.

"Yes, my dear. Expand those horizons. Open your mind to every possibility and let yourself go. Then call me when you need bail money and a lawyer."

"Gee, Uncle Cy, aren't you worried that I might generate negative publicity if I get arrested in the hills of Kentucky? You know for something outrageous like running moonshine? Maybe you could hook me up with some of the old family connections to get me started?"

"Are you kidding? Publicity is publicity, baby girl. Your book sales have tripled in the last two days. Head to the hills and work on quadrupling them. And my connections are long gone. I told you when I left that dying county I cut all ties. You're on your own. Go find your own trouble."

"YOUR MOTHER LOOKED like she'd swallowed about eight lemons in quick succession. I thought for a moment she was actually going to hurl all over my new hiking boots. She really hates me, doesn't she?"

Emily was driving in typical Emily style—full throttle. Her lead foot was matched only by her mouth in terms of speed. I wasn't sure if the roaring V-8 under the hood of her new Tahoe would be able to keep up with her motor mouth. She needed a Corvette or Porsche to even get close.

We were into hour four of our seven hour drive to Kentucky. At the rate Emily was driving, we would make it in five. The scenery had whizzed by and the few times I tried to look out the window made my stomach churn with motion sickness.

"You should have seen her face the day I moved out. I believe she did actually toss her lunch before the last box was loaded. She's just overly protective. After all, it's been just the two of us against the world since I came along. Well, and Uncle Cy, but that isn't the same. Her maternal instincts are always in high gear which is only natural. And she doesn't hate you. How could anyone hate you? You are a regular ball of sunshine."

Emily threw her head back and laughed, releasing some of her ebony locks from the messy bun piled high on her head. "I've been called a lot of things but a ball of sunshine? That's a new one! I guess I need to work on my evil, dark side."

"You, dark? Emily, you couldn't be mysterious if your life depended upon it. You just exude happiness and pep. I'm the brooding one of this duo, remember?"

Emily grinned, her perfectly white teeth stood out against her deeply bronzed skin. I smiled in response, remembering the three years of torture she went through during her early teens when she wore braces.

"No doubt. But we will change that this weekend, I promise. I plan on giving your mom a real reason to despise my innards."

We exited the freeway. Emily finally let her foot off the pedal and eased out of hyper-speed, pulling into a small gas station. The tires barked as Emily tromped on the brakes. She must have read my mind because my bladder was about to burst from all the water I had been drinking. The tires screeched to a stop in front of the ancient gas pumps. I was glad I wore my seat belt or my face would have connected with the dashboard.

"If your plan is to jar depressing thoughts out of my head, it's working. Better yet, if I suffer a concussion, perhaps I will forget the last week in its entirety. Shall we back up and try again?" I climbed out of the truck, my feet thankful to no longer be shoved against the floorboard stepping on imaginary brakes.

Emily dismissed my comeback with the flip of her hand while she began pumping gas.

"My plan is to get you high, drunk and laid, and not necessarily in that order. If ever there was a human being on this planet that needed to cut loose, it's you."

This time the loud laughter came from me as I walked inside the store to find the restrooms. I had only experienced one out of the three debaucheries and there was no way I planned on completing the trio. My mind was already playing tricks on me. There was no telling what it would do if chemically altered. Besides, the only sweaty farmhand that I wanted to feel on top of me was halfway around the world in the desert.

Ten minutes later we were back on the road, the Tahoe eating up the blacktop after bladders were emptied and the tank topped off. We munched on junk food that was probably clogging up our arteries, maybe taking off several minutes of our lives, but we didn't care. Our conversation was kept light and on subjects that we could easily discuss. No politics, no religion, no breaking headlines, no authors passing out on live television. We treated each other to the easy jabbering of two best friends that hadn't spent time together in months and played catch up. Well, *one-sided* catch up. As usual, Emily regaled me with the tales of her flamboyant life in college, the breakup of yet another short-lived collegiate romance and the latest fashion forward outfits she purchased at some overly priced boutiques.

For me, it was Heaven. Idle chit-chat and mindless drivel was just what I needed to keep my thoughts away from the events of the past few months.

When we started the windy trek through the coal-filled mountains of Kentucky, Emily slowed down as we wound through the steep roads. Mountains ripped apart by dynamite to carve out the curvy highway towered on each side of us. Dark green kudzu wrapped around everything in sight. The strong vines clamped around telephone poles, road signs and fences, completely oblivious to the constant tactics of the locals to kill their invading grip on anything that didn't move. The devouring was slow, methodical and unstoppable. I felt a strange kinship with the choked out items as they were slowly absorbed by the hungry kudzu.

My family hailed from the deep roots of this rugged country. Both my parents were born and raised in the miniscule mining town of Martin, which had fallen on hard times after the coal boom rescinded back in the early '60s. Once all the black gold was stripped from the rugged hillsides by greedy corporations that cared nothing about the broken shell they left behind, the town nearly died.

The fall of the local economy destroyed numerous families when the mining companies shut down, leaving uneducated and unemployable men with hungry mouths to feed at home. Faced with no choice but to either escape all they had ever known or resort to a life of crime, their options were bleak. For many, the lure of easy cash proved to be too strong and moonshining and pot farming in the dense hills became the underground economic lifeline. Illegal or not, the new business ventures kept children from starving in the small community.

Not everyone fell into temptation. My Uncle Cy, who was ten years older than my mother, fled the poverty when he was drafted into the military during the Vietnam War. Once he was gone, he made good on his promise to never return. After surviving the jungles in Asia, he discovered he had a knack for marketing and editing, and found a low-paying job in the publishing industry and never looked back.

The Moncrilles and McManns were part of a handful of families that stayed true to the morals and ethics of the previous generations who survived the harsh terrain of eastern Kentucky. My mother's family, the McManns, owned the only general store in the county for years. It was on its fourth generation of owners when my mom and Uncle Cy came along. He was to be the fifth owner, but when Uncle Cy opted not to return, that duty was passed to my mother. That ownership never happened either.

My mother told me she fell in love with Bobby Mac Moncrille the moment she heard him sing *Amazing Grace* off key in church when she was about ten years old on Christmas Eve. It was the first time she had ever seen him in church as the Moncrilles were extremely poor and rarely ever left their holler. Bobby Mac had never attended school, forced to work on the farm since he had been a small boy while his father worked in the coal mines. When his father lost his leg in a mining accident, Bobby Mac became the "man" of the house. He began to come into town a few times a year to trade his homegrown commodities for other staples from my Grandpa McMann.

But a massive fire destroyed everything at his family's farm when it burned to the ground the night before. Mom said their shack had been struck by lightning during a rare winter thunderstorm. It left my father an instant orphan at the age of thirteen. My father only survived because he had gone outside to the barn to grab some more firewood. The church service that night was dedicated to not only celebrating Christmas, but also coming together as a community to help out Bobby Mac Moncrille, who literally was left with nothing except the soot-encrusted clothes on his back. Grandpa and Grandma McMann left the service that night with Bobby Mac in tow. They offered him a job at the general store and a warm room in the back to sleep in.

Soon, Bobby Mac was running the place, giving Grandpa McMann a chance to relax in his old age. When my mother turned fifteen she became Mrs. Bobby Mac Moncrille.

When she first told me she had married at fifteen and dad was only eighteen, I didn't believe her. The thought of all the responsibilities that entail being married resting on the shoulders of two teenagers made my skin crawl. Mom would just smile whenever the subject came up, a whimsical expression crossing her face at the memories. Her face would soften for a brief flash, revealing real emotions when she spoke of my father. A lump in my throat surprised me. I knew better than to start reminiscing about the tragic life of the father I had never known. I swallowed the sadness down and forced myself to look out the window.

My chest tightened as we passed the sign that read *Welcome to Floyd County, Kentucky*. Emily was definitely right—I needed a vacation and this was the perfect place to take it. Every summer since I could remember had been spent here. My mother still owned the cabin she was born in, built by the hands of her own grandfather from the strong pines that dotted the landscape. When my first royalty check rolled in, we spent a month having the entire place gutted and redone making it a comfortable getaway for us both. I wrote my first poem sitting against the knotted pine in the backyard when I was six.

Even though I wasn't born here, I sensed an intense draw to the place. A primal pulling from deep within that told me I was home. An inexplicable peace enveloped me, cradling me in its warmth. It was a strange sensation, and one that I never could understand. My mother said it was because the blood of my ancestors ran deep into the land and flowed through my veins, calling out to me—generations of hardworking and devoted souls who never gave up, even against the most dire circumstances.

Whatever it was that encapsulated my soul, I didn't care. I just enjoyed the sensation as Emily made her way across the bridge into the main part of town. My thoughts were interrupted when she stopped in front of McMann's General Store and started gabbing.

"Whew! Now I remember why I haven't been here in a while. The smell is gross." She dramatically fanned her face with her hand. "That's just awful."

"I've told you a hundred times what that smell is. Don't you remember?" I unlatched my seatbelt and fumbled for my purse. We needed to get a few supplies before we headed out to the cabin. Since our trip had been so spontaneous, I had neglected to call Mrs. Langston, our closest neighbor over two miles away, and ask her to run by the place to prepare it for our visit. When we left New York I realized I needed to call her, but Emily had convinced me not to, stating the less people that knew I was in Martin, the better.

I didn't argue with that logic.

"Of course I do. Sulfur mixed with something underground produces that aromatic rotten egg stench. I forgot how bad it was. Please, please tell me that the water at the cabin isn't going to smell like that? The last time it took me three weeks to get that reeking mess out of my clothes and hair."

"You are such a drama queen, Emily. But don't worry," I said as I stepped out of the truck, "we have plenty of bottled water. You can just wash your hair in Evian."

She slammed her door shut and locked it, laughing as she did. "Oh, I can really claim the title of 'diva' now that I will be washing my hair in fancy French water."

"Hey, I forgot to leave the window cracked a bit. Will you throw me the keys, please? I don't want Furby getting too hot while we shop."

"I can't believe you made me drag that cat all the way from New York," she replied, a hint of irritation in her voice while she trudged back to the truck and cracked the windows. Once completed she shot me a wicked smile as I held the door open to the store for her. The loud bells that hung from the ceiling clanged loudly, announcing our presence.

"That cat is pampered. And you call me a diva." She laughed, her voice reverberating throughout the ancient walls of the small community store.

"He is like my AmEx—I never leave home without him," I shot back, followed by a playful hug. "And thanks for letting him ride in your new truck. At least he didn't chatter the entire time. He was the quiet one."

"Well, I'll be dammed. If it ain't our favorite author come fer a visit."

The heavily accented voice echoing throughout the store was the owner, Mr. Randall Sneed. His craggy, weather-worn face crinkled into a warm smile from behind the counter. Even though his family bought the store over twenty years ago when my mother left town, he kept the McMann name.

An ex-coal miner, he was one of the few citizens that lived on the up and up.

"Hey there, Mr. Sneed. Great to see you again," I replied. I stepped around the long wooden counter to give him a hug. His strong arms encircled my neck, the smell of aftershave and tobacco enveloped me and immediately reminded me of Mitchell's scent. Not only did the smell bring back a rush of childhood memories but also an ache in my heart for Mitchell. I wanted to ask if he'd heard from him, but opted to steer clear of that conversation. I was already teetering on the verge of a breakdown. If he had bad news to share then I preferred to be blissfully unaware.

"Step back and let me look at ya, girl," pushing me back after his forceful hug. "Yep, same as last time—you need some sun and to eat some good ol' southern food. That high falutin' stuff ya New Yorkers call food don't seem to pack any calories. Dontcha worry though, my lil' gal. I got some fresh steaks hidden in the back just for you. I 'spected you would be payin' us a visit."

I forced my eyes not to roll at his comments. Instead, I looked over at Emily for a bailout. Obviously, Mr. Sneed had watched my first and last interview, and expected me to flee the city, which was exactly what I was doing. The flush of embarrassment rose up from my chest and caused my tongue to lock in place. Thankfully, Emily came to the rescue. She sauntered up to the old man and stuck out her hand.

"Mr. Sneed, I'm Emily Carson, Karmen's publicist and official bodyguard for the weekend. Karmen needs a chance to recuperate and breathe from her hectic schedule, and she told me that this lovely town was the perfect place to accomplish just that. Off the map and hidden away from the prying eyes of the media trolls who might come sniffing around. If they follow her scent here, we would appreciate it if you helped keep our little secret by telling them you haven't seen her."

Mr. Sneed's dark blue eyes squinted with immediate distrust when Emily first clasped his hand. A distaste for outsiders spread across the wrinkled skin. He looked at me with one eyebrow raised and I responded by nodding my head in astonished agreement. Emily continued to woo him after their handshake was over. She pointed her slender finger to the books behind him on the counter.

"I see you are already an avid supporter of our darling Karmen by the vast display of books here."

Mr. Sneed continued to eye Emily with suspicion then followed her gaze to the stacks of books for sale on the shelves. My cheeks grew hotter. I sensed some tension leave his face as his old eyes moved across the numerous titles that I had autographed for him over the years. It was a long standing tradition that I send him a pre-release copy so he could brag to his friends. He was such a kindly old man. How could I not indulge him?

"Yes ma'am, we all is right proud of our lil' gal. Them there's my personal collection, signed by her hands 'fore anyone else got one."

"Oh yes, Karmen is quite the treasure to us all. And we should all aim to keep it that way, shouldn't we? She can't possibly autograph any more books for you if the press won't leave her to write in peace, now can she?" Emily dangled the bait in front of poor Mr. Sneed, her words coming out like sweet honey. Her New York brogue had been replaced by a seductive tone tainted with a hint of southern drawl that she had honed over the years. It looked like Mr. Sneed was lapping up the honey.

"No ma'am, they surely won't let her rest a wink if'n they knew she was here. That's why I was 'bout to climb up there and move 'em books. Told ya, I figured Mz. Karmen would be payin' us a visit. Sure 'nough, I was right."

Mr. Sneed grinned, his dry lips curled back over his crooked, tobacco-stained teeth. His attempt at a smile looked more like an evil sneer for a brief second before the emotion made its way to his watery eyes. He waved us off with his gnarled hand and turned to the small, decrepit ladder that I hadn't noticed earlier. Dust balls wafted around him as he began his slow climb to reach the top shelf and it creaked in protest under his weight. It looked old enough to be a remnant from when my grandparents owned the place. Knowing Mr. Sneed and his tight grip on his pocketbook, it probably was.

"Ya'll just grab whatcha need, don't pay me no never mind. I'm just gonna fetch these books then hide them real nice while ya'll grab some vittles. And don't forget those steaks in yonder, Mz. Karmen. They's delicious, and just what you need to feel right as rain. And dontcha be afeared 'bout them reporters. This ol' boy is just like this small town—he knows how to keep a secret."

Emily grabbed my arm and forced me to move away from the counter. Whenever embarrassment hit me, I tended to freeze up. Sort of like a deer caught in headlights—terrified yet unable to move or run. At least this time I didn't have a panic attack and pass out onto the dirty hardwood floor.

"Thank you, Mr. Sneed. I just knew we could count on you keeping our little secret. We'll just grab a few things and then be out of your hair."

He grumbled a reply, but I couldn't make out what he said. Emily yanked me to the back of the store, her other hand covering her mouth before her laughter escaped. The look of triumph on her face was hysterical. The tightness in my chest loosened finally and I smiled while we made a mad dash through the few rows of mundane, everyday items that we needed for the cabin.

We could hear Mr. Sneed as he moved stuff around up front, his low grunts rather comical as he removed the books from their special place of honor on the shelf. Emily snatched a large box of toilet paper and whispered, "Nope, no corncobs for me. This Diva don't play that!"

Unable to control myself, I burst out laughing and nearly dropped my armload of groceries. Thankfully, Emily had a better sense of balance and cat-like reflexes, and helped me steady everything before the items crashed to the floor. We unloaded our booty at the counter and waited for Mr. Sneed to ring us up. I noticed all my novels were now gone and all that remained was a dusty outline of where they had been. The rickety ladder was gone as well, and Mr. Sneed was nowhere in sight.

"Where the hell did he go?" Emily said, her voice low but her irritation high as she shifted from one foot to the other. "I've got to pee and I don't want to do it here."

A shiver of fear danced up my spine the instant the last syllable left her mouth. There was only one exit in the back, and he would have walked right past us to use it. If he went out the front door we would have heard the bells. The only other exit was the big plate glass window in front that he obviously didn't go through.

I swallowed the rising panic that crept through my insides and looked around for signs of additions to the interior since my last visit, like a new door or window. I even scanned the aged pine floors for a trap door, anything that would ease the alarm welling up inside me. Seeing nothing, I turned back to the counter, intent on telling Emily that we could just leave some cash and come back later to settle up.

Instead, I just gasped.

The bright sunlight was gone, blocked by dark shadows that pulsed and vibrated against the window and the walls. Thick, cold vapor entwined around my legs and snaked up and over the counter. The air around me turned frigid, my breath a wisp of frozen, white steam. Low, rhythmic chanting echoed all around me. The haunting sounds felt as if they were trying to get under my skin and embed the voices within my soul. The ethereal hums terrified me and I desperately wanted to shake my body and remove their invading presence. I tried to move, but my limbs were locked. Only my eyes functioned.

The wall where my books had sat was gone, replaced by an ebony nothingness that throbbed and writhed like swirling black tar. I looked down and watched in horrified awe as the viscous vapor wound its icy tendrils around my body. The mass moved over the counter and crawled up the walls. The soupy mist that covered the entire room wafted toward the darkness and disappeared into the gaping space. The same force that pulled the freezing fog into oblivion was drawing me in as well. The chanting grew louder and my skin tingled from the cold vapors and the toxic murmurs that urged me closer.

"The time is nigh, Karmen. Come, see!"

I wanted to scream. I wanted to run. I wanted to close my eyes and will the images to disappear. I had to be free from the raw terror that coursed through me, to take back control of my shuddering limbs. To rid myself of the heavy cloak of evil around me. I needed to be anywhere but trapped inside this living nightmare that seemed so real. My entire being was transfixed on the unfathomable images that held me captive with its macabre melody.

Transfixed in horror, I watched the edges of the blackness begin to pulse and turn a vibrant mixture of orange and red that ebbed and flowed like roiling lava. The mist intermingled with the other colors and began to form a shape.

A human shape.

"Come, Karmen. Unleash your gift. We are ready. He is ready."

My tears turned to ice as they raced down my cheeks. Unable to break the spell, I watched in dread as the shape became a fully formed being from the throbbing mass. The torso shifted and shook as arms, legs and a head emerged, then took on solid form. The skin turned whiter than fresh snow and gleamed like a beacon in the dark store, the intense heat emanating from it chasing away the frosty temperature. Blond hair sprung from the head and slid quietly down the skull, and stopped just at the base of the neck. Sinewy muscles flexed as the torso shifted and stretched followed by the loud crack of bones as the thing craned its neck from one side to the next. The body structure left no doubt that it was a man.

Black cloth appeared to grow out of the naked skin and covered his frame from head to toe. Bulging and twisting around every inch of his body it bubbled out of him until he was encased in a suit of black. The room was now stifling, banished by the creation of molten lava into this…this *thing*. The pressure in the room changed in a split second, filling the air with the burning stench of sulfur and snatching my breath away.

He turned and faced me. His impeccable clothes a perfect fit and his face shimmered brighter than the noonday sun. The light was so intense I couldn't make out any discernible features. I realized I could move when my arms shot up from my sides to shield my eyes from his radiance. Although I couldn't see his lips, I heard his words resound inside my head. His voice was the most beautiful and terrifying thing I had ever heard. The syllables caressed my spirit like warm silk then clamped like boney fingers around my mind.

"I am. Follow me."

"YA'LL FORGOT TO fetch that meat. Mz. Karmen looks like she could just pass out any second. I'm here ta tell ya, that gal needs to *eat!*" Mr. Sneed punctuated his words by plopping two thick slabs of wrapped meat on the counter. "Yes'm, it's a right good thing ya'll stopped by so I could give her a fillin' up. She shore does need it."

In a blink everything changed again. The sounds, smells and images from just a nanosecond before were gone as if none of it ever existed. I sucked in a huge, cleansing breath and put my shaking hands on the counter to steady myself. Waves of nausea washed over me and it took all my concentration just to remember how to breathe.

"It's been a really long trip, Mr. Sneed. Thank you for your thoughtful gift. I will make sure she eats it," Emily replied, then scooped up the sack of groceries with one hand and latched on to my arm with the other. "Thank you for the steaks and for removing her books. Those nosey reporters would hound you until you cracked if they thought you were a fan. Take care."

As Emily led me out of the store, my body began to tremble even more. I felt disjointed, like my nerve endings were disconnected from my muscles. Emily sensed my unsteadiness and pulled me closer, leaning her body into mine for support. The tinkling bells sounded again as we exited the door and made our way outside toward the truck. Without a word, she helped me inside the cab and then ran around to the driver's side and climbed in, squealing tires as she backed out onto the highway.

I still couldn't form any words. So many thoughts whizzed through my mind that there was no way I could verbalize them, let alone pluck out one of the speeding images to focus on. If Emily didn't already know the way to the cabin, we would have been in trouble.

We rode the next fifteen minutes in silence even though I sensed she was dying to ask me what was wrong. Emily navigated the winding back roads with ease until we finally pulled up in front of the cabin. The sprawling trees on each side of the place encased the entire house in a comforting cocoon, the branches nearly touching at the peak of the roof. Just seeing the place made my blood pressure slow down. The evil that had engulfed me at the grocery store waned, and I finally loosened my death grip on the seat.

Emily was out the door in a flash with groceries in hand, her normally perky voice tinged with worry. "Stay put, doll. Let me unload all this and I'll be right back for you."

I didn't respond except for the slight nod of my head, my eyes focused on the trees that covered Bailey Mountain. Two trips later, the backseat was completely empty with Furby safely inside. Emily opened the door and clasped my cold hand in her warm one and didn't let go until we were inside and seated on the couch. Her eyes clouded over with worry as she searched my face for answers except my blank stare didn't offer any.

"Just rest a bit, sweetie. I'll go rustle something up in the kitchen. Mr. Sneed was right—you do look a tad pale. Here, drink some water while I throw together a sandwich. I'll be right back."

She pressed her water bottle into my hands. Like an obedient child, I nodded again and held on to the cool plastic, unable to find the muscle coordination to bring it to my lips. That's when I noticed my knuckles were white.

Emily bounced up from the couch and disappeared into the kitchen and began rummaging around. I sat and stared at the small living room that resembled its original design in shape only and worried about my sanity. Was I truly losing my mind? Were these episodes minor tremors in preparation of the major earthquake that would shatter my connection with reality? Was I doomed to break and spend the remainder of my life locked inside the impenetrable walls of a psychiatric ward medicated to the point that all I was capable of doing was drooling?

If the events of the last few weeks were any indication, it looked like that was the direction I was heading.

Emily appeared in the doorway, her lips smiling but her brow furrowed with worry. "An early dinner is now being served, my dear. What is the Kentuckian expression? 'Time to get the feedbag on?'"

For the first time in the last half-hour, I felt the connection between my thoughts and my body meld and discovered that I could move. I gave her a weak smile, slowly stood up and walked into the kitchen. Furby crunched on his bowl of cat food loudly in the corner, oblivious to the fact that his owner was about to lose her grip on sanity.

Two delicious looking sandwiches about six inches high graced the small table that butted up against the picture window. Emily had thought of everything and I was grateful she was here with me. Although I didn't relish the idea of my best friend being forced to watch me slide into insanity.

"I believe the correct expression is 'time to strap on the feedbag.' But I've lived in New York long enough that I could be wrong," I said, sitting down on the old wooden chair that my grandfather made over seventy years ago. Emily pointed at my plate while she poured me a glass of Pinot.

"Whatever. Just eat. And drink. And I won't take no for an answer. If you clean your plate and drink your wine, I have a surprise for dessert. Guaranteed to make you relax."

"Wine? Emily, you know I don't…"

"Today, you do. No excuses."

I didn't have to force the smile that appeared this time. My gratitude for our friendship made it happen on its own.

TWO HOURS LATER we had both unpacked our bags and settled in for the night. My blood pressure had finally returned to normal and I could feel and control my extremities after a long, hot shower. I knew Emily was concerned about me since she let me take one first. Normally, she would have commandeered the bathroom until she primped and preened herself into her version of presentable, which generally meant being dressed and coiffed to the hilt. While I was rinsing the shampoo out of my hair, lauding her kindness in my mind, reality kicked in when she rapped on the door and requested I leave her a few dribbles of hot water.

It was still warm outside, the sun just setting over Bailey Mountain. I heard the swing creak on the front porch so I grabbed my glass of wine and headed out to join Emily. The air was crisp and a slight breeze greeted me when I stepped outside.

She smiled, concern and love radiating from behind her luminous eyes, along with apprehension. I eased into the swing next to her and felt my face begin to burn from shame. She had given me enough time to prepare myself for the looming questions that she had arduously kept at bay for the past three days. I braced myself for their onslaught and wondered if I could actually share with another person what had been happening to me.

Emily surprised me when she reached into her jeans pocket and pulled out a pack of cigarettes. She smiled demurely and winked as she extracted one that looked frail and sickly, and waved it in front of me.

"Here's dessert as promised."

"Is that what I think it is?"

"Gee, you aren't as sheltered as I thought. Now," she said, holding the joint to her lips and lighting up, "I know you are virginal when it comes to hitting it up, but trust me, if ever there was a person in this world that needed to enjoy the effects of THC it's you."

The rank smoke swirled around Emily's head and I crinkled my nose.

"God, that reeks. Smells like a dead skunk. No way I'm letting that thing near me."

Emily exhaled a huge plume of white vapor and laughed.

"Hey, the stronger the skunk, the better the funk."

Emily held out the stinking mess and watched in silence as I stared at it. The wispy tendrils of smoke twirled from the burnt end like fingers and danced around my face. Never had I even remotely considered imbibing in any type of substance. The two glasses of wine I had already drank was my first experience with alcohol.

My mother had drilled it into my head how dangerous "losing control of one's mind" was since I was old enough to comprehend the English language. Plus, being homeschooled and a virtual inmate with a prison guard for a mother kept me quite sheltered from the temptations of the world. Even when I moved out on my own I never felt the urge to rebel doing drugs. Truth be told, I was terrified of them and of what my mother had warned me about—losing my ability to write.

But I had lost it through no fault of a foreign substance traveling through my veins. Not to mention my mind had already taken a hiatus from reality. The two things I feared the most had already occurred on their own. So what was I exactly endangering? Would it really be all that awful to have a sudden urge to eat an entire bag of potato chips?

"If I end up suffering a brain meltdown it will be your fault." I leaned over and pursed my lips together waiting for her to bring the thing up to my lips. It was so damn small I was afraid I would drop it. I kept my personal opinions about the hypocrisy of her behavior to myself. The so called "Christian" that Emily proclaimed to be was laughable. Here she was, not only engaging in illegal activities, but encouraging another to do the same

"Now this would give my mother a reason to hate you for sure."

"I'm certainly not going to rat you out. Just take a big breath in and hold it. You're gonna cough, but that's okay. Hold it in as long as you can."

I spent the next ten minutes gagging, coughing and whining about the stench, the burn in my lungs, and the fact that she drove all the way from New York to Kentucky with illegal narcotics in her truck. At the fifteen minute mark I began to feel the effects. The tension in my neck was almost gone and my jaws were no longer clamped together from anxiety. I took a sip of wine and let it sit in my mouth for a few seconds to put some moisture back.

The sounds of the forest seemed louder than before, the melodious symphony of cicadas, birds and other creatures lulled me into a state of tranquility. Maybe it was because we were out in the country safely tucked away from the hustle and noise of the city or because I was high as a proverbial kite, but I felt calm. Emily's giggles brought me out of my mental foray into the woods.

"You should see your eyes, girl. They are positively glowing. You look evil!"

"Yours aren't much better! Don't even start, you *wanted* me to do this, remember?"

Emily straightened up and pulled her legs under her. Her glazed eyes swept over me, taking in my inebriation with gusto. She reached out and clasped my hand and gave it a gentle squeeze. "Karmen, all joking aside. As your best friend I have to say you're scaring the pants off me. What is going on? And please don't tell me it's nothing. What happened during your interview? You looked like a deer trapped in bright headlights before you passed out. And today? I've never seen anyone look so terrified in my whole life."

I don't know if it was the marijuana, my worried friend's imploring, or both, but the words finally broke free. They had been building for so long inside my head that the pressure had become unbearable.

"I only looked scared because I was petrified. I think, oh God I don't know, that either I am suffering from paranoid delusions or maybe a brain tumor or something."

Her grip intensified but her demeanor remained calm. "Expound on that please."

"I don't even know where to begin, Emily. It's all such a complicated, unfathomable monstrosity."

"Hey, it's okay. Tell me. I'm here and I'll listen. We'll work through it no matter what it is."

"If I'm going to unleash this story, I'm going to need more wine. And so are you."

Wednesday Night

"EVER SINCE I WAS LITTLE THE WORDS JUST…WERE. I wrote my first poem the summer I was six leaning against that tree right there." I pointed toward the tall oak about sixty yards away. "It seemed just as natural as breathing or walking to me. I never went anywhere without a notepad, recording anything that came to my inquisitive mind.

"You know from personal experience that my mother instilled in me a love for reading and writing, just like I said during my interview last week. I read about ten books a week during my teenage years devouring each volume she placed in front of me."

Emily smiled at the memory. "Yep, I remember thinking you were going to go blind before thirty because you read so much."

"I felt *safe* inside the pages of a book. Lost in a world that didn't exist yet feeling more alive than I did in reality. And I wanted more than anything to create the same feelings in others. It was beyond a desire or obsession. It was…I don't know any other way to describe it other than a hunger. Remember the night I turned sixteen? It was one of the few times you were allowed to spend the night and I let you read my journal notes of *Shrewsbury?*"

Emily nodded, enthralled, the curiosity apparent even through the red haze of pot we smoked.

"The look on your face while you read satisfied my hunger—for a moment. But as soon as you went to sleep, I tried to relive the rush I got from watching you enjoy what I wrote except nothing happened. The hunger growled inside of me. The need to satisfy it overwhelmed everything. That night I prayed that whatever was out there controlling our puppet strings would satiate the gnawing and allow me to experience the sensation you gave me when you read my book."

Emily cocked her head to the side. "You *prayed?* Well, that's a first. I thought I was the only one of this duo that believed in a higher power."

"I said I *prayed. I* didn't say I *believed,*" I replied with a smirk. The only time Emily and I ever argued was over religion. Her family was Episca-teryian-olic-something-or-other and she had been shocked when the subject was first broached between the two of us years ago that I was a non-believer.

"Two days after I requested divine intervention is when things started to get, um, a little weird."

"Weird how?" Her eyes peeked over the rim of her wineglass after a hefty slurp.

A shudder of fear spread through me. I had never told a living soul nor admitted out loud what I was about to reveal. "Don't laugh. Promise?" I pleaded. I followed that up by draining my glass in one big, unladylike gulp.

Emily's gaze was soft and her warm hand returned to hold mine. "Of course not, Karmen. It's okay, tell me."

I reached over and took a hefty sip of her wine before I continued. *Jesus, where do I start?*

"You've read the original version of *Shrewsbury* and what was published. They are very different as I'm sure you noticed."

Emily nodded in agreement. "I assumed it was from the magic of having an uncle for an editor."

I let out an exasperated sigh. "If you only knew how much I wish that was the reason." I stood up, my body unable to confine my nervousness into one spot. I walked across the expanse of the porch to the table that the wine bottle sat on and refilled our glasses. I handed it to her, averting my eyes from her probing ones. Emily waited in silence while I gulped down more liquid courage and paced the wooden porch like a caged animal.

"Two nights after my birthday, I had a dream. A very vivid dream. The kind that takes place in real life surroundings, giving the illusion that it is really happening. William Shakespeare appeared in it and started to talk to me, telling me he wanted to help me write. His bodiless head floated over my bed for what seemed like the entire night, some of what he said I heard and some of it murmured so softly, almost like he was chanting, that I couldn't decipher his words.

"When I woke up that morning I felt exhausted. My neck and shoulders were in knots and my head was throbbing. When I got up to use the restroom, I noticed my computer was on, which was odd because I remembered turning it off before going to bed. When I got closer to the screen I noticed a document was open. Not just any document but a four hundred page one. The cursor was blinking at the end of the last word. When I scrolled up to the top, I panicked."

While I had been talking, Emily had chugged her wine and gotten up and poured another drink. As she settled back into the cushions of the swing, she asked in a quiet voice, "Why did you panic, Karmen?"

"Because the title at the top was *Shrewsbury*. A four hundred page story that I had absolutely no recollection of writing or the slightest clue as to how it got on my computer."

Emily's lips broke out into a huge grin and she burst out of the swing and loped across the porch in three long strides. She grabbed me around the neck and hugged me, spilling both of our glasses with her enthusiasm.

"Oh sweetie, you were simply sleepwalking. Or, in this case, sleep *typing!* While odd, I have heard other stories of people performing all sorts of things like driving, swimming and such. All this worry, this fear of going nuts or having some brain issue, needs to be put to rest. Right now. You're fine, just a little odder than I always thought."

"You didn't let me finish. That's just the tip of the iceberg." I pulled away from her warm embrace. "You'll need to sit down for the rest."

Emily's demeanor immediately shifted to worry. She started to speak but once she looked into my eyes she sensed my apprehension and returned to the swing. She nodded for me to continue.

"At first I thought I was still dreaming and looked around for Shakespeare's floating head except it wasn't there. I willed myself to wake up. I snapped my eyes shut and waited for the dream to end. To my horror, I heard the soft tap of the keys and the temperature of the room dropped so fast my ears popped. That first gulp of frozen air forced my eyes open and back to the screen. There were new words on the screen that said: *'Thou hath awakened, 'tis not a dream. Thy gift, which 'twas requested from thy supplications and prayers, has been bestowed. And so it begins. William'*

"Terror hit me so hard I threw up. I wanted to run from the room screaming but seemed inexplicably drawn to the words on the screen. It was like the cold air held me captive in the chair—I couldn't move. The sensation of invisible fingers holding my head in place, forcing me to read, filled me with dread. It was like being a moth pulled to the flame—something deep and sinister controlled me and I had no choice.

"I had read about two hundred pages when I heard my mother coming down the hall. I looked at the clock and realized it was almost noon and that I had been reading for hours. Suddenly, I found my limbs were free and I shut the system down then fled to the bathroom and jumped in the shower."

Emily's face had turned a strange shade of pale as she listened. "Go on," she urged.

"I don't know what I was thinking. My thoughts were coming in spurts and the only thing I could seem to truly latch onto was getting under the hot water and washing away the cold and fear. It never occurred to me that my mother would decide at that moment to snoop around on my computer. She found the file and read it, then gave it to Uncle Cy.

"I was furious with her at first and petrified at the same time. I wanted to tell her to delete it, that I had no recollection of typing it. She gushed on and on about how great it was and in the midst of her ramblings, I realized the hunger I had felt before was gone. I let her comments override my fears and pushed aside the true way the book came to be and thought like you—that I wrote it in some sort of sleep-mode."

Emily pulled out another joint and lit up. "Hang on. I can tell from your tone this is about to get wicked." She inhaled deeply then stretched her arm out toward me. I reached out then hesitated. My head was already spinning. Time to slow down before I passed out. If I was going to let all this out of me, I needed to be somewhat sober The wine was enough. It only took a few minutes for her to smoke it down to a small nub before I continued.

"It's funny how you can lie to yourself so many times that it becomes quasi-truth. During the next year, I convinced myself that my interactions with Shakespeare were just an extension of my dream and that I *did* write the book. But my subconscious knew the truth. I think that's why I started having panic attacks. When anyone asked me about my writing process the truth reared its ugly head inside me. It was like a safety valve and it worked. I used my attacks to steer clear of interviews.

"Nothing happened again for almost a year-and-a-half. Then Faulkner came to me in a dream one night, again just as a floating head that carried on a conversation that I only vaguely remembered. When I woke up book number two was on my computer. And so it went off and on for the next few years. Dante, Steinbeck, Shelley, Hemingway, Twain, Poe. I would get visits from dead authors in my dreams then wake up to a completed book with no memory of typing it."

"May I stop you here?" Emily said, her voice a whisper.

"Sure, I need a break. And more wine. My throat is dry from all this yapping." I walked over to the table and topped off my glass, wincing when I realized I didn't walk a straight line.

"Do you think it's possible that the dreams came to you as a form of creative expression? You've read all those author's books at least twice if not more. Plus you've mentioned several times to me that they were your favorite writers. Maybe you just absorbed more than you thought when you read their books and the way you released it was through your dreams?"

"At first, yes, I did give that serious consideration. I pushed aside the fact that all their writing styles, genres and subject matters they wrote ranged from one spectrum to another. But when I woke up and looked at my computer screen it always matched. You've read the reviews—most of the critics have commented in one form or another that my books are eerily similar in depth, prose and style to a particular author. *Dead* authors."

"So, you think there is more to this than mere coincidence?"

"After the experiences of the last five weeks you better believe it." Wobbling over to the swing, I plopped down next to Emily, the alcohol and THC removing my normal inhibitions, and leaned my head onto her warm shoulder. "Way more."

Emily stroked my hair while the night rolled over Bailey Mountain. In the darkness, the fireflies dancing on the cooler air were our only light.

"Five weeks ago the dreams crossed over into the real world."

Emily's fingers stopped in mid-caress. "What?"

Sitting up, I drained my glass then stared at Emily's disbelieving eyes.

"The fire at my apartment wasn't started by Furby knocking over a candle in the kitchen while I was in the bathroom. Thankfully it was a completely plausible scenario and one the fire investigator bought. However, the truth of the matter is that it started when I hurled a lit candle across the room at Alexandre Dumas."

"Come again?" Emily replied, unable to hide her shock.

"Let me backtrack here. Two years ago the dreams stopped and so did my words. Poof! The vapors of creativity vanished up in smoke. Not only did the dead stop writing my bestsellers, but *I* couldn't form a full sentence to save my life. No little tinkling ideas, no lines of poetry, hell, not even a grocery list! Right after you left for college I sort of sunk into a depression, I guess. It only got worse when Mitchell and I broke up and he left for Iraq. I tried everything to jumpstart the words, but they sat in silence, locked away inside of me. That is until the day I sat at my desk and wished for my gift back. A few seconds later, Alexandre Dumas was standing in my kitchen."

Emily blinked a few times as if she was ensuring *she* was awake and not dreaming the conversation. Her quizzical stare was damn near laughable. "Are you sure you weren't…"

I held up my empty glass and stopped her.

"Yes, I'm sure I wasn't dreaming. He was as real as you are right now. He spoke in French yet I understood his words, *'Le temps est venu. Votre destin vous attend,'* which means 'The time has come. Your destiny awaits.'

"I had never experienced the raw terror his words elicited from me. I knew I had to be hallucinating because there are no such things as ghosts or the dead chatting with random people in their kitchens. I closed my eyes and fought the image in my mind, straining to retain control. I tried to convince myself that my eyes were playing a trick on me. But when Furby started hissing, I opened them again and realized he saw something, too. His back was arched and his teeth barred as he sent out a warning growl before hightailing it into my bedroom.

"My response was a screaming fit and I threw the first thing I grabbed which was a lit candle. Even though Dumas was a solid form it sailed right through him. He vanished into thin air and the fire roared to life. I ran into the bedroom, grabbed Furby, and ran."

"Oh…my…God…" Emily eked out, her voice as shaky as my hands.

"Yeah, 'oh my' is putting it mildly. It gets worse."

Emily gulped.

"After the fire things seemed to just hover, like I was in a holding pattern or stuck in neutral. The dead didn't come back, but neither did my writing ability. My dreams were normal, if there is such a thing. No more dead novelists popped in to take over my mind, although a feeling of unease surrounded me.

"I felt like I was being smothered if that makes sense. Mom and Uncle Cy were pushing hard to get me to start making the media rounds since *Madness* was such a hit. And you know me, I *hate* dealing with that sort of thing. I was also worried about Mitchell. It's been almost a year since I've heard from him. I know we aren't technically dating anymore, but still…"

A tear slid down my cheek at the thought of Mitchell. Emily smiled at the mention of my former one-and-only boyfriend.

"Of course you felt smothered. With all the pressure you've been under it's no wonder you're experiencing such—"

"Stress-induced hallucinations? Yeah, I thought that as well even after my meltdown on television. But…" My voice hitched and I knew once I spoke the words there would be no turning back.

Emily reached out and touched my shoulder. Her tender fingers gripped my arm. "But what, Karmen? What did you see at your interview? What else happened?"

Here it comes…the cat is clawing out of the bag, never to be replaced.

"I…I was holding it together, praying that Renee would stick to the limited scope of questions I had prepared prior to agreeing to do the interview. When she veered and started asking how I came up with ideas, I felt the panic attack coming. I deflected the first probe. And when she asked about my writing process that question did it. That's when everything changed."

Emily's grip grew tighter on my shoulder. "Changed how, sweetie?"

I tried to hide my fear by being flip with my response. "Well, the lovely Renee Jackson's face sort of mutated into a montage of the dead that had been visiting me. Then it said in a gravelly voice, *'It is time, Karmen. Time to fulfill your destiny. We have prepared you well. Go, write it.'* That little moment is precisely when I fainted."

Even in the moonlight, I could tell that Emily's face blanched. Her mouth formed that small 'o' that people make when they are shocked and at a loss for words. The warm hand she had on my shoulder flew up to cover her mouth. I decided to drop the rest of the happy news of my slide into insanity.

"After that fun experience, I truly thought it was stress-induced. I *felt* the anxiety attack coming before she transformed into the living dead. And when you showed up in my room later that night insisting we get away for a few days, I wanted desperately to believe that was all I needed—a vacation. A mental break from the world I found myself confined in. As soon as you mentioned this cabin," I stood up and started walking down the porch steps and onto the cool grass, "for the first time in years, I felt… calm. Like this place is where I belong, hidden away in these dense woods so no one can hear me scream."

The swing creaked as Emily arose and followed my steps out to the grass. I stood with my back to her, ashamed of the tears that streaked my face. She stopped in front of me and lifted my chin with her hands, forcing me to look at her.

"What happened today at the store, Karmen?" Her voice was firm, probing.

The chill of the night air whispered through my hair and made my skin prickle as the goose bumps sprouted on my arms. I gently pulled my head away from Emily's hands and started walking toward the outcropping of sweet birch trees that lead to the endless forest that made up Bailey Mountain. A few were dead from either lack of water or some malaise from insects and stood like bare bones, their gnarled limbs frozen in time.

I trod in silence through the slippery grass, the mist from the mountain already had settled on their tender blades, until I was almost at the edge of the mountain. I could sense Emily right behind me, and knew I needed to answer her question, but I felt the strange need to move away from the cabin before I did. It was almost as though I didn't want to tarnish my connection with my family's ancestral home with my insane words.

Emily came up behind me and waited in silence for me to answer.

"When we were at the counter the temperature dropped and then the wall behind the counter vanished and what replaced it…well, describing it is damn near impossible. The wall turned into this black, gooey tar-like glob that moved like it was alive. It writhed around and then I heard chanting. You know, deep and rhythmic like cloistered monks do in movies. At first it was just indecipherable murmurings, but then I distinctly heard '*The time is nigh. Come, see! Come, Karmen. Unleash your gift. We are ready. He is ready.*' Then it amassed together and created a form—a human form—that glowed like the sun. It had turned into something like lava. He turned to me and said, '*I am. Follow me.*'"

Emily's gasp was suppressed only because her right hand was clamped over her mouth, her left around her waist, like she was holding her shriek inside her belly. I smiled weakly at her, tears of relief at releasing my secret sprinted down my face.

"Welcome to my nightmare. Fun, isn't it? Right now I'd wish for only one thing—for you to say that you saw it, too. Judging by the look on your face that isn't the case."

Thankfully, my best friend didn't bolt and run screaming. She simply stepped over closer and wrapped her long arms around my neck and hugged me in silence. The cool evening mist that swirled around our feet left our legs damp, but that was nothing in comparison to what my sobs did to Emily's shirt.

THE UNBURDENING OF my soul took about two hours, two joints and two very large bottles of white wine. After my deluge of tears finally dried up, Emily went inside and brought out a snack and more alcohol. By the time midnight rolled around, we were thoroughly trashed.

I was curled up in bed with Furby nestled in the crook behind my knees, his soft fur keeping my legs warm. Emily snored loudly next to me in a drunken stupor. By the time we decided to call it a night, she was the one that required assistance getting inside. I had struggled and pulled to get her up the steps and through the door, giggling and mocking her considering this had been my first drunk and her umpteenth millionth.

Once we staggered through the threshold, she let go of her death grip on me and lunged for the kitchen sink. I guess her violent vomiting took a lot out of her because she ended up crawling to my bedroom, which was the closest. I was too lit myself to protest and had motioned for her to join me.

Truth be told, I was glad she was in here even though she was sawing logs so loud I was afraid the paint on the walls would start cracking. Normally, I was a loner that preferred my space except tonight I didn't want to be alone.

Emily's only response earlier was that she didn't know what to think. She wanted to sleep on it and discuss the subject in the morning. I nodded in agreement because now that I had finally released what I had kept bottled up inside for so long, I was exhausted as well as extremely buzzed. We didn't discuss my troubling visions anymore, opting instead for light-hearted banter like guys, clothes and sex.

With a wicked grin on her face, Emily had told me all about her crazy college exploits with the local male population at her college. Nights filled with drinking, crazy sexual acts and other forms of debauchery. I had laughed but secretly wondered what the state of our world was coming to if this was how our future ruling generation passed their time. Then again, hadn't all past generations done the same? That would explain why the world just kept collapsing a bit deeper into a sinkhole of filth.

I stared out the window into the darkened night, the sprawling backyard bathed in the silvery tendrils of the full moon. Other than Furby's shallow purr and Emily's nasal symphony, it was quiet. In my youth the cabin had creaked and moaned due to its age at night, scaring me silly in the darkness of my room. After its full makeover it was as solid as if it were brand new.

An invisible warm blanket of security enveloped me, loosening my muscles from their previous tautness and I began to relax. Part of me wondered if the state of bliss I was feeling was from the booze and bud. Another part, something down far deeper, knew it was because I belonged here.

I was home.

As my sleepy and drunk mind tried to ponder the necessary steps it would take to make all the arrangements to take up permanent residence here, I began to drift off.

I wasn't sure if the orange glow that meandered above the forest trees or the cadenced chanting that delicately enchanted my ears was real or imagined.

5

Thursday

THE SMELL OF BACON AND COFFEE WOKE ME FROM my peaceful dream state. I stretched and opened my eyes to the bright sunshine that streamed through the window. Even though my mouth felt like it had been packed full of cotton and my head throbbed from too much wine, I still felt like a new woman. I hadn't experienced a night of restful sleep in years.

Noticing I was alone in my bed, I retreated to the bathroom to wash the stuffing out of my mouth then followed the intoxicating smells of a country breakfast to the kitchen. Emily was going to spoil me rotten with all her culinary skills since mine were limited to items that could be heated in the microwave. My mother was even worse. Her solution was dining out whenever possible. I think she chose that route because the thought of washing a dish made her cringe.

There was another faint scent tickling my nose that I recognized but couldn't quite place. My stomach growled with anticipation of food, and the pounding in my head told me I needed to down some aspirin and water to ease my hangover.

Once out in the hallway, the lure of food and medicine abruptly vanished when I heard laughter coming from the kitchen. My heart leapt in my chest and I stopped dead in my tracks when I recognized the deep, baritone voice of Mitchell's laughter intermingled with Emily's dainty giggles.

The one and only man I had ever loved was here—his musky aroma was the smell that eluded my memory earlier but the laugh that was embedded in my heart gave him away.

My hands instinctively flew to my head and felt the gnarled mass that was my hair. Then I glanced down and looked at the skimpy blue Baby Doll I was wearing. I felt heat rush up and spread across my cheeks. It had been over a year since I'd last seen Mitchell. There was no way in hell I would let his first glimpse of me after such a long time be when I looked like something Furby drug in after a night of carousing in the woods. Finding my muscle control again, I spun on my heels and flew back to my room.

Fifteen minutes later, I felt a smidgeon more presentable than before. I had thrown on a pair of jeans and a T-shirt after slathering myself with some tropical smelling lotion, then combed my unruly hair back in a ponytail and finished with a dot of mascara and gloss on my face. I smoothed the wrinkles of my shirt with shaking fingers and walked into the kitchen.

The sight of him took my breath away. His muscular shoulders and biceps strained for release from the thin cotton shirt that was stretched tightly across his back. The dark brown hair that I used to curl around my fingers when we shared our innermost thoughts after dramatic love-making sessions was gone, shorn down to his head in typical military style. The last time we had spoken was the day he left for active duty in Iraq. What a horrible day that had been. It damn near broke my spirit when we decided to part as friends, each free to travel down their own perspective path and, if fate would allow it, see what happened when his active duty was over. His dark brown eyes were harsh that day, his words clipped and to the point. I shuddered when I recalled my bitter retorts as well, hurled across the airport like daggers to wound his spirit just as he had wounded mine.

I blinked and forced that day and those painful memories out of my head. What was done was done. What mattered was he was here now, and I knew exactly who to blame for that.

"Good morning, sleeping beauty. My, you look much better than I thought you would after all you drank last night," Emily teased as she flipped the bacon, splattering grease all over the counter.

"Wish I could say the same about you." I shot her a look before Mitchell turned around, then grabbed the spatula from her, shooing her from the pan. Her impish grin lit up the room and I contemplated smacking her in the face with the hot utensil.

"Aren't you going to say hello to our guest? Where are your manners, girl?" Emily prodded, her eyes dancing with delight at my nervousness.

"Well, of course. But I wanted to save the bacon from turning into a pile of ash. How hospitable would it be to serve that?" I set the spatula to the side and turned to face Mitchell. "Good morning, Mitch. Wonderful to see you."

The chair screeched as he pushed it back and stood up. He seemed taller, more bulky. His eyes never left mine as he crossed the floor in two strides before giving me what could only be called a bear hug.

"Karmie! My God, but ain't you a sight for the sorest of eyes! Just as gorgeous as ever, and I see that smart mouth of yours ain't let up one bit, has it?"

His smile was the most beautiful thing I had ever seen, but I couldn't let him know that. "Mitch, please, put me down. I'm not a pecan that needs to be cracked."

For the next twenty minutes, the three of us sat in the cozy dining room and slurped down an artery-hardening meal, complete with hand-turned butter. Mitchell's mother had been famous throughout Floyd County for her butter before she passed away eight years ago. Mitchell took on the role of cook and housekeeper after she died. Her culinary skills weren't lost on him as she had taught him well. His butter was just as rich and sweet as his mother's had been.

Surrounded by my closest friend and the love of my life, the fear and stress that had been my constant companion for the last six years melted away like the butter on the hot, home-made biscuits. All the unexplained happenings had to have been stress-induced because now that the unbearable tension was gone, I felt refreshed, revived and stronger than I could ever recall feeling.

Maybe my writer's block was what was driving my brain to release my creative thoughts in such an odd way. Or maybe having so much pressure on me, some personally induced and some forced upon me by others, had reached such an epic pro-portion that the only escape was insanity. Whatever it was, it didn't seem to matter anymore. Emily had been right—I had desperately needed to get away. To be free of the confines my writing had trapped me in. Free to explore the other aspects of life and attach myself to the real world, not the ones I created inside my head.

Even in my youth, this tiny town, full of eccentric, eclectic people that were bound together just as strong as the moonshine that cooked in the hollers and the coal that rested below the mountains, gave me a sense of strength. Generational ties that held families together through adversities that would have bro-ken the spirits of weaker people had somehow migrated down to me. The lush land and breathtaking landscape could also be cruel and heartless. Your bloodline had to be hardy enough to survive and pass along the strength to the next generation.

But it was home. It's where my roots were, and as I gazed upon the dense forest outside, I felt the call to stay. Maybe once I drew from the well of strength of my family's heritage, my words would begin to flow again. Maybe I could work part-time at McMann's General Store and soak up some local lore. Perhaps I could coax the local patrons into sharing some stories of their ancestors that I could turn into a great book.

Emily and Mitch swapped stories about the events in their lives for the past year and I just absorbed the magical moments, as was my way. Being a writer, I was always the quiet one in a room, insistent upon listening, grasping every nuance, inflection, and sensory input. I would kick the crap out of Emily later for not telling me before she invited Mitchell over. Who was I kidding? Emily had set the surprise visit up for my birthday so I really couldn't tear into her. But I decided I could bite into Mitchell just a nibble for being back in the states without informing me that he was home.

Then it dawned on me that he was back before his deployment ended, and I doubted the Army let active duty soldiers just randomly leave to go home to celebrate the birthday of someone they *used* to date. I ignored the fact that he and Emily were jabbering.

"Mitchell, when did you get back? You should've called me. You have no idea how..." I stopped short, wishing my mouth had an off switch.

His lips twisted into a sly grin as he slowly turned his head toward mine.

"Why Karmie, were you goin' to admit that ya'll was worried about me?"

His sultry voice sent shivers down my back and blood pounding to my cheeks. God, between the accent and the richness of his smooth cadence, I feared that any minute I would just launch myself across the table and ravish him on the floor. Thankfully, my fear of displaying my affection in front of Emily overrode my rampant hormones.

"Well of course she was worried, you hillbilly buffoon. All of the people that cared about you were. But, Karmen has a point—when were you going to let everyone know you were back? Tsk, tsk. Not fair letting us all worry about bullets whizzing by your shaved little head every night when you were safe and sound on American soil," Emily said, then playfully slugged Mitchell's enormous bicep.

I couldn't take my eyes off the darkly tanned muscle that now sported some sort of black, symbolic military tattoo that flexed with each movement. Man, it was getting really hot in the kitchen. Coffee was not going to help so I chugged on my cold milk, gulping it so fast it made my head hurt.

Mitchell knew me well enough to recognize that I was about to spontaneously combust. I felt the heat of desire race through me and briefly wondered if this was what had been driving me insane the last twelve months—not feeling the touch of Mitchell's hands on my body. His eyes were full of passion, the lids hooded and a faint bead of sweat glistened on the bridge of his nose. The intense stare of his gorgeous eyes never left my own as he responded to Emily's question.

"I've only been back for two weeks and was a bit tied up with takin' care of the funeral arrangements 'n such. Once that was all over, I planned on callin' on Mz. Karmie the other night, but I saw on the news what happened, so I figured she'd be a'comin' down here pretty soon. Sure 'nuff, here she is."

My tongue was still held captive by his smoldering eyes but thankfully, Emily's was not.

"Oh, I feel awful now! I didn't realize someone in your family passed away. I'm sorry for your loss, Mitchell."

The second Emily's words left her mouth, the red hot longing I had was replaced by icy fear. Mitchell only had one surviving family member left, and if he had just died…

"Thank you, Emily, for your kind words. Uncle Randy lived a long life, but since I am the only kin left, his passin' last week and this here wound," he pulled back the collar of his shirt, exposing an angry red scar across his shoulder, "got me out of the burnin' desert—permanently. So, I'm hangin' up my combat boots and puttin' my cowboy ones back on. Good thing I worked in the store as a kid or I'd really be up a creek. I think I can recall enough to keep the place up and runnin'. Karmie, you remember that summer we met after you dropped a can of…?"

Mitchell's question trailed off when he looked my way. Two pairs of eyes stared at me but I was unable to move. I couldn't even open my mouth to release the scream of terror that wanted desperately to escape. The blood drained from my face and surged into my stomach in one giant *whoosh*. My body started trembling uncontrollably, my vision began to blur. I hung on to the last mental string of consciousness and forced my eyes over to Emily, fighting the waves of nausea that threatened to drown me.

"Karmen, oh God, what's wrong?" Emily said, immediately rising from her seat. In a flash, she was crouched down next to me, her hand clasped around my clenched fingers.

Tears flowed down my face and the few precious moments of tranquility I had experienced earlier were gone. I stared at the worried eyes of my best friend and realized that something much deeper was going on, and that I wasn't the only one affected by the menacing presence.

"Mr. Sneed is Mitchell's uncle, which means you and I bought groceries and had a conversation with a dead man yesterday."

"I DON'T GET what ya'll are tryin' to tell me here. It…it just sounds like you two are out of your minds. I mean, come on! It's not possible."

Mitchell, Emily and I were huddled together in the living room, their faces both deathly white against the backdrop of the tan walls, and I'm sure my own reflected the same pallor. For the last hour and a half, Emily and I had explained everything in vivid detail, starting with my first dream and ending with our stop at McMann's Grocery Store yesterday. Mitchell tried to follow, but bless his country heart he was finding that to be an impossible task. Emily and I had run over each other with our stories, sometimes talking at the same time. No wonder he was confused. The look of frustration on his face would have been comical had we been discussing a subject that wasn't so damned creepy.

"I'm sorry, Mitch. I know it's a lot to swallow. Believe me when I say this isn't any easier for either of us," I said, taking a sip of water. I closed my eyes for a brief moment, trying to envision the cool liquid travelling through my veins to soothe my frayed nerves.

Too bad it wasn't working.

Emily piped up next, her voice oddly quiet and shaky. "Easy? *Easy!* That's putting it mildly, Karmen. I talked to a dead man yesterday. It's like we are living in some *Twilight Zone* episode or something. If I didn't know any better, I would start tearing this place apart for hidden cameras or microphones because it sure would make one helluva episode on a reality show. I'm living inside the 'I see dead people' movie and I don't like it one bit. Not at all."

I sighed heavily and tried to force some semblance of rational thought. Unfortunately, that was impossible. "At least I know that I'm not crazy or have this massive lump of foreign tissue pressing down on vital parts of my brain," I said, trying to inject some levity into the situation.

Emily snorted with disgust. "You know I love you girl, couldn't love you more if you were my own flesh and blood, but there are some things that I just don't want to share with you. Your ghostly visits top that list."

"This just don't make no sense, ladies. You both are tryin' your damndest to convince me that some *unnatural* force is playin' around here. The whole kit and caboodle! Ghosts, demons, evil gurglin' tar…"

"Now hold on, Mitchell. I never said anything about demons. It's only been…" I was shocked by his use of the word demons.

"Ya'll tryin' to tell me you don't recognize your description of the guy that grows his own clothes out of his lily white skin after comin' to be from oozin' tar? That's a demon risin' straight up from the bowels of Hell itself if I ever heard tell. Come on, Karmie. You're too smart not to see that. I know you don't believe in an afterlife, or any sort of religious teachin's, but that don't make them any less real."

I stared up at the ceiling wishing that the answers would just magically appear. He was right and I knew it. I never have believed in all that religious mumbo-jumbo about Heaven, Hell, a being that makes us do bad things or even one that created us. Religion was a creation of weak human minds that wanted something, or someone, to take the place of rational thought and acceptance of our own choices in life. And the catalyst for most of the major battles that have raged across the world for centuries as each sect attempted to gain dominance. Just like the one that had taken Mitchell, and countless others, across the sea to the deserts of the Middle East. How convenient was it that when something went according to one's wishes that they sang hallelujahs and praises to an invisible being that floated around in the stratosphere?

Better yet, what better way was there to explain your faults and mistakes by claiming "the devil made me do it?" It was a pathetic crutch that small minds invented to ease their own fears and trepidations or invade other countries under the crux of doing "God's work."

That's what I had told myself ever since I had been capable of rational thought. That is, until today. There was a small portion of me that was happy that my cheese hadn't slid off my cracker, but another part almost wished that I was going insane because the otherworldly option was freaking me out.

"So tell me, oh wise and powerful Oz, what do you think is happening here?" I replied, throwing the ball up in the air and hoping that Mitchell had a plausible answer that would keep it afloat and not come crashing down on us all.

Mitchell cleared his throat then stood up and walked over to the picture window. He stared for a few moments in silence, his back erect and his eyes never leaving the woods. He let out a long, heavy sigh, his words slow and methodic. "I would say a night of too much drinkin' and smokin'…"

Emily bristled with anger and sprung up from her position on the couch. "Hold on there, bub. You must have missed the part where Karmen explained that she started experiencing all these, these *phenomenons* over six years ago! Plus, I was completely sober yesterday when we stopped by the store to shop. I certainly didn't hallucinate talking to your…uncle. I can prove… oh yeah! I sure can prove it. We bought some groceries *and* he even gave us some meat that's wrapped in 'McMann's Grocery' paper. I'll show you!"

Emily bounded into the kitchen.

We could hear her clanking around in the cabinets and the creak of the refrigerator door when she opened it, her voice nearly an octave higher with excitement at proving to Mitchell that neither of us had lost our marbles. "See, here it is….. *Oh my God!*"

Mitchell and I almost collided as we ran into the kitchen at the sound of Emily's ear-shattering scream and glass breaking.

Emily was no longer standing in front of the open fridge door. She had climbed up onto the counter across from the mess on the floor, her entire body trembling. Her screaming abruptly ended as she clamped her hand across her mouth. The other pointed at the floor.

I stopped at the door frame and followed her petrified gaze. Mitchell continued into the kitchen and knelt down to study what was left of the plate of meat that had splattered all over the hardwood floors where she dropped it. Revulsion seeped through me, every nerve inside on edge. I stared at the rotting mass of what once was two thick slices of prime grade beef that was to be our dinner this evening, courtesy of Mr. Sneed.

The *dead* Mr. Sneed.

What rested on the floor no longer looked like two plump, juicy steaks ready for the grill. Slimy, white maggots crawled through the open holes of the blackish-green meat, the consistency of the rank mess close to Jell-O. Mitchell poked one with a fork and pushed aside the paper that bore the name of the store and then turned his nose, the stench immediately making his eyes water.

"What the hell?" He stood back up and moved over to stand in front of Emily and me as if his bulky frame would shield us from the monstrous goop on the floor.

Emily was in no shape to form a cohesive string of words. She buried her head in my shoulder and was softly crying. My arm encircled around her as pity for her creased my brow. It was one thing to live inside your own torment, but quite another to see a person you love experience the same, especially when the circumstances seemed to revolve around you.

"Those were parting gifts from our shopping excursion yesterday. Your dead Uncle Ralph brought them from the back—said they were special steaks just for us. At this point, I think Emily and I just became vegetarians."

"Well, Karmie, I think I gotta answer for ya," Mitchell said. He lifted Emily's limp frame off the counter and carried her into the living room. I followed after him. "I ain't got no clue what the hell is goin' on here. I don't rightly know what to make 'bout all ya'll have said. What I do know is this—I've seen plenty of men scared out of their wits in combat, and they all had the same look in their eyes there as Mz. Emily does. I can't say I understand 'cause all I've seen is some rotted meat, but I believe ya'll have experienced somethin'. I'm just not sure what. This kinda stuff is way above my pay grade, but I'm stickin' with my original guess—this here's somethin' evil."

Emily's trembling intensified with Mitchell's words. I hugged her closer and stared out the window. I felt somehow responsible for her terror and wished I could wipe away her fright.

And my own.

AN HOUR LATER, Emily had finally stopped shaking. We all had moved outside with the hope that the warm sunshine would help defrost our frozen fears, but so far, it hadn't worked. Mitchell had gallantly cleaned the fetid mess in the kitchen while I tried to console Emily on the porch. Although her quaking had ceased, her tongue seemed locked to the roof of her mouth. She hadn't spoken a word since the discovery of the rancid meat in the kitchen. She just stared out into the forest, her eyes not focused on anything in particular. I sensed she wanted to be alone with her thoughts so I obliged her.

I walked over to Mitchell, who was standing on the other side of the porch. His forehead was knitted with worry as he watched both of us from his perch on the railing.

My hand gently caressed the fabric of his T-shirt that covered his war injury, a tingle of thankfulness skittered up my arm, grateful the wound missed his heart.

"Why didn't you call? Or write? Do you know how much I worried?" I whispered as I sat down next to him.

His eyes had lost their sparkle from earlier. Sadness and regret swam behind them along with a healthy dollop of confusion. "I could ask you the same question, Karmie," he whispered.

Hearing my pet name whispered in my ear almost brought the tears again except I refused to let them spill. Enough of them had soaked my lonely pillow during the last year.

"I think the story I related earlier should explain that. I've had a lot going on," I said with a sarcastic retort.

"Ditto." His voice was uncharacteristically hard, but the warmth of his hand that cupped my chin wasn't. His strong fingers lightly stroked my cheek.

"You're okay now, right? There's no permanent damage?" I pulled my face from his hands. His touch always had an effect on me, and I needed my wits sharp.

"I'm good. No stray bullet can take out this tough farm boy. Only thing that can kill me is a dagger to the heart. Know anybody that's got one of them?"

A weak smile crossed my lips. I understood his thinly veiled reference to our breakup.

"Nope, I sure don't. My weapon of choice has always been words."

"Ain't that the truth! You could mow down high cotton with one sentence."

We both laughed quietly, the tension finally broken between the two of us.

I yearned to melt into him, to feel his arms embrace me inside their muscled fortress, shielding me from the fear that was my constant companion. I needed him to offer the perfect, plausible explanation as to what was happening. Or better yet, kiss me until I woke up from this nightmare. My heart craved to go back to that day in the glen years ago. A passion-infused day when we first discovered the secret spots of ecstasy on each other. The entire afternoon was spent exploring the wonders of our love on the soft grass of my family's farm.

But those days of youthful bliss were gone, destroyed by events that threw a thick, concrete barrier between the two of us. His decision to join the military led to countless nights of constant fighting. I couldn't, and *wouldn't*, comprehend his barbaric need to slaughter people just because they happened to be of an ethnic heritage that didn't sit well with the ruling elite of the world. Or worse, the poor souls that lived on top of black gold that someone with greedy paws wanted to snatch up as their own.

And he couldn't grasp why, at the ripe old age of twenty-one, I wouldn't agree to up and marry him and settle back into the coal-filled foothills of Martin. His argument had been that I could write from anywhere, which was true, but at that particular time in my life the thought of leaving the hustle and bustle of New York for the quiet life in rural Kentucky made me want to vomit. The mental images I conjured up of me chasing little rugrats around the house, my hair unkempt and wild from neglect, and my thunderous thighs rubbing together as I tried to keep up with the brats was enough to override the feelings I had for Mitchell.

When I declined his proposal he abruptly decided to enlist in the military. Three months of long-distance arguments over the phone and email ended our relationship since neither of us would budge on our drastically opposite stances.

Like an idiot, I stood silent and let him go. I was unwilling to let go of my own stubbornness and my fear of the unknown. I had been angry at myself for allowing another individual to crawl around inside of me like he had done so effortlessly—hell, I wasn't always comfortable living in my own skin. Why should I let someone else wander around?

Except a lot can happen in the span of over seven hundred plus days. For one, I grew up and two, my recent paranormal experiences changed everything. I had kept silent for so long, unwilling to share with others what I had thought were the dark imaginations of my creative mind or some medical disease. But since discovering that another person, a sane, normal person, was also experiencing the strange happenings, I felt a tremendous sense of relief.

The eyes that captivated my soul from the moment he first looked at me held me now. The world around us seemed to melt away as I felt myself begin to fall into them, diving face-first into the pools of his soul. In the back of my mind, I heard the swing creak and the gentle footsteps of Emily as she left the porch and went inside. A small tugging in my heart told me I should go check on her, but I was already swimming in the waters of my love's heart.

"There wasn't a day that went by that I didn't think about you," Mitchell whispered, pulling me into his warm arms.

I forced the lump of tears in my throat back down. My voice was uncharacteristically husky and muffled as I buried my head into his massive chest, "Me either. Oh Mitchell, I did miss you. Terribly. You have no idea how much I worri—"

His kiss was tender and heated. I felt my knees weaken as I soaked in every sensation.

Now that was love worth fighting for. Never again will I quiet the longings of my heart. When this was all over, if he asked me to marry him again, I would. In a heartbeat.

Dazed and unsteady by the rush of emotions, we both pulled away from our embrace, afraid of what might happen next. My eyes never left his. I watched the hunger in them follow me back over to the swing. Space was needed before we consummated our separation on the porch.

Lost in thought, my fingers gently rubbed my swollen lips, the images of the past and present mingling through my mind. How in the world could it be possible for one person to experience such a wide range of emotions at one time? Fear, stress and worry comingled with the overwhelming sense of love and happiness.

Mitchell let out a slow whistle, pulling me back to reality. "Karmie, are ya okay?"

I shook the cobwebs of the past out of my head and stared into his questioning eyes. "Sorry, just thinking about our situation here. I'm not sure what direction I should go next." My voice was barely a faint whisper. I'd hoped that Emily hadn't heard me, but that thought was quickly quashed.

"We, Karmen. What direction *we* should go since I'm now involved in this wickedness." Emily turned her watery green eyes our way, her face still sickly pale. On trembling legs she slowly walked down the steps out into the yard. After walking about ten feet she stopped and raised her arm and pointed to the forest. "That's where we go to find answers, Karmen. Don't ask how I know, I just do."

"What in tarnation are ya'll talkin' 'bout?" Mitchell said, then grasped my hand and pulled me up from my seat. We trudged down to join Emily on the grass. "Ain't nothin' out there but trees and—"

I thought I was the only one that heard the thrumming vibrations in my ears, but then I saw the look of terror on both Mitchell's and Emily's faces.

Emily began to shake again then lowered her outstretched arm and backed up a few steps. "See, told you. Something's out there. And whatever it is—whoever it is—is calling to us. I feel the pull, don't you?"

I felt the compulsion as well. It rattled deep within me, coursing through my veins like some unholy forest siren. I felt the rhythmic vibrations underneath my feet as it grew louder. Mitchell's grip tightened and I felt his gaze through my peripheral vision as he stared a hole through me.

"Guess we are going hiking this afternoon, guys. At least it's a nice, sunny day outside. Uncle Cy told me I needed to commune with nature while I was here. Seems he isn't the only one that thinks that is a good idea."

FORTY MINUTES LATER, our single file trio tromped through the thick piles of kudzu that wound around every immobile object in the forest. Thankfully, the eerie chanting stopped the minute we crossed the threshold of trees at the edge of my yard. None of us had spoken a word since our journey began, each lost in thought as to just what in the world we were doing out here—and what we might find.

Ever the southern gentlemen, Mitchell led the way, his sharp, silver machete slicing through the knotted vines that hung from the trees with ease. His truck had been full of an arsenal of military equipment ranging from the massive blade to night vision goggles and all sorts of other tools of destruction. They made me cringe when he had rummaged through the various items in search of the tools he felt necessary for our voyage into the woods.

A twinge of pride pricked my heart since he opted not to abandon what probably seemed like two crazy broads and decided to join us on the quest of madness. Of course, I hadn't needed to try and sway his opinion to tag along since he had heard the same haunting sounds that Emily and I had earlier.

I was doing my best to keep up with Mitchell's fast pace through the woods. Emily was right behind me, her left hand clamped around my back belt loop and her right hand on my shoulder. Her fear seeped through her hands onto my clothes and melded with my own. Mitchell came to a dead stop in front of us, his hand motioning for us to freeze. His practiced eyes scanned the area, which had grown darker the deeper we went into the forest. I sensed his apprehension and tried to follow his gaze, looking for any signs of something amiss.

"What's wrong?" Emily whispered in my ear.

"Shhh," Mitchell growled.

Like deer frozen in stride when they sensed a predator approaching, the three of us turned into human statues. The only movement was our eyes as each of us nervously scanned the unfamiliar terrain. After about thirty seconds, Mitchell came back to life and stepped over to us, his voice low and husky. "Ya'll hear that?"

"Oh God, what is it, Mitchell? I don't hear a thing," Emily said.

"That's just it—nothin'. Woods ain't supposed to be quiet."

He was right. I hadn't noticed it because I was focused on keeping my balance while Emily clung to me for dear life. My ears strained to hear the rustle of a leaf, the chattering of a squirrel, the chirping of a bird. I was greeted by deafening silence.

Mitchell stood directly in front of us, firm and stiff like a sentry guarding the castle gate. His voice was low but in the stillness of the silent forest it sounded like he was yelling. "Somethin' ain't right…we should get outta—"

A howling wind blew around us with gale force, nearly knocking all three of us off our feet. Emily clung tighter to me, her head burrowing into my shoulder. Mitchell sheathed his machete and started to herd us the way we came, but the force of the air made moving a difficult task. Leaves, twigs, debris and dirt slammed into our bodies, the peppering rubble blocking the remaining rays of sun from the tree canopy, immersing us in near darkness.

"Come on! We gotta move!" Mitchell yelled over the turbulent breeze, his hands gripping my shoulders as he tried to force me to move.

Before I could respond, the hurricane simply stopped. It was like being inside a blender turned on high and then someone pulled the plug from the wall. The churning debris fell to the ground all at once, barely making a sound as it landed on the cushy kudzu. Even though it was no longer blocking the light from the afternoon sun, the darkness hung on. The peculiar silence that had stopped us before was back and we each took a second to shake off the remaining leftovers from our hair and clothes.

"What the *hell* was that?" Emily muttered, picking a stick from her knotted hair with shaking hands.

"A slight gust?" I replied. I wiped the leaves from my own hair, once again hiding my fear through sarcasm.

"Ya'll are worried about a rush of air when it's almost dark—at 2:30 in the afternoon?" Mitchell said. He produced a flashlight from his back pocket and clicked it on, surveying the trees that surrounded us. The thin beam of light barely made a dent though the thick darkness.

"Hey, I…" Emily whined before letting out a loud gasp.

Her response didn't faze me because I had already felt what I knew she was gaping at behind me. Red-hot warmth shot through my ribcage from the back and then spread throughout my body in the blink of an eye. Burning embers of heat wrapped around my insides, the invisible aura tugged at my soul with uncaring control. I felt the glow inside me before it appeared all around us, the orangey haze illuminating the entire area with a throbbing, flame-like shimmer.

I could tell from their facial expressions that Emily and Mitchell were screaming at me, but their voices were barely above a faint whisper. They were drowned out by the thrumming vibrations that surged through me and the heavy chanting from before. The forest floor was sucked back; the dirt, leaves and kudzu vanished, leaving us standing on a two foot wide trail of fresh, black earth. As the chanting grew louder and the ground continued to quake beneath me, indentations that looked like footprints appeared on the path. When they stopped right in front of me, the heat dissipated and a cold chill enveloped me.

"*Come. Elios awaits. Fulfill your destiny. Bring your sacrif—*"

"Karmen, *now!*" Mitchell screamed. His rough hand stung as he delivered a slap that brought me out of my fugue state. I blinked the tears away and felt the terrifying energy leave my body. My knees gave out and Mitchell caught me before I hit the ground. He scooped me up and flung me over his shoulder, grabbed Emily's hand, and ran back to the safety of the cabin, the woods whizzing by in a blur as their feet pounded the ground.

What in the world was happening to us? I succumbed to the welcoming darkness.

THE THROBBING IN my temples woke me from a dreamless slumber. When I opened my eyes, I was greeted by utter darkness and for a moment, alarm bells rang inside my head. The last thing I remembered was being in the forest as wicked winds and dark chanting surrounded us. For a split second, panic ripped through me. How long had I been unconscious? Was I still in the forest? Where were Emily and Mitchell?

Relief washed over me when I recognized the soft pillow under my head and the warmth of the comforter. I was safe inside my room in the cabin. Except the room was still pitch black, not even a single star shown through the window to help, which meant I had been asleep for hours. I tried to recall what happened after the wind kicked up, but I was drawing a blank. I had no idea how, or when, we made it back to the cabin. Chunks were missing from my memory My nerves had passed the point of being on edge.

Furby purred quietly next to my head, and I reached up to stroke his soft fur. My movement stirred my bedmate, which to my surprise, was Mitchell. His light snoring filled the room with his presence and the heat that radiated from his body immediately comforted my nerves.

Unwilling to depart the warm confines of bed, I decided to remain under the covers. My body was exhausted. Every muscle ached and my head pounded relentlessly. I tried to push past the pain and concentrate on the crazy events of the past two days. It was one thing to feel like I was losing my mind but quite another to discover that the strange activity was now reaching out of my mind and tainting others.

What in the hell was going on? Why do the dead keep telling me to write?

Nothing made any sense. It simply was not possible to converse with the dead. They were just that—dead. Unlike the hokum that pervaded the entertainment industry, the paranormal was mythical, unreal musings of warped minds. A pathetic attempt to make a statement of a particular societal issue under the cover of something that didn't exist—like a love story that touts abstinence and loyalty written under the ruse of vampires and shapeshifters. Or the demonization of human sexuality during the Victorian era by interweaving sex with bloodletting and death.

And the worst travesty, at least in my opinion, was the fictional work purportedly by sixty some different writers. Works compiled over centuries that convinced meager minds that their destiny was controlled by some unseen entity that created the world then seemed bent on destroying it because we didn't conform to his ideals.

I needed to be rational about this. I tried to conjure up my staunch perceptions, to use my knowledge and not succumb to my emotions, but after today, that wasn't going to happen. I wanted to believe that my internal paranoia was so strong that somehow the negative energy that my mind created had managed to escape and seeped into the neurons of Emily and Mitchell. Could my own sickness somehow have pulled them into my lunacy through simple osmosis? The problem was that rational was just as far stretched as coming to grips that we were all experiencing something that wasn't from our plane of existence.

And that the paranormal did truly exist.

Mitchell's snoring grew louder and pulled me out of my dark meanderings. I gently poked his side to persuade him to roll over. I smiled, thankful that he had made it home safe and in one piece. It disappeared just as quick at the thought of him being drawn into the fray of whatever was going to happen next.

I had never admitted to anyone my true feelings for Mitchell—not even to him—but I was deeply in love with him. In all the books I had read throughout my life, they all spoke of a love like this that in reality seemed impossible. How ironic to find it, to feel as if you really were missing your other half. The yin to your yang. And it scared the crap out of me.

Finding out I had almost lost him forever to a bullet made me physically ill. Even with all the drama surrounding us at the moment, I took comfort in the strength that his presence had always brought since I was sixteen.

My head still thumped. I needed aspirin. Gently I climbed out from under the covers and tiptoed toward the bathroom, careful not to disturb Mitchell. Trying to navigate through the blackness was impossible and I stubbed my toe on the edge of the bedframe. I tried not to cuss out loud as the pain shot up my leg. I felt the warm trickle of blood drip from my big toe and limped into the bathroom.

I flicked on the light after shutting the door. I was shocked when I discovered the nail was split in half and oozed bright, red blood. Quickly, I grabbed a hand towel and threw it on the floor to stand on while I rummaged through the medicine cabinet for peroxide and bandages. There wasn't much except one miniscule Band-Aide and some alcohol that looked like it had been there since my childhood. I hobbled over to the bathtub and turned the water on to rinse my foot.

The cool porcelain of the tub greeted the naked backs of my thighs, instantaneously wiping away the sleepy cobwebs in my head. Wincing as the water and alcohol splashed across my foot, I heard the door creak open. Furby poked his delicate head through the opening and sauntered in, eager to see what I was doing. He hopped up on the other end of the tub and watched, his cat curiosity forcing him to ignore the fact that water was involved. He let out a small meow that almost sounded like a chirp.

"Hey, my little hairball. Look what Mommy did…humans aren't nearly as graceful in the dark as you sneaky felines are. Looks gross, huh?"

His enormous eyes stared back at me and his little, hairy form gave me a sense of tranquility. At least he wasn't losing his marbles.

The bleeding finally stopped and my toe was wrapped in the funky bandage. I turned off the water and eased off the edge, ready to head back to the warm bed that awaited me in the next room.

"Come on, Furby. It's time for…"

I froze as I watched his entire body arch in defense. Every hair stood on end as he laid his ears back, bared teeth hissing a cloud of vapor.

The room temperature had dropped and I felt the bone-chilling fear hit me. It didn't take Furby's alert to let me know that something or someone was behind me because I sensed the evil. I froze.

No, you face whatever it is, Karmen. Somehow you opened a door, a portal, an entryway of some sorts, and that means only you can close it. Turn around and face your fears before your loved ones get in too deep.

I closed my eyes and inhaled slowly, purposely and deeply, then controlled the release of my breath. It was now or never. I straightened my shoulders and clenched my fists. I willed myself to be strong and turned to face whatever was behind me.

I was prepared for another encounter with the dead author's society, perhaps even a ghost, but not what greeted my eyes, which was nothing. The bathroom was only occupied by me and Furby. I would have laughed but the room was getting colder.

"Show yourself, whatever you are. Stop playing games and just tell me what you want." My words sounded bolder than I actually felt. The temperature dropped again, the floor underneath my bare feet like a block of ice. My thin nightgown offered no protection against the frigid air, and I began to shake so hard my teeth chattered.

Silence. Even though I was freezing, I realized I wasn't in danger. Nothing was jumping out to get me. I leaned over and scooped up Furby from the edge of the tub and stepped toward the door. Anger swept over me. I was sick of this twisted mind game. Enough was enough. If fear truly fed a monster then I wouldn't show it any longer.

"Really, that's all you got? Just some arctic air, swirling wind, disembodied heads and the ability to frighten my poor cat? Well, I'm tired of it. Leave us all alone and go pester someone else!" I shouted, bolder than before.

I grasped the door handle and yanked it open a few inches when it slammed shut on its own accord. The force nearly knocked me off my feet and sent Furby sailing across the tile floor. The cold fingers that held my head the day of my interview were back, the grip so forceful it took my breath away. They wound around my body and pushed me against the back wall, holding my head in place and forcing my gaze to remain on the wall next to the door.

The surprise attack left me momentarily stunned. I should have been scared but I wasn't. I was angrier than before, the heat of my rage flowed through me as I tried to free myself from the invisible grip that held me hostage. Hot tears of anger and madness raced down my face, and I tried to open my mouth to release the obscenities that were trapped inside. I couldn't. The frosted, invisible fingers were tightly clamped around my jaw.

My bravado vanished when the bathroom wall began to move. It bulged and contracted as if it were breathing. The tan paint began to crack and crumble as a thick, viscous vapor spewed out of the crevices. The white mist converged into a large, oozing mass. The stench of sulfur and decay assaulted my senses. The room was eerily silent except for Furby's incessant hissing and growls. The noxious haze began to solidify, pulsating and shaking as it rose into the air.

This isn't happening. I'm dreaming again. Wake up, Karmen! Oh Mitchell, Emily, please, someone wake me up!

In a flash of light, the same figure from the grocery store stood in front of me but this time he was naked. His gleaming body illuminated the room with a brilliant glow of white light. His radiance temporarily blinded me, my eyes crushed closed as I fought to remain lucid. The freezing air was replaced by an intense heat that I felt not only against my skin but inside of me. I fought back with the only weapon I had—to keep my eyes shut and will myself to wake up.

"Karmen, fear not, for I am with thee. The Angel of Light has come to set captive souls bound in darkness free. God of this world, bringer of peace. Open your eyes, child, and behold my beauty."

The words weren't just spoken—I *felt* them. They were like an entity that settled over my entire body, burrowing under my skin as they adhered to every part. I was repulsed by the overwhelming sensation of doom as his words echoed in my mind, yet captivated by the powerful charisma of his voice.

The otherworldly shackles suddenly released me and I collapsed, my head striking the edge of the sink on my way down. Blackness and the alluring voice swirled around me.

"Your words shall usher in the New World, my child. They will tickle the ears of the masses, and they shall harken to them and they shall be drawn nigh to me. Listen, and record my sayings, child, for the time has come.

6

Friday Morning

JACOB ABSHIRE DID NOT WANT TO ANSWER THE phone. When he recognized the number of his lead deacon, he felt a twinge of guilt when he opted to let the machine pick it up. He would call Russell back when his head was clearer.

He had been immersed in deep meditation and prayer at his small dining table with his morning coffee. The small parsonage was his refuge and his safe haven for over twenty-two years.

On the table in front of him were the tattered family photos of his wife and daughter. They were taken in Florida the day before their fateful trip to Martin, Kentucky. Frayed and faded, the smiling faces that stared back at Jacob still brought fresh pain to his heart.

Grief was timeless and Jacob felt a lump in his throat as he picked up the delicate paper and placed a soft kiss on each face. His trembling lips whispered, "I love you," and Jacob gently placed them back inside the thin leather casing he kept them in. Once safely tucked inside, he unzipped the backpack at his feet and placed them in the side pocket. It was the last thing he needed for the journey he was embarking upon. Jacob knew that the old photos were just that, photos, but he felt that he needed them for strength.

Jacob wiped away a lone tear of sadness. He glanced around the meager surroundings that had been his home for years. The small, old farmhouse that sat on the property adjacent to the church was a place filled with a plethora of memories. Countless lonely nights had been spent behind the walls, his life as pastor at Forest Hills Baptist Church the only thing that kept him from losing his mind.

Jacob's eyes settled on the painting on the dining room wall of a beautiful garden with the words *Come unto me, I will give you rest* that was given to him by one of his church members a few weeks after the accident. His attention shifted to the heavy quilt made by several women from the church's quilting club that rested over the back of his recliner. The vibrant colors and intricate pattern a sweet testament to the loving hands that had created it, and the hope that the warmth it would provide his body could spread inside his soul as well.

Yes, the small, close knit community of Martin had welcomed Jacob with open arms. Each congregation member had offered something to their young pastor to help the broken man heal after he had suffered such a wretched beginning in their town. Jacob formed a weak smile when his stare settled on the kitchen counter, recalling that his first two years as pastor came and went without him every having to cook a meal.

The church had stood behind their broken pastor, even when Jacob succumbed to the Devil's drink. The first three years after Deborah's and Sarah's passing, Jacob found his only solace rested inside the dark bottles that Kentucky was known for—Jack Daniels whiskey. It took another four years of vigilant prayer and the help of another recovering alcoholic that had thirty-one years of sobriety, Russell Cocker, to finally bury the insatiable desire for liquor. Russell's dark experiences with the tainted drink helped Jacob to confront his heartbreak and lone-liness that threatened to destroy Jacob and his ministry.

Russell became like a second father to Jacob over the years, their tight bonds formed over twenty-two years ago, the night that Jacob's life had crumbled on the side of a dark, curvy road. When Jacob awoke for the first time in his hospital bed, Russell was there at his side. Russell took care of the funeral arrange-ments and stayed with Jacob for weeks while he recovered from his broken bones and shattered heart.

Jacob eventually found quiet solace in his role as pastor. Over the years, he watched the small children recite verses and baptized countless souls as they came to know the Lord. He had performed dozens of weddings and numerous funerals. He held Alcoholics Anonymous meetings every Tuesday and Thursday in the comfort of his home so church members wouldn't feel uneasy spilling their vile deeds within the Lord's house. Even those who attended that weren't Christians felt it was plain wrong to sully the building with their stories.

Jacob decided to head to the restroom and splash some water on his face before he called Russell back. He had sat in the uncomfortable wooden chair at the dining table too long, his lingering limp from his shattered leg more pronounced as he padded down the hallway. Once inside the bathroom, he tried to wash the memories of his past away with the cold water. All he succeeded in doing was soaking his salt and pepper hair and his shirt since his hands were still shaking.

He went back to the bedroom and grabbed the items of clothing and sat on the edge of the empty bed to lace up his hik-ing boots. He looked at the crisp sheets and wrinkle-free com-forter and felt a stab of loneliness poke at his stomach. The one and only time a female ever shared his bed had been over fifteen years ago. Another damaged soul that drowned her sorrowful life with alcohol at the bar in Manchester County—the same place Jacob thought he could hide his own descent into the bottle.

For a few months, his nights were filled with the drunken debauchery that his flesh had craved. Rayna's warm frame, when nestled against his skin after a night of passion, would help lull him to sleep. His mind would pretend that Rayna was really Deborah, but his heart ached with the guilty knowledge that she wasn't. They had an agreement that she would always be gone in the morning so his parsonage would not see her, yet the lustful images from the night before still adhered to Jacob's alcohol-soaked mind. When sober, the guilt would tear at his heart, not only for his betrayal of his wife, but because he knew he was committing the sin of fornication. After three months of reveling in his flesh, Jacob reached out to Russell and pulled his shattered spirit out of the bottle. His bed had remained cold and empty ever since.

Jacob shook the demons of his past away and grabbed his clothes off the floor. He shut the bedroom door behind him and headed back to the kitchen. He secured his few outfits in the backpack and reached for the phone to call Russell. While he waited for the call to connect, Jacob stared at the black bag next to him as his thoughts drifted over what had prompted him to leave today.

The accident site where his beloved wife Deborah and their daughter Sarah went to meet the Lord still was marked with a simple white cross. Each anniversary of that horrific day, Jacob went to the woods for a few days to commune with the Lord after placing fresh flowers under the marker. His yearly retreat to plead with the Lord for mercy, grace and strength to continue on in the wretched world, despite his earthly body's pining for Heaven and to be reunited with his family, were his private reflections on just what his faith meant to him.

But there had always been another small item that he would address each year with the Lord after his prayers and supplications for his family were over: the answers to his reoccurring dream.

A dream that began after the accident and visited him several times each year. At first, Jacob thought the young woman fleeing from an unseen attacker through the dark woods had been an older version of his daughter. The coppery, curly red hair she had looked exactly like Sarah's. Jacob thought the terrifying visions stemmed from his internal torment from the accident.

After the fifth time the dream happened, he realized the girl wasn't his daughter. He felt the dream was sent by God and while praying about it he was led to a verse in the Bible that morning from Acts 2:17:

> *And it shall come to pass in the last days, saith God, I will pour out of my Spirit upon all flesh: and your sons and your daughters shall prophesy, and your young men shall see visions, and your old men shall dream dreams.*

Somehow he knew she was a real, live person that needed his help. The disturbing visions left him with a sense of duty to the faceless woman that was at the center of them. The dream was always the same and never changed. Jacob would awaken from it with an inexplicable connection that he had felt with the redhead as she ran through the ominous woods, feeling her terror as if it were his own. He knew in his heart of hearts that there was something the Lord wanted from him. He sensed he was supposed to help her, but he wasn't sure how.

For years when Jacob would lie prostrate on the ground during his yearly retreat deep in prayer to the Lord, his last request had always been the same—for the Lord to show him what Jacob needed to do for the young woman that haunted his slumber.

Finally, only hours earlier in the predawn minutes of the morning, he awoke with the answer to not only who the poor terrified soul was, but also what his role in her life was to be.

When she ran from whatever was chasing her this time, she turned around and screamed *'Help me.'* Jacob finally saw the face that had eluded him for over twenty years. He immediately recognized her from the covers of her numerous books that graced the shelves of his library—Karmen Moncrille.

When Jacob awoke with a start and found himself covered in sweat after the dream earlier, he immediately had leapt off the bed and raced to the bathroom, releasing the wave of nausea that overwhelmed him. His fifty-eight year old body had been electrified, his feet were antsy and hands jittery when he came to terms with the fact that the now identified woman he was left on this earth to save was a famous writer.

This lost, forlorn soul had recently suffered some sort of breakdown on live television less than a week ago and came to her family's hometown to rest. Or she was here to hide from the media in the hills and hollers of Kentucky. Whatever the reason didn't matter to Jacob. He lived in a town with a population of less than one thousand; everyone knew what was going on in a matter of minutes. The phone lines would burn up from one wagging tongue to the next as the town shared the latest news over the telephone. Jacob hadn't given it much thought when his secretary remarked two days ago that "the McMann girl—Shasta's daughter" was back in town.

Of course, with the events of the last five hours, all that had changed.

Jacob had paced the floor after his morning commune with the Lord, packed and ready to leave. He knew after his first stop at the mile marker where his earlier life had ended, he would head to the farm where his new destiny awaited. He wasn't only looking at the pictures of his family but also the old maps of Floyd County to determine which road to take to Karmen Moncrille's family farm when Russell had called.

Jacob was careful to keep his voice under control and to reflect a nonchalant.

"Mornin' Pastor. Ya'll packed and ready for your vacation?"

"Sure am, Russ. However, I think this year I'm going to extend my vacation longer than just a three-day weekend. Would you be able to conduct the Wednesday night service?"

There was a long pause before Russell replied. "Well, course I can. Not a problem. Ya'll know me, I ain't afraid to preach the truth anytime, anywhere. Got lots of sermons just waitin' to be released to the flock. Ya know what I'm sayin'?" Russell replied.

"Thank you, Russ. It means a lot to me to know I can always count on you. I have some things I need to take care of and I'm not sure how long it will take." Jacob cringed at his words. He was a man of God and tried his best to conduct himself accordingly. He tried to set an example of how a follower of Christ should act. Although he wasn't flat out lying, he wasn't telling him the truth, either.

In all the years he had known Russell, he had never once lied to him. Even during the early years when Russell spent hours listening to Jacob pour out the pain in his heart at the loss of his family. Jacob's pain was embedded so deeply inside that extracting it was nearly impossible except in his silent petitions to God and to the patient, willing ears of the kind-hearted soul that was Russell. Jacob had never held anything back, revealing to Russell all of his inner torment, self-doubt, anger and questions about not only the death of his wife and daughter, but his role in the world as well.

How could he explain the mysterious woman from his dreams that he felt compelled to rescue? Russell would think he had finally snapped, and as Jacob fiddled with his coffee while he stared out into the bright morning sun that streamed across Bailey Mountain, he wondered the same thing.

"Jacob," Russell's voice was low and sympathetic, "take all the time ya need. I'll handle things here, dontcha worry 'bout that. Ya'll just get done what needs gettin' done. But, before ya go, I need to share somethin' with ya."

Jacob stood up and headed to the counter to refill his coffee, needing more caffeine to set his legs in full motion. Jacob could tell from the tone in Russell's voice that he was worried about him. He hoped Russell wouldn't ask any probing questions. Jacob took a sip of the hot coffee. "Sure thing, Russell. What is it?"

"I don't rightly know how to say it where it'll make any sort of sense, so I'll just spit it out. I had a dream 'bout you last night and when I woke up this mornin', I felt the Lord weighin' down on my heart to keep ya in my prayers. And I don't mean the normal way of prayin' for someone that's sick or in need of some guidance. I mean a heavy sense of urgency for ya safety. I ain't gonna pry, Jacob, 'cause I know it ain't none of my business. But I do know this—He has a mission for ya to do, and it is the kind that requires the fervent prayers of your brethren.

"What I'm sayin' is I got ya covered on that end. I won't stop until ya come back. I'm a sinner, just like everyone else and nowhere near righteous, but my prayers will be just as fervent as if I were a saint."

Jacob was so stunned his coffee cup slipped through his shaking fingers and crashed to the floor. The hot liquid sprayed all over his pants but he didn't notice the pain. He was too shocked by Russell's words. It took a few seconds for Jacob to recover his faculties and find his voice after he swallowed the lump in his throat.

"I...oh Russell. Truly, the Lord does work in mysterious ways. Thank you for sharing that with me and of course for your prayers. You just answered another one of my own by assuring me that I am not losing my mind. I'll admit that the thought that I was teetering on insanity has been lurking around the corners of my mind."

"Crazy? Why Jacob, ya is the sanest man I know! Now, ya listen here, and listen up good. I don't know what the Lord has in store my friend, but I do know this—that doubt is simply ol'

Satan fillin' that head of yours with lies and half-truths. Don't listen to that ol' snake's ramblin's or let his sneaky ways lead ya off the path the Lord has set ya upon. I feel the pull of the Spirit that whatever the Lord has in store for ya is big, and He laid it on my heart to tell ya these things. Now, go do His work. I'll feed the flock."

Jacob felt warm tears lingering behind his eyes. The strength and conviction of his closest friend was truly a blessing from God almighty, and infused him with renewed vigor for his journey.

"Bless you, my friend. I have a feeling that what I'm about to do will be the hardest thing I've ever faced. I promise not to falter in my faith," Jacob replied. His heart pounded in his chest but his hands were steady now. "I also know it is my cross to bear. If you don't hear from me again…"

"Then I'll just wait and let you tell me the story in Heaven, my friend. Godspeed."

Before Jacob could reply, the line went dead. He cradled the silent phone in his hand and stared at it, mesmerized by the unexpected conversation. He pulled himself back to the task at hand to finish his prep work on locating the best route to the Moncrille farm. He buzzed around the kitchen, cleaned up the mess he had made earlier and finally sat back down at the table to study the map. A few minutes later, Jacob was satisfied that he knew where he was heading. He folded and stuffed it into the side pocket of his backpack. He double checked the contents to be sure he hadn't forgotten anything. Once Jacob was satisfied he had everything needed, he knelt down by the table and prayed for strength and guidance, then grabbed his car keys. He made one last round of the house checking to be sure everything was secure.

He finished in the living room and stopped at the large bookcase that housed volumes of Bibles and study material. Two entire shelves were dedicated to end time prophesies penned by various authors. Although several of the writers differed in terms of their opinions about when, or if, the church would be called to Heaven in the Rapture spoken about in *1 Corinthians 15*, they all agreed that the world would end after the seven-year rule of the Antichrist. They also concurred that a new one would be ushered in by Jesus Christ after the end of the seven-year tribulation that the remaining inhabitants of the planet would endure.

Jacob ran his fingers over the spines of several of his favorites, his passion for studying eschatology the last ten years had almost become an obsession. *No, not an obsession—preparation.*

After all his years of study, he still hadn't picked a side. Pre-tribulation, mid-tribulation or post-tribulation viewpoints each had strong positions for their stance. All Jacob knew for sure was that the end *would* happen, whether the church was still here to endure it or not wasn't his call to make.

Images of news reports flooded his vision. The technology was available for the Mark of the Beast that each person would have to receive in order to buy or sell. A simple chip implanted either in the forehead or hand that would control every aspect of human lives had already been developed, just not implemented. The twice destroyed Temple Mount in Jerusalem, the most valuable and sought after piece of real estate in the world, was the constant focus of all three major religions. The financial state of the world hung in a precarious balance. Famine abounded. The world had abandoned their Creator and replaced Him with countless idolatrous replacements. The last prophecy that needed to be fulfilled was a brokerage of peace in the Middle East that would be sealed when the Antichrist orchestrated it.

Jacob closed his eyes and silently recited the verses ingrained into his memory from *Matthew 24*, when the disciples questioned Jesus about the end of the world:

> *³ And as he sat upon the mount of Olives, the disciples came unto him privately, saying, Tell us, when shall*

*these things be? and what shall be the sign of thy com-
ing, and of the end of the world?⁴ And Jesus answered
and said unto them, Take heed that no man deceive
you.⁵ For many shall come in my name, saying, I am
Christ; and shall deceive many.⁶ And ye shall hear of
wars and rumours of wars: see that ye be not troubled:
for all these things must come to pass, but the end is
not yet.⁷ For nation shall rise against nation, and kingdom against kingdom: and there shall be famines, and
pestilences, and earthquakes, in divers places.⁸ All these
are the beginning of sorrows.⁹ Then shall they deliver
you up to be afflicted, and shall kill you: and ye shall
be hated of all nations for my name's sake.¹⁰ And then
shall many be offended, and shall betray one another,
and shall hate one another.¹¹ And many false proph-
ets shall rise, and shall deceive many.¹² And because
iniquity shall abound, the love of many shall wax
cold.¹³ But he that shall endure unto the end, the same
shall be saved.¹⁴ And this gospel of the kingdom shall be
preached in all the world for a witness unto all nations;
and then shall the end come.*

He felt the stirrings inside of him—he sensed the end was
near. Perhaps even in his lifetime. As a faithful servant he didn't
question when, why or how. He simply believed and waited.

As he backed his ancient Chevy truck out of the short
driveway that led to the quaint parsonage that had been his
home for nearly twenty-three years, he wondered briefly if he
would ever step foot inside the welcoming walls ever again and
actually wished he wouldn't.

Jacob was ready for his role to be called up yonder. He
hummed the old hymn as he drove down the highway that once
ruined his life. This time, he felt it would redeem it.

Friday Morning

"KARMEN? KARMEN, ARE YOU ALL RIGHT? OH MY God, what happened? You're bleeding! Hold on, let me get a rag. Don't move."

I groaned in protest to the intrusion of my blessed unconsciousness. The volume of Emily's voice sounded like nails down a chalkboard. She needn't worry about me moving. My head throbbed as if Thor himself had slammed his sledgehammer into it. I struggled to pry my eyes open. The bright light made the jackhammering inside my brain even worse.

"Turn the light off," I said as I raised my arm to cover my face. Emily's hand forced my arm back down while the other applied a cold compress to the side of my head.

"I will not. I need to see if you need stitches first. Hold still." She knelt down next to me and brought her face within inches of my own.

"Stitches? Why would I need stitches?"

"Because you have about a four inch gash on the side of your head sitting on top of an egg-sized knot, that's why." Her warm fingers gently prodded my hairline.

"Ouch!" I yelped, jerking my head away. "How in the hell did I cut my head open? I kicked my foot on the bedrail not my head."

Emily motioned toward the sink. "Judging by the blood there, I would say you decided to head butt the sink. Looks like you lost. Guess you forgot that porcelain trumps flesh and bone."

"Is the blood fresh?" I sat up to look. A wave of dizziness tried to stop me, but I ignored it.

"It still looks sticky but it isn't dripping. You should be more care…what happened to your foot? Jeez Karmen, you're a mess! And why in the world did you decide to write on *paper* in the bathroom?"

"It's called trying to navigate your way around a room in the dark. Damn near lost my toenail." I followed Emily's gaze to the floor. "Write? What the hell are you…"

Before me was a pile of white parchment paper on the floor with a red fountain pen lying on top of the delicately scrolled words. I reached out and picked up a single page and noticed it was written in another language. It looked like Latin.

"Your mom is really going to hate me now that I've let her only child crack her head wide open and almost lose a toe in some unfortunate bathroom accident." I wasn't amused at her humor and shot Emily a look of irritation, then reached out with both hands for help to stand up.

"Like my mother is going to blame you for my clumsiness. It's not like she doesn't know I possess the coordination of a sixty year old drunk. I'll simply hide the evidence with my hair when we get home. As for the foreign words on those papers, I have no earthly idea. What a shock, huh?"

Emily's laugh was forced and sounded fake, which matched the look on her face perfectly. I ignored her and walked over to the bathroom mirror to survey the damage.

"Okay, spit out whatever you have to say, but remember, if it's about me and Mitchell, I don't kiss and tell. And don't start asking questions about that," I motioned at the few sheets of paper on the floor. "because I can't think about that right now. I'm sure it's some literary masterpiece written at the instructions from the dead to be dealt with later."

Emily's face reddened, her eyes darting over to the opened bathroom door then back down to the floor. She lowered her voice to a quiet whisper. "Your mom is *here.*"

I spun around and faced her then motioned for her to shut the door.

"What? When...?"

Emily closed the door as quietly as she could then turned on the water to rinse out the bloodied rag. "I don't know when she arrived. I just know she is here. When I woke up and went to the kitchen to make coffee she was already sitting at the table drinking some. Scared the bejesus out of me. Of course, after everything that has happened in the last forty-eight hours, I guess I am a little on edge. And now this."

"Great, just freaking dandy. The last thing I need is to have her under my feet and asking questions. How am I supposed to figure out what is going on with her here?"

"We, Karmen. How are *we* supposed to figure this out? Remember, whatever is going on isn't just hanging out in your head anymore. It's busted out of your noggin and spilled over into reality. Mine and Mitchell's reality."

I reached over Emily's head and opened the medicine cabinet and grabbed the aspirin, quickly downing four. Two for the current headache and two in preparation for the onslaught of another one, compliments of my mother

"Let me take a quick shower and wash all this blood off. Will you bring me some clothes and stall her?" I turned on the water in the tub. "And put these in my suitcase, will you please?"

Bending down I scooped up the ramblings of a mad woman and handed them to Emily.

Emily shut the sink off and handed me the rag and took the papers. "Sure thing. Oh, and by the way, you might want to hurry. She's chatting up Mitchell right now. If you want to revive your relationship with him, I suggest you make it quick. When I left her in the kitchen she was dressing him down for not calling you while he was in Iraq. He looked appalled."

I moaned and shooed her out of the bathroom. The last thing any of us needed right now was my mother's incessant babbling. It wasn't that I didn't love her. But trying to keep her occupied while we figured out why the dead were terrorizing all three of us was another stressor that we didn't need.

While the hot water cascaded down my tense muscles, I tried to remember the events of the night before. I remembered waking up next to Mitchell and then nearly ripping off my nail on the way. After that everything was blank. I had no recollection of dreaming or visions. Nothing to shed light on how the fancy papyrus sheets and fountain pen got on the floor. I sure as hell didn't bring them with me. I had anything associated with writing at home until I figured out what was going on.

I couldn't shake the uneasy feeling that something was wrong. Part of me wanted to try and decipher the words on the pages to see what message the dead had sent, but the other part was screaming to burn the pages and let it go. I opted to do neither until I dealt with the other problems that required my immediate attention.

Ten minutes later I was dressed and all the evidence of the previous night was hidden. My sore toe was stuffed inside my tennis shoe and my hair styled to cover the bruise. I glanced in the mirror and cringed at the dark circles under my eyes knowing my mother would immediately see them and start worrying about my health. I hoped that Emily had thrown away the empty wine bottles and hidden her stash of weed. If my mother sensed any use of narcotics or alcohol, she would completely flip out.

Having a restful vacation just flew right out the window.

Dammit.

"WELL, IT'S ABOUT time you graced us with your lovely presence, sleepyhead," my mother cooed. She rose from her spot in the kitchen to greet me with a kiss and to get a closer look at me.

"Morning, Mom." I quickly kissed her cheek and returned her hug and scooted over to the coffee pot, busying my nervous hands while I poured a cup. "Gee, did you miss me that much? I've only been gone for two days."

She clucked in mock irritation. "Why Karmen, of course I missed you! But that isn't why I trekked all the way from New York back to these hills. A very important day is coming up on Monday. I haven't missed the first twenty-two, and I'm not about to miss the twenty-third."

I had to force myself not to roll my eyes. Geesh, it wasn't like twenty-three was a pivotal birthday or something. After the extravagant celebration she hosted when I turned twenty-one, she couldn't have topped it if she tried. Maybe she just wanted to come and veg out on the farm with me and Emily.

Yeah, right.

"Come, bring your coffee and sit down. Have some bagels, fresh from Breinstein Bakery. Well, they were fresh when I bought them," she said, pointing to the dining area. Mitchell and Emily sat on opposite ends of the table, each doing their best not to laugh. Emily stared out the window and Mitchell examined the contents of his coffee cup, but both of them watched with amusement. For a brief second, I thought about tripping and flinging my hot coffee over the both of them, but then decided the aromatic liquid would serve me better if I drank it.

I followed my mother and sat down, turning my head so the sunlight was on the back of my hair and not my face. As usual, she was dressed impeccably, every hair in place and her jewelry, although minimal, was crafted by the finest designers. Looking at her outer perfection always made me feel self-conscious about my nonchalant attitude toward clothes and makeup. Her uptown haute couture and snobbish attitude didn't fit with the roots of her upbringing, and even though the cabin had been totally renovated and updated, I felt her tension just sitting in the place that reminded her of her humble beginnings.

The wheel of ideas to get my mom out of the cabin and onto some project was spinning around in my head faster than a hamster high on cocaine. Unfortunately, the manic pace produced the same results—nothing. I decided to stuff my mouth with a stale bagel instead.

"So darling, when were you going to tell me that Mitchell came home all the way from Iraq just to celebrate your birthday?"

I choked and concentrated on not spitting my breakfast all over her four hundred dollar shirt. "Mom!"

She held up her manicured hand and stopped me. "Karmen, don't talk with your mouth full. It's not ladylike."

I managed to swallow the remaining food and took a heavy swig of coffee to chase it down before I responded, doing my best to keep my anger under control. Before I could respond, Mitchell interjected.

"Ms. Moncrille, as I was tryin' to tell you earlier, I didn't come home to celebrate Karmen's birthday, though that is a lovely idea." He spoke slowly with carefully chosen words, his eyes locked on my mother. "I came here to take over the store after Uncle Randy passed away."

It was rare my mother was ever taken aback, and when it happened, it was usually hilarious. But there were limits to what even I considered humorous and death ranked up there at number one.

Mom's hands instinctively fluttered to her ample chest and she let out a small gasp of shock. "Mitchell, I'm so sorry. Randy was a good man. When did this happen? Did I already miss his services?"

"Yes, ma'am. It was last week. He's restin' at Turner Cemetery out on Highway 25 if you would like to go pay your respects."

Mom was no longer looking at Mitchell and turned her gaze back on me. Mitchell winked, and I wanted to kiss him for his brilliance to get my mother out of the cabin for a while. My excitement was short lived.

"Karmen, did you know this?"

"Yes, mother, but I just found out..."

"Don't trifle me with your excuses. A longtime friend of the family passes and you can't even take two minutes out of your *vacation* to call me? I'm appalled at your lack of ..."

That was it. I'd heard enough. "Mom! Enough. I didn't call you because I only found out yesterday, which just so happened to coincide with the surprise visit by Mitchell. I was not aware that he had returned from Iraq or that anyone with connections to us had passed away. I would have told you. I am not some heartless, unfeeling person for God's sake."

My outburst caused the room to fall silent. Even Furby had stopped crunching on his breakfast in the corner and scurried off to hide. I rarely ever yelled and certainly never directed my anger at my mother. Emily and Mitchell knew the reasons behind my short fuse, but my mother didn't, and I immediately felt guilty for lashing out at her.

"Karmen, I realize you are under a great amount of duress after your botched interview and the recent turn of events during the past two days that you *so eloquently* just shared with me.

However, I don't believe that is all that is bothering you. Would you kindly fill me in... What happened to your head!"

During my tirade, I must have loosened the bandage on my temple because I felt the warm trickle of blood race down my face. I watched it land on the wooden table. Before I could answer, the rapid fire questions I had been dreading exploded out of her.

"Karmen, you're bleeding! How did you cut yourself? Do we need to get you to the hospital? Emily, Mitchell, why didn't you inform me that Karmen was hurt? Why..."

"Mom, please. If you will stop for just a moment and let me talk, I'll happily answer all of your questions."

Emily rose and went to the sink and grabbed a dishtowel, then snagged a few pieces of ice from the freezer. She wrapped the makeshift compress tight and silently brought it to me. I smiled half-heartedly and held it gently against the knot that was not only bleeding again, but throbbing in time with my rapid, irritated heartbeat.

Mom narrowed her and gave me a curt nod to continue.

"I had to use the restroom last night and I stumbled in the dark and hit my head on the sink in the bathroom. It's deep, but not enough that it requires stitches. The impact sort of rang my bell, and I still have a headache, so I apologize for snapping at you. You know me, klutzy as ever."

I should have let Emily or Mitchell explain because I wasn't a very good liar. Mom instantly knew I wasn't telling the complete truth. I could see it in her eyes. She didn't say a word. She leaned over and motioned for me to move the ice so she could inspect the wound. As she poked and prodded with the ease that comes only from numerous times of performing the same task on an accident-prone child, she shifted her feet under the table. Her high heel caught the edge of my big toe and I jerked in response.

"What's wrong with your foot, Karmen? I suppose you hit that, too?"

I gave her a sheepish grin in response.

Mom stood up and placed her hands on her hips as she took turns staring at us. After what seemed like an eternity, she grabbed her empty coffee cup and sauntered over to the coffee pot for a refill. For a minute, I thought she was going to let it go, but I knew I couldn't get that lucky.

"Karmen, I believe that there is something you aren't telling me, and that it is a very *important* something. Is it because we need to be alone to discuss whatever it is, or are you three conspiring to keep me out of the know? Spill. I've got all day."

I felt the burning stares of Emily and Mitchell, but I refused to look at them. I found myself almost mesmerized by my mother's probing eyes, her worry and love overriding her maternal irritation. Something inside of me nudged me to come clean, to tell her the truth. After all, she was my flesh and blood, the person that had doted upon me ever since I took my first lungful of air.

I sighed heavily, a signal that both Emily and Mitchell sensed was my resignation and the fact that I was about to drop the paranormal bomb on my mother. Mitchell shook his head while Emily opted for a verbal plea.

"Karmen, don't. She won't believe…"

Mom was across the kitchen floor in two long strides. She sat back down and grabbed my hand, shushing Emily with the other.

"Karmen, I'm here baby. I promise to believe whatever you have to say. What is it? What's going on?"

I looked at Emily and Mitchell for support. Hot tears welled up in my eyes as the enormity of sharing our perverted secret hit home. Once I spoke the words there would be no turning back. What if I dragged my mom into this paranormal realm by telling her? Then again, if there was one person, other than Uncle

Cy, that was completely grounded and could help us find a plausible, rational explanation for what was going on, my mother was at the top of my list.

Emily and Mitchell both rose from the table simultaneously, their movements swift and almost choreographed with perfect precision. Emily motioned with her eyes to head to the porch, and I knew she was right. The last two times I unleashed my story, I couldn't keep my feet still.

And I knew this time would be no different.

"Come on, Mom. Let's take the coffee and head out to the porch. This story is going to take a while."

I HEARD MITCHELL'S stomach growl with hunger. We had been outside over four hours as one by one we each recounted our recent bouts with the supernatural. I went first, then Emily and then Mitchell. Exactly in the order everything had happened, from beginning to end. The only thing I held back was my still unknown nighttime escapades in the bathroom that produced the garbled words in some odd language. I wasn't quite ready to drop that just yet. I wanted my mother to digest everything we had just thrown onto her lap.

For the first time I could ever recall my mother had been speechless. She never once interrupted. She simply listened while her senses took in every nuance and word we said. Her face displayed a roller coaster of emotions from disbelief to shock to fear. When Mitchell finished his last sentence her face was unreadable. She held her emotions at bay while three eager sets of eyes stared at her, awaiting her thoughts and opinions.

She took a sip of cold coffee. Her keen eyes never broke the stare with mine.

"I believe you and Emily have something else to share? There's a look."

Jesus, she was like a human lie detector. Were we that obvious? "There's no look, Mom," I said, hoping she would just drop it.

"Honey, one day when you are a parent, you will recognize the look a mile away. I see it shining like a beacon on both of your foreheads. You've already told me enough to give me nightmares until I'm one hundred, so please don't hold back now. How can I help resolve this if you keep what could be important facts from me?"

Emily and I immediately exchanged glances, both of us on the same wavelength. I nodded my head and she disappeared inside. I turned my focus back to my mother. "You're right, and I'm sorry. We weren't trying to be evasive, we just…well we don't know what to think about this latest twist."

"Honey, maybe once the final, most recent piece is put on the table, we all can work together to solve this puzzle?"

"The problem with that is I don't remember anything. Again." I plopped down next to her on the swing. She reached out and held my hand. I had a flashback to two nights ago when I was in the very same spot telling my darkest fears and experiences to Emily.

Emily came out and handed the folded papers to me. I saw her hand was shaking. While I fumbled to open up the pages, she sat next to Mitchell on the railing. The look of confusion on his face almost made him look like a little boy for a split second.

"Like I said earlier, I did wake up in the middle of the night. The next thing I remember was the bathroom becoming incredibly cold. Then nothing until Emily came in this morning. And we found this."

A shudder of fear made me jerk as I handed the papers to my mother. Her eyes were wide with confusion as she gingerly grasped the pages.

"What did you write, Karmie?" Mitchell said with concern. He walked behind my mother and tried to read over her shoulder. His perplexed look when he saw the foreign language was just as strong as my own had been.

"That's just it, Mitch. I have no idea. Again, not only do I have no recollection of writing anything, but I seemed to have learned another language overnight. I think, but I'm not sure, that it might be in Lat—"

"Latin," my mother finished. Her lips moved in silence as she read the dainty script.

My mouth hung open in shock. I didn't think my mom's reaction to our tale of paranormal visitations would make her bolt for the hills, but I also didn't expect her to be so calm.

"You read and understand Latin? Wow, I'm impressed. So tell us, what does it say? Is it a cure for cancer handed down from the sages of past generations, or am I prophesizing the next apocalypse or something?" I replied sarcastically.

"Well, I *used* to be able to read Latin, but this—well—it's a mess. The sentences make no sense. There are just a bunch of jumbled words with no cohesive flow or meaning, almost like it's written backward or missing sections or something. And I don't believe these marks here and here," she motioned to some strange looking symbols on the pages, "are anything I have ever seen before."

"Why doesn't *that* surprise me?" I said, my irritation rising. The message, and the messenger weren't doing a very good job.

"Perhaps it isn't Latin at all. After all, it's been years since I have read anything written in the ancient language." Mom stood up and walked to the front door.

"Mitchell, is there still a fax machine at the store?"

"Yes, in the back. Why?"

"Because I believe I know someone that could translate this, but I need to fax it. I don't think reading it over the phone would work. Would you mind driving me? I'm sort of sick of being behind the wheel."

"Sure thing, Mz. Moncrille. Let me just go get my keys," Mitchell said as he held the door open for my mom. They disappeared inside and left Emily and me on the porch.

We both looked at each other and our silence spoke volumes. Each of us lost in our thoughts and my mother's strange reaction to our stories.

"Karmen, don't you worry about all of this honey," my mom said as they came back out. "We'll get to the bottom of it. I believe that once these words are deciphered," she waved the paper in her hand, "that will be the start. Will you two please lay off this stuff until I get back? That might help you both keep things in better perspective."

Mom held Emily's bag of weed in her other hand, dangling it like a slow moving pendulum. Emily looked like she wanted to crawl under the nearest rock, but I just fumed. I *knew* she would think all of this was just some drug-induced paranoia if she found the dope, which Emily obviously didn't hide very well. Or, Mom was just a phenomenal sleuth. Either way, it didn't matter because she found it and the quizzical look about our stories danced across her face. Her smug look of triumph caused me to explode.

"This has *nothing* to do with that!" I shouted, trying to yank the baggie out of her hand. She was faster than I gave her credit for and moved her hand at lightning speed. The look of doubt on her face enraged me. I leapt to my feet and faced her eye-to-eye, forcing my voice to remain low as I growled out my response.

"Let me make this crystal clear because I obviously failed to do so earlier. Up until two days ago, I have never ingested any type of drug except an occasional aspirin. And apparently you didn't hear the first part of my story where I said that the *dead* have been visiting me and writing my books since I was sixteen. I shouldn't have kept that secret to myself for so long, but to be honest, I thought I was crazy."

I shook with fury—from all the fear, panic and rage that had been bottled up inside me over the past six years. The repressed feelings finally had peaked and flew out of my mouth in one uncontrollable outburst, delivered within inches from my mother's pale, surprised face.

"And after what Emily and Mitchell have experienced *when they were stone cold sober, I might add,* I am filled with relief at the knowledge that I'm not insane, and terrified of what all this means at the same time. So please, stop treating us like we're drug addicts that are suffering from wild hallucinations, and *help us* figure out what is going on before I truly *do* lose my mind. Or worse. Right now I'm pretty freaking scared that something horrible is about to happen."

Mom's eyes were wide pools of shock. She stuttered at first, completely taken aback by my display of raw anger. She opened her mouth to answer, but her words were drowned out by the Gregorian chants that suddenly surrounded the cabin— the eerie humming louder than it had ever been before.

Bet she believes us now.

Panic lit a fire under her feet. Mom spun around and practically shoved Mitchell down the stairs to the truck. They left a cloud of gravel and dust in their wake as he drove like a bat out of hell to town. I couldn't hear my exasperated sigh over the loud, incessant chanting.

I glanced over at Emily, both hands clamped down over her ears in a vain attempt to muffle the noise. Her entire body was trembling, and despite the rising fear within me, I overrode it with the waves of regret I felt for putting Emily in this situation. The anger from only minutes ago raged back, fueled by remorse for involving my loved ones and overwhelming feeling of helplessness that threatened to swallow me whole.

"Leave them alone! It's me you want, so *tell me what you want from me!*" My lungs expelled the words with such force that I almost collapsed onto the steps of the porch.

The instant the last syllable left my throat, the chanting stopped. The only sound was the thumping of my heart and Emily's soft sobs. I turned and held her close as we tried to comfort each other.

Friday Afternoon

KIROLY ADAMIK STARED OUT THE WINDOW INTO the expansive sea of white, cumulous clouds that floated underneath the roaring engines of the Airbus A380. Prince Al Fashawan of Dubai had insisted that Kiroly make his triumphant trip to the U.N. Headquarters in New York in style, especially after the successful outcome of their meeting yesterday. Kiroly smiled at the memory, his perfectly white teeth glinted in the late afternoon sun that streamed through the small window.

The aroma of the freshly prepared meal of curried lamb and other Middle Eastern delicacies still lingered inside the enormous cabin, along with the sour attitude of the chef. The Prince had spared no expense in supplying Kiroly with every possible pleasure or need on his long flight, including the use of his personal cook. The stocky, rotund man had been incensed when Kiroly had waived off the dinner earlier and stormed off in a huff. Kiroly's smile curved into a wicked smirk. He never forgot a face or name, and Kiroly had plans for the pompous blowhard once they landed at JFK. The insolent prick would never cook another meal when Kiroly finished with him. Prince Al Fashawan would have to procure the services of a new cook.

Kiroly took a slow, deliberate sip of the remaining champagne in his glass. Food wasn't of interest to him tonight, and after the events of yesterday, he knew it never would be again. But, he was in the mood to celebrate his victory, and his change, with a bottle of Armand de Brignac compliments of the grateful Prince.

The other gifts the Prince had supplied Kiroly to pass the long, thirteen hour flight with were six of the Prince's favorite voluptuous party favors. The luscious, young women were ripe for the picking and ready to satisfy any fantasy that Kiroly might have. His Hungarian blond locks, lithe, muscular frame, translucent blue eyes and charming personality worked like a magnet not only on women, but men as well. The horny sluts had practically drooled when he first boarded the flight hours ago.

The six-pack of wanton whores had retired to the large master suite after Kiroly's rejection of their advances, their disappointment almost as palpable as the chef's anger. Kiroly hoped they were keeping themselves occupied by screwing the demoralized chef back into a state of bliss, since that would be the last bit of human contact he would enjoy before he ceased to exist in this world.

The fleshly lusts of most men, even the ones that liked to tout themselves as pious and pure, would have been too difficult to dismiss when the sexy sirens turned on the charm. They had been eager; however, Kiroly simply wasn't swayed by their open sexuality and eagerness to please.

His diabolical desires lay elsewhere and besides—he was no longer a man—he only inhabited the body.

What the soul of the former Kiroly had hungered for was absolute power and nothing less. At only thirty years old, his meteoric rise to the rank of Prime Minister of Hungary then achieving the rank of President of the European Council at age twenty-seven quickly became a legend throughout the world. His charming wit, insightful problem solving skills, and incredible intelligence naturally drew people to him, even as a small child in Hungary.

It was, after all, what he was born to do. And Kiroly finally got what he had sacrificed and prayed for all his life.

He was the Antichrist. At least his flesh was. Kiroly's soul was destroyed and sent to the abyss for eternity when Heylel penetrated his flesh yesterday.

The in-dwelling of Kiroly's physical body had been as simple as stepping inside a well-worn suit. As it should have been— Heylel had transferred his spirit into countless men over the millennia. It was one thing to invade the dreams or worm his way into the weak minds of the inhabitants of the earth, laughing as they heeded his suggestions of indulging in their wanton needs. It was quite another to completely control the host from the inside after obliterating their soul.

Kiroly's charisma negotiated the highly secretive meeting with the figureheads that assumed they controlled the Middle East. His slick tongue and effortless ability to lull both warring sides into a false sense of security brought them all to the negotiating table to talk. But it wasn't until Heylel's spirit absorbed Kiroly's flesh that the actual agreement was solidified with ink, the signatures of the dueling sides hesitantly scrawled on the dotted lines.

The signed treaty that would bring peace to the Middle East for the first time—ever—was now locked securely inside the steel-encased attaché in the seat next to him. Heylel's announcement to the world that he had procured a lasting, seven-year peace pact between Israel and Palestine would be announced in front of the U.N. General Assembly on Monday afternoon. The broadcast was scheduled to be on every single news outlet for the entire globe to watch.

Heylel was beyond ecstatic. Over the centuries he had come close to taking what was rightfully his, but each time he overtook the body and soul of his chosen instrument, he was met with opposition. Heylel felt his anger well up, the heat so intense that wisps of smoke wafted from the singed skin on his hand. He immediately checked his anger and focused on his triumph of securing the covenant with the multitudes. The next to last item, and one that had never been accomplished before, was the last remaining obstacle before the roaring lion took over the world.

This was his destiny, his time to reign supreme over the Earth and all the mite-like inhabitants. What his essence had pined for since the moment of his creation. Yet, he had been punished by the One who made him for striving to live up to the potential he was given, which was a complete oxymoron.

The human's beloved phrase, *The Lord giveth and the Lord taketh away* was, after all, said to him as Michael tossed him out of the heavens. The Supreme Being of the universe had a sick perception of fairness. After all, it wasn't *his* idea to be created by *Elohim* as the most beautiful and wisest of all the angels. Why was he banned from the glory of Heaven for taking pride in the endowments bestowed upon him?

It mattered no more. Heylel had unleashed his anger at his punishment on the pathetic souls that *Jehovah* loved so much. They were like warm molding clay—so simple to manipulate and form into any twisted shape he desired that it almost wasn't fun anymore. Humans were feeble minded yet more full of pride than Heylel ever had been. The more he suggested a new form of cruelty or debauchery, the more they latched on to it and ran, blinded by their own dark desires and insatiable appetites.

The last two hundred years had produced the biggest leaps in humanity in terms of technology and knowledge, but it also brought a complete and utter denial of not only the concept of God—which didn't bother Heylel one iota—but the dismissal of His *coming* as well. Ingrained human instincts that recognized from birth their existence has been numbed by the onslaught of what the stupid humans liked to call *knowledge*.

After his ascent to power and his upcoming speech at the U.N. on Monday, all that would change. The words written that would alter the hearts and minds of the disbelieving masses would bend to his will the minute they were spoken from his lips. The world would know, without a shadow of doubt, who ruled it.

And the entire population would cower at his feet once he spoke the lie that would enslave them. The little bitch he had been terrorizing by invading her dreams needed to finish. She was the chosen one. Heylel had watched the sacrifice that his devote followers, Elios and the others, made to gift her with that role. After Heylel's visit with her last night, he knew she had written it, but he also knew that the words were unintelligible drivel until the final sacrifice was made.

Heylel decided to enjoy some fleshly lusts. It had been a long time since he felt the quaking of a woman under him. It was just an added bonus that there was a male to ravage as well. Besides, it would occupy his time while he waited for the completion of the ritual. Once he possessed the flesh of his chosen vessel, his power was limited. When he was in the ethereal realm, he had the ability to stalk the minds of his prey across the globe, but when encased inside the bonds of flesh, he did not and that agitated Heylel even more.

Heylel could hear the practiced, coy giggles of the wenches in the other room, followed by a slight groan of pleasure from the chef. The face that once belonged to Kiroly Adamik grinned as he stripped off his clothes and headed to the bedroom. Wouldn't they be in for a surprise when he revealed his true self?

As he reached the door and clasped the handle he was stopped by the notification from his private phone. Only one person had that number, and they knew they weren't to use it until it was time. In the blink of an eye, Heylel was across the cabin and snatched the phone to his ear.

"My trusted one, you have news for me?"

"Yes, my lord. It has been sent to you on the secured server. The offering will be tonight. Then, my king, you shall reign supreme!"

Heylel's excitement could no longer be contained inside the confines of the pitiable flesh. He had to release his exuberance, and he knew exactly how he would do that. His fiery eyes never left the bedroom door.

"Excellent work, Elios. Well done, my servant. I suggest you celebrate, as I shall. It's been quite a while since I have enjoyed the sensations of the flesh. Prince Fashawan was kind enough to supply me some entertainment. I believe I shall indulge."

Heylel disconnected the call, and his vile yearnings overtook him. When he opened the door the women were all draped around the bed, each taking turns with the frumpy chef. They startled as he entered the room, the stench of death following him in plumes of white smoke that seemed to leak from his every orifice.

He smiled, exposing his elongated, yellow teeth, and releasing more putrid smells into the room. "Ladies and gentlemen, welcome to your worst nightmare."

Their screams of agony paled in comparison to the growls of pleasure from Heylel.

Early Friday Evening

MY FEET HURT FROM ALL THE PACING. I PADDED back and forth like a caged jungle cat across the expanse of the porch, waiting for Mitchell and my Mom to return. They were gone for hours and Emily and I were both starting to worry. I looked at my friend curled up into a tight ball on the Adirondack chair at the far end of the porch. In the fading glow of the late afternoon sun, her disheveled hair and streaks of makeup had run down her face making her look like a war refuge. Pangs of guilt at seeing her so upset were eating away at my insides.

"I'm going to get some water. Do you want some?" I said, pausing at the screen door. Emily immediately rose to her feet and walked over to me. Her eyes betrayed her fright.

"I need something to drink, but water wasn't what I had in mind," she said through forced laughter. I held the door open and she stepped inside. I knew that she hated being left alone and I couldn't blame her. We were wide awake yet living a nightmare.

We hadn't spoken much since Mom and Mitchell left for town. Both of us were wrapped up in our own thoughts, desperate to put the odd puzzle pieces together. None of this made any sense. Supernatural phenomenon was strictly for the movies, not reality. But that was the only explanation—we were experiencing something from another realm. Hopefully, some answers would be gleaned if Mom was successful in getting the nonsensical words transcribed.

I headed to the fridge and snagged a bottle of water. Emily went straight to the cabinet and grabbed a wine glass and froze in place, refusing to open the refrigerator door. Her enormous eyes pleaded with mine for help.

"Oh, sorry. Here," I said and grabbed a bottle of Riesling. "Guess this means I'm cooking dinner as well, huh?"

"I don't plan on eating anything. Maybe ever again. You're on your own for food. Sorry," Emily said, snatching the cold bottle from me and filling the glass to the rim. "I plan on just drowning my stress in booze. It always worked when my heart was broken, so I'm hoping it works just for our current situation.

"Emily, you need to eat. Let me fix you a sandwich," I said, reaching past her to retrieve the bread. "If you drink as heavily as I suspect you plan to then you are going to have an intimate relationship with the toilet all night if you don't put something in your stomach first."

"Hey, at least if I'm puking, I won't be thinking about anything else. Wish I still had a bit of smoke left. Now *I'm* the one that needs to relax." She took a huge gulp of wine. "I also understand why our priest keeps wine stashed everywhere. You need to be on the sauce when dealing with evil spirits."

Had Emily made that sort of comment any other time, I would have railed on her about the absolute absurdity of not only the priesthood, but also the consideration of evil spirits. But, after the events of the past few days, I held my tongue.

"Come on, I don't feel like hanging out in the kitchen. Gives me the creeps." Emily brushed past me into the living room. It looked like I wouldn't be fixing her something to eat after all.

"Let me grab our sweaters. It's starting to get chilly outside," I yelled over my shoulder as I veered off toward our rooms. "Hang on."

She stopped at the door and waited until I came back. Once outside, we settled back onto the porch swing, each instinctively scrunching closer together, just as we had done when we were little.

"Karmen?"

"Yes?"

"May I tell you something without you getting all pious and huffy?" Emily said into my shoulder. Her words were muffled since her head was buried against my skin. I sensed her apprehension and kept my sarcastic comments to myself.

"Of course. Spill."

"I know you don't believe the same way I do, and the thought of Heaven, Hell and an afterlife makes you cringe, but I truly believe that you are in danger. Not just physically, but spiritually. We generally don't discuss religion, but this isn't about one belief system over another. Sometimes, I get confused by all the differences that each sect preaches so I try to just stick with the basics. I believe in God. I believe that when we die, we live on in one or two places, the location determined by the way we lived our lives on Earth. But what I want to bring home here is the fact that all this strange activity is centered around you. And, quite frankly, I am scared for you."

Emily sat up straight and clutched my hand, her fingers trembling as they wound around mine. I wanted to interject, but kept my lips sealed and let her ramble. Her eyes locked onto mine as she continued with renewed fervor.

"The simple facts are that you have been visited, and possibly led by, beings that don't exist in our world. Call them ghosts, call them demons, call them whatever you like, but whatever you decide to name them doesn't change the facts of what has happened. You said it yourself that the dreams started a little over six years ago. You were given words, no, *books*, in them. You experienced visions that changed your life and made you a household name. I'll admit when you first told me I thought maybe you had been sleepwalking since you said you had no recollection of writing the stories. But then the dreams broke the plane into your reality—and then ours. The underlying question that we need to figure out is why and what this...this *contact* with the other side means."

I sighed heavily and stood up. She was so emphatic, so sure of herself and her beliefs and I was still waffling back and forth about mine. As her friend, I accepted her views although I didn't agree with them. But she was right about one thing. I needed to determine *what* I was supposed to be writing and why.

I was saved from having to formulate an answer when Mitchell's truck horn blared as it sped up the driveway. Thank goodness, because I wasn't sure what I would have said.

"It's about time! Let's hope Mom has some answers." I jumped down the stairs and ran out to greet them, Emily right on my heels.

"May I at least exit the vehicle before you accost me, Karmen?" my mother said, her voice heavy with irritation. I could immediately tell from the furrowed lines on her forehead that she didn't know any more than when she left.

"Hey, will ya'll help with the groceries? Your mom damn near bought out the Piggly-Wiggly," Mitchell said, his smile bright but his eyes full of concern as he looked at me.

Emily and I helped lug the plastic sacks from the back of Mitchell's truck as I watched my mother walk slowly up the steps toward the house. Her posture was all wrong. She looked dejected, her carriage of a defeated woman. Never had I seen her look anything but regal and poised. I scrambled up the steps and followed her into the house, determined to find out exactly what she did today.

"MS. MONCRILLE, THAT was 'bout the finest meal I've had in years! Nothin' like some rib-stickin' southern cookin', I'll tell ya. MRE's keep ya fit, but not satisfied."

Mitchell patted his swollen belly and smiled. At least one of us had an appetite. Emily managed three bites of mashed potatoes to go along with her nearly empty bottle of wine. I kept down one chicken leg and a few bites of green beans, but that was it. Mom had a full plate but simply pushed her food around, giving the illusion that she was eating.

I stood up and took my plate to the sink and started the job of cleaning up the enormous mess she had made while cooking.

"All right Mom, you've stalled for two hours now. I need to hear what you found out today."

"*We* need to hear," Emily interjected.

Mom remained seated at the table. Her amber eyes scanned ours. She nodded and brought her plate to the sink and put it down into the soapy water. Holding up a slender finger, she signaled for us to wait while she retrieved her bag.

Emily and I busied our hands with the dishes while Mitchell cleared the table. The air was thick with anticipation and worry. Mom returned with the crinkled pages clasped in her fist.

"Leave these until tomorrow. I'm going to fix a strong pot of coffee and we are all going to sit down and discuss the contents of what you wrote, Karmen. And trust me when I say it's going to be a long night. I'll bring the coffee out directly. Please wait for me on the porch. Bring blankets."

"THE WORDS SEEM to be Latin-based, with a smidgeon of Arabic and Hebrew. Some of the symbols took a while to determine their origin, but the consensus is they are an ancient form of hieroglyphics."

I was sandwiched between Emily and Mitchell on the swing, a long afghan covering our laps. Mom sat across from us as she poured steaming coffee then gently handed a hot mug to each of us.

"The placement of the words seems haphazard, but we believe it is some sort of coded message. It might take some time to translate after we figure out *how* to decode it."

I took a sip of coffee and let those words sink in. "We? Who did you send the fax to, Mom?"

"Uncle Cy," she said as she settled back into the chair.

I almost dropped my coffee mug. Why hadn't *I* thought about that? Of course! Uncle Cy was the most intelligent man I knew, and if he couldn't figure out the words he certainly had the contacts to for help

Unable to sit still any longer, I flung the blanked back and stood up. "So, what *could* he determine?"

Mom ran her hand over the paper that sat in her lap, smoothing out the wrinkled pages. She hesitated, gathering her thoughts. The woman that I had always known was cool-headed and never flustered. But the woman that sat in front of me wasn't, and that scared me almost as much as everything else.

Mitchell and Emily saw her fear and they looked just as worried. Mitchell, the saint that he was, reached his hand over and patted my mom's shoulder.

"It's okay, Mrs. Moncrille. Tell us. Whatever it is, we'll work through it. We'll stand together and face whatever it is, dontcha worry none about that. This ol' boy don't run from anybody or anything that tries to mess with his gal."

Mitchell turned his face toward mine for a split second and winked. I felt the love hit me right in my heart.

For the first time in my life, I saw tears in my mom's eyes. I knew what she was about to tell us would change all of our worlds forever. I took a heavy gulp of coffee then knelt down in front of her.

"What did Uncle Cy figure out, Mom?" I whispered, my own tears appearing in response to hers.

She cleared her throat and blinked several times. Her answer was a garbled whisper, her eyes filled with pain and terror as she looked down at me. "That something evil has been unleashed by you and it's coming to seek and destroy."

"Why would something want to seek and destroy Karmen?" Emily asked in astonishment.

Mom looked at Emily. "Not just Karmen. All of us."

I lost my balance and fell onto my ass on the cold hardwood. My vision started to spin and the sounds around me faded. Gone were the voices of my mother, Mitchell and Emily that I heard mere seconds before. They were replaced by the infernal chanting and the numerous voices of the dead screaming in my head...

"It is time, Karmen."

"Time for what?" I screamed before the darkness took me over.

THE ODDLY FAMILIAR sound of meowing in the distance woke me up. My head was fuzzy and when I opened my eyes, my vision was blurred. I tried to sit up and when I moved my stiff limbs, a wave of nausea slammed me back down. I turned my head and clawed my way to the edge of the porch and wretched violently.

My throat burned like I had just swallowed a flaming sword. I remained still and gulped the cool night air into my heaving lungs and willed the cobwebs to disappear. After a few seconds, I felt the dizziness pass and sat up. I waited for my eyes to adjust to the darkness. Panic already had begun to well up inside of me when I realized I was alone.

"Mom? Emily? Mitchell?"

The only thing I heard was another meow. I looked up and saw Furby sitting on the windowsill, his furry feet pawing at the glass. I rolled over onto all fours and maneuvered my wobbly legs under me. I pushed aside the urge to vomit again and stood up. Stumbling, I made my way to the railing and held on for support while I scanned the vast expanse of my yard for signs of life.

All their vehicles sat silently in the driveway. I breathed a heavy sigh of relief when I realized they were still here. That relief was quickly replaced by irritation. *Why did they leave me on the porch alone? The last thing I could remember was eating dinner and I didn't recall drinking any alcohol, so why was my memory so foggy?*

Anger overrode everything else and I stormed inside, ready to give them all a piece of my pissed off mind. "Anyone care to explain why I was left on the porch like yesterday's garbage?" I yelled out to no one in particular. Furby jumped off his perch and trotted over to me, his huge tail wrapping around my legs. I bent over and picked him up, hugging him tightly to my chest as I headed to Emily's room.

"Emily, why in the hell did you..."

I snapped my mouth shut when I realized her room was empty, her bed untouched. Her purse, keys and luggage sat in the same spot as before. The green-eyed monster of jealousy reared its ugly head as the images of her in bed with Mitchell exploded inside my head.

No, stop it Karmen! There is no way that either of them would do that to you. Besides, your Mom is here. A parental figure in the next room is not exactly an aphrodisiac.

"All right, guys. This is so not funny. After everything that has happened, you want to freak me out even more? Come on, fun's over." I opened the door to my room and froze in my tracks when I saw it was also empty. My bags sat silently next to my mother's, unopened. Setting Furby down, I ran into the bathroom only to find the same—nothing.

I felt the cold, icicle-like tentacles of fear race through me. The only place left was the kitchen. *Please, let them be sitting there having a middle of the night snack attack or something. Maybe Emily convinced my mom and Mitchell to light up and they are all suffering a case of the munchies...*

The hallway seemed miles long as I slowly walked to the kitchen. My gut roiled with fear because I *knew* that they wouldn't be there. I closed my eyes and steadied my resolve as I came to the threshold that led to the kitchen.

My heart sank when I was greeted by unoccupied chairs. *Where were they?*

In a last ditch effort, I dug my cell phone out of my back pocket and tried Emily's number. It rang several times then went to voicemail. The same thing happened when I tried Mitchell's and my mom's phone. A sense of dread hung over me. Not only didn't they answer the calls, I didn't hear the phones ring inside the cabin.

I walked back into the small living room and sat down. Furby immediately jumped into my lap and began doing happy feet, pushing and prodding my legs with the pads of his paws to find a comfortable spot. At least *he* was here.

Absentmindedly, I stroked his soft fur while I rationally tried to determine what was going on. I needed to think things through methodically rather than jumping to wild conclusions. The vehicles were still here. Emily's and Mitchell's keys were still here. That meant wherever they went they went on foot. I looked at my watch, surprised it was three a.m.

Did they go for a walk in the woods? Maybe Mom wanted to see the spot we told her about the other day. No, no way. I could see Mitchell doing that, and maybe my mom since she grew up here and probably had no apprehension of the woods. But Emily? The poor thing was already on the verge of a breakdown and I couldn't imagine *anything* would convince her to hike back there again, not even in the daylight.

So, where the hell were they?

Lost in thought, I zoned while I stared out the front window. The moon illuminated the tops of the trees and bathed the front yard with its silvery rays. The stars were twinkling like bright fireflies in the distance. But there was something else that caught my eye.

A hazy shade of red.

The second I noticed the amber glow, Furby let out a deep, low growl. His ears flattened and in one swift movement, he dug in his back claws and leapt off my lap and scurried away into the darkness.

"Damn, Furby! Those things are like little daggers! What's gotten into..." then I stopped cold. The wicked sounds of the infernal chanting enveloped me. The deep vibrations were so loud that the floor and walls started shaking. Pictures and knickknacks fell off the shelves and shattered as they crashed onto the floor. I could hear glass breaking in the kitchen. The noise grew to a fever pitch, so loud that I clamped my hands over my ears just as Emily had done. Just when I thought my eardrums would explode, the mutterings stopped. I took a deep breath and lowered my hands from my ears, my eyes open again and drawn to the pulsating glow that emanated from the trees.

"*Karmen!* The booming voice was Mitchell's, and it was the most horrific sound I'd ever heard because it was full of pain. "*Karmen, help us!* The dual screams of my mother and Emily turned my blood into ice.

The tortured pleadings of my loved ones tore at my soul. Whatever that wanted something from me had them. Red-hot fury ripped through me. I would do whatever I needed to in order to save them.

But, I had to find them first.

I ran to the kitchen and grabbed a flashlight. I raced back through the house, nearly yanking the screen door from its hinges to get outside. I hit my full stride after the first fifty yards. The night was silent—too silent. Not even a bug made a blip. I concentrated on my breathing and in seconds, I was at the edge of the tree line that led to the heart of the woods.

The chanting from earlier had stopped, but I felt a strange vibration under my feet, like a small electrical current running beneath me. It pulled at me like an invisible string attached to my soul, coaxing me to continue forward.

"Mom...Mitchell...Emily...? Can you hear me?" I screamed into the darkened path ahead of me.

"Karmen, help us!"

When I heard all three voices unite as one, all worry left me and I bolted. My feet ate up the path as I ran. I ignored the small brush that poked and stabbed at me, oblivious to the scraps and cuts they were making on my exposed skin. I kept my focus on the reddish-orange glow that shimmered ahead of me, ignoring the burning pain in my lungs and legs. As I drew closer to it, the air grew hotter and the pungent scent of the forest disappeared. It was replaced with a horrendous stench.

I broke through the tree lines and found myself facing an open expanse of ground. At the center of a large circle was a massive, glowing slab of rock—the source of light that had been my guide through the woods. My heart skipped several beats when I realized there were bodies leaning against it, as well as encircling it. People wearing dark robes and swaying back and forth, their heads tilted back toward the heavens, their hands reaching in the same direction.

Fear kept me frozen in place, my shaking legs firmly planted and my heaving lungs unwilling to let words escape my mouth. That was until I realized Mitchell and Emily were the ones bound and gagged against the rock. *Oh God, where was my mom?*

"Whatever you want from me, I won't do it until you let them go." I was surprised at the strength in my voice. Allowing the words to escape gave me renewed vigor so I began walking toward the enclave. "And all deals are off if you have harmed one hair on any of their heads. Now, where is my mother?"

The tallest figure standing at the head of the stone laughed. His deep, baritone voice sent shivers down my spine, but I refused to let it stop me. I was only ten feet from the circle and even if I had wanted to stop, I knew I couldn't. It was like some otherworldly force was controlling my body.

"Such spirit you possess in the face of fear. Your father would be proud of you."

The mention of my father stopped me in my tracks, as well as the odd familiarity of the voice. I swallowed the lump in my throat and concentrated my focus on counting the robed figures around me. There were twelve, plus the one that spoke to me. Since I was closer I could hear the light sobs coming from Emily and the labored breathing from Mitchell. My eyes swept over them briefly, noting that both were bound with rope around their hands and ankles, and that they were naked and covered in dirt. Their shredded clothes rested less than five feet away from them.

What did they do to them? To my mother?

I wrenched my eyes away from Emily and Mitchell and focused my attention back to the altar. From my peripheral vision, I watched the twelve that encircled the stone stop swaying. In unison they all shed their robes. The one closest to me turned around, her white body shimmered under the moonlight, illuminating her face. Instant recognition of the beautiful features made my throat dry and my entire body tremble.

"Karmen, do not fear, my child. I'm right here. Come, all will be revealed to you now."

My mother stood in front of me, naked as the day she was born. Her hair spilled over her bare shoulders and glimmered in the light. She held her slender arm toward me, beckoning me to join her. Relief that she was alive had been replaced by the repulsion I felt when I noticed that her eyes and face were hard as stone.

"What…what are you doing, Mom?" I stuttered.

"She's helping us usher in the New World, my dear," said the man next to the altar. His voice hit me like a freight train, barreling through my soul and left a gaping hole in its wake.

"Uncle Cy?"

I couldn't breathe. My mind was gridlocked. I watched in horror as my mother and uncle joined hands and walked over to me, a look of triumph passed between them as they appeared to float over to me. I shook uncontrollably from their touch as their naked arms encircled my shoulders, although I was unable to move away. The electrical vibrations that I had felt earlier were stronger now, almost magnetic. They held me firmly in place on the cold, damp grass beneath my feet.

"Darling, your time has come. We have waited for twenty-three years for this moment. You were chosen, don't you see? Your gift, your talent, your *destiny*, was bought with a great price."

Mother's words were spoken in a calm, quiet voice but they still sent panic racing through me. The air froze as she spoke, her hot breath producing wisps of milky colored tendrils of smoke.

"My destiny? Bought with a price? What are you talking about?"

The thing that looked and sounded like my mother stroked my hair and purred into my ear.

"We are about to introduce you to something truly spectacular, truly magical. And no, I don't mean the fairytales and hokum about witches, vampires, fairies and such. Those things are mere mortal escapes from reality created by the rambling minds of individuals that can't, or won't, accept the reality they live in. What I'm talking about is the power that will rule the world. You see, our family belongs to this ancient group of worshipers," she said, her arm motioned toward the remaining members of the group. "Entry is by birthright and passed down from one generation to the next through the sons and daughters. Or, like in your father's case, admission is granted through the ultimate sacrifice."

My mind was reeling as I tried to make sense of her sick words. The subject of my father rarely ever had been broached between us. All I had ever really known was that he had died before I was born in a car accident and that my mom had left the sleepy town of Martin right after his passing to live with Uncle Cy in New York.

The knot in my stomach jerked tighter.

"He didn't die in an accident, did he?" I whispered.

She was on the other side of me now, her cool hand pressed against my elbow as she slowly guided me toward the altar, her other hand gently stroking my knotted hair.

"No, he didn't. Your father was gifted with words and he so desired to be the chosen one. But it wasn't his destiny. He wasn't from the proper lineage, you see. He even tried to sidestep the requirements by sacrificing his own parents, which did gain him entry into the fold, but nothing else. His destiny was to allow the privilege to be passed on to his child through his willingness to die. So, twenty-three years ago, this very night, he sealed your fate with his precious blood that I spilled."

I felt my knees buckle underneath me at her words. Hot tears streamed down my face. I recalled all the childhood memories of the story about the tragic fire that killed my grandparents, how my parents met afterwards, told in a loving voice full of sad memories by the same woman that held my arm. Her strong fingers dug into the flesh on my elbow and kept me on my feet. Her voice turned hard.

"I didn't raise you to be a weak, blubbering fool, Karmen. I didn't watch the love of my life die in front of me, from my own hands mind you, just to listen to you cry. You are a Moncrille, Karmen. You were born to set things in the order they were meant to be. *And you will do just that. Tonight.*"

I looked into the eyes of the woman that had been my rock ever since I could recall. Childhood memories whizzed by in a blur and suddenly I realized that my entire existence had been a lie. The eyes that stared back at me were lifeless, dead. No love, no compassion, no soul existed behind them.

This can't be happening.

"He killed his parents, and you killed him to be a part of this?" The simple bewilderment at the absurdity of grown adults believing in this sick, twisted fairytale suddenly made me furious. *"Why?"*

Uncle Cy moved closer, his strong hands cupped my face and forced my attention over to him. Normally, his eyes were the color of baby blue but tonight they were as black as the coal that Kentucky was known for.

"Listen, little one," he began, his voice low, melodic. "How many times have we discussed the awful state of the world? Countless hours we have conversed, lamenting the senselessness of it all. The anger we both feel at the lot in life of those who live in squalor and filth while others sleep on satin sheets and eat caviar. How many times did you share with me your own guilt of the vast wealth you have accumulated—which fueled your desire to give so much of it away to charity?"

As Uncle Cy spoke with eloquence and candor, I heard his words but *felt* them flow throw me at the same time. Behind him, the pulsating light began to shift colors from the previous deep orange to a vibrant crimson, its liquid movements synchronized with my pounding heart.

"Remember the disgust we shared when we heard about how despondent souls commit atrocities over their dread of losing their possessions? The wails of the orphaned, their parents lost to them forever from addiction, shootings, poverty or simply abandoning them to pursue a variety of selfish lusts? Streets are littered with human trash and the world turns a blind eye, too busy focusing their sights on their own needs.

"We have seen countries wage war with each other over the natural resources that lay under the ground. Bodies vaporized, corpses rotting in the streets from bioterrorism. Technology has advanced so far that we have weapons that are capable of destroying the entire planet—and are in the demented hands of world leaders that could snap at any time. Bloody battles have been waged for centuries over which religion interprets the mind of God correctly. We are humanity, united by the bonds of DNA, yet we seem doomed to separate and segregate each other by our outward appearances and differences. And to covet with insatiable desire what our neighbors have."

Uncle Cy's words flowed over me, caressing and probing deep inside my heart. As they always had, they calmed my mind and seeped into every neuron. A feeling of deep warmth spread through me as his melodic voice lulled me into a state of calming bliss.

Yes, yes. I understand.

"You can end all of that. Your words have that power, my dear. They are the culmination of all the supplication and prayers from centuries of worshippers that have awaited His coming. Once they are spoken by Him, the world will forever be changed. No more war. No more sickness. No more frivolous fighting that accomplishes nothing except to breed more hate. Poverty obliterated with us all on even, common ground. Freedom will truly reign supreme. The freedom to live as each diverse heart wishes with no limitations or restrictions attached. Imagine it, Karmen: true liberation from the bondage of guilt. The words were given to you and, once spoken, will set the captives free."

As I stared into the limpid pools of Uncle Cy's eyes, I felt his words pierce every part of my heart, mind and soul. While he spoke, images of all the death, destruction, famine and pain caused by man's inhumanity to man appeared in my mind. For the first time in six years, I felt joyful exuberance overtake me. If my words could be used to rid suffering of the world, wasn't it my duty to use them?

"There is just one caveat, dear," Uncle Cy said, his voice tender yet authoritative. "You must be willing to step into this circle with a heart full of love for mankind and make the sacrifice that will give your words their life-force. There's power in the shed blood of an innocent. Are you willing, my child?"

My mouth was dry and my heart seemed to have stopped beating. I felt like a spectator watching myself from a distance. I watched my head nod yes involuntarily and saw the smile that broke out across Uncle Cy's and my mother's faces.

"Shed your earthly encumbrances and step forth into the inner circle," my mother whispered behind me. I never took my eyes off Uncle Cy as I did what was asked. Once I was unclothed, Uncle Cy motioned for me to come closer. In his hand he held a long, silver dagger. He extended his hand and the blade tip touched my forehead.

"Sister, do you make this offering of your own free will and enter into this blood pact with open eyes?"

"I do," I heard myself say.

"Now, you must choose your sacrifice," he said, his eyes darting over to Emily and Mitchell. They were terrified, their faces white from fear. I felt a twinge of sadness for them. Hadn't they been listening to what Uncle Cy said? They were witnessing the end of tyranny!

Uncle Cy handed me the dagger.

"Sister, you must offer up the one that you love the most. Which one shall it be?"

"Him," I said, pointing the dagger at Mitchell. Immediately, the other members of the circle converged on Mitchell and picked him up and deposited his writhing body on the altar. The smooth rock was a vibrant burgundy, throbbing in tune with my own heartbeat. Uncle Cy and my mother moved next to me in silent unison. The electrical surge under my feet spread up and through my body, warming my soul from the inside.

"Sister, offer your sacrifice as you say the words, *'Let the truth be known.'*"

I stood over Mitchell and looked into his eyes, then plunged the knife deep into his heart.

"Let the truth be known."

Late Friday Evening

"MS. MONCRILLE. MS. MONCRILLE! CAN YOU HEAR me? Are you all right?"

A cold hand patted my cheek with fervor, the unfamiliar male voice quiet yet insistent. Instantly awake, I bolted upright and moved away from the man that was crouched down next to me. My heart throbbed in my chest as I stared at the stranger from the other side of the porch. He didn't attempt to follow me nor did he seem agitated or angry. He simply sat down on the steps as he watched me with concern.

Trembling and mind racing, I stole a quick glance down at my hands, expecting to see them covered in blood. To my surprise, not only were they clean but I was still fully clothed. Glancing around the porch, I saw no one but the nameless stranger. The vehicles were still parked in the drive, along with a new one I assumed belonged to the man sitting on my porch.

It was a nightmare! Thank goodness. No wonder I felt so out of sorts.

I felt the hackles that had been standing at full attention earlier on the back of my neck finally recess a little. The sudden drop of adrenaline levels in my system overwhelmed me and I was overcome by a sickening wave of dizziness. My legs felt like watery Jell-O and I gripped the railing next to me tightly with both hands to steady myself. I forced my breathing to slow down. *It wasn't real...it was just a dream. Mom, Emily and Mitchell are inside sleeping. You were just sleepwalking.*

My eyes snapped back open when I heard Furby meowing. I cut my vision to the left and started shaking when I saw him on the windowsill, his little paws patting the window as he clamored for my attention.

Just like in the dream...

"Ms. Moncrille, please, don't be frightened by my presence. My name is Jacob Abshire. I'm the pastor at Highland Heights First Baptist Church on Highway 67. Have been for over twenty years now and, well—I know this is going to sound utterly ridiculous—but God sent me here to protect you. From what, exactly, I'm not sure. I am just following where He leads me."

My vision began to blur as the blood pounded inside my head. Instead of responding to him, I leaned over the railing and tossed my dinner into the bushes below.

Just like in the dream...

I caught a glimpse of movement behind me. When I finished retching, a wrinkled hand held out a cold washcloth in front of me. I didn't realize he was standing right next to me and I screamed at him as I backed up against the railing.

"Get away from me!"

Oddly, he looked wounded by my outburst. Something about his countenance, a sincere look that graced his soft, craggy features told me he meant me no harm. His luminous eyes held no malice behind them, only concern and sympathy. His body language never changed as he continued to stand in the same spot, the rag still clasped gently in his hand.

"Ma'am, I mean you no harm," he said as he set down the washcloth on the railing and eased over to the front steps, "You probably think I'm some crazy, old man, but on my life, I promise you that I am telling the truth. I'm just as nervous as you are, believe me."

I leaned over and snatched the rag and wiped it across my face and neck, never taking my eyes off his back. Part of me wanted to know why he was here, but I had other things to concern myself with. First and foremost on my list was waking everyone in the house up to tell them about this latest nightmare. I didn't have the time or the patience to deal with some whack job. It wouldn't be the first time that I had been stalked by an overzealous fan. At least this one seemed harmless.

I noticed his head was turned away from mine and I followed his gaze. He was staring out into the woods—woods that were lit a brilliant red. The hazy glow jutted up from the epicenter of the woods and languidly danced across the night sky.

No sound escaped my lips as I dropped the washcloth and ran inside. I tore through the house, screaming out the names of my loved ones, struggling to tamp down the overwhelming sense of dread that churned inside of me. Even while I ran, I knew I wouldn't get a response from anyone because my heart knew where they were. Tears were streaming down my face by the time I ended back up in the living room and I felt Furby winding his soft body around my trembling legs.

"Every time, the dream was the same. I saw a faceless young woman running through the woods at night, terrified by something chasing her in the darkness. I never could see what was chasing her while she ran. Each time I had the dream—I never could see her face, either. That is, until two nights ago. God laid it on my heart years ago that the dream was actually a vision of things to come. And now they have. So, here I am."

Through my tear-filled eyes, I watched the old man from my spot in the living room. My mind reeled from the bombardment of thoughts. My hands and feet were tingling and my mouth felt like I had swallowed a wad of cotton. *Was I still dreaming? I had to be…*

"I know you must be scared out of your wits, but if you will allow me to explain further, perhaps we can figure it out... together"

"Stop. I don't have time to talk to you, Mister. I've got to find..."

"Abshire. Jacob Abshire's my name."

I wiped my tears on the back of my hand and forced myself to think like a rational person. So far, everything had been just like the dream. I woke up on the porch; I vomited; the vehicles were parked in the drive and everyone was missing. Even Furby had been pawing at the same spot on the window. The only difference was the presence of Mr. Abshire. I shut my eyes for a moment and tried to recall what happened next.

I called their phones...

Mr. Abshire was still resting in the same spot, his back toward me, so I reached around and grabbed my cell phone out of my back pocket and tried all three numbers. Each one rang in my ear, but I heard nothing inside of the house. Fresh tears rolled down my cheeks and I crumpled onto the couch, then Furby jumped up into my lap.

If the chanting starts next...

My fingers clutched the cushions so hard my knuckles turned bone-white. I set my jaw and waited for the haunting sounds.

None came.

Renewed hope sprang up inside of me and I loosened my grip on the couch. True, the events up until this point had matched my dream, but it was just that: a dream. My overactive imagination had run amok after all the events of the past three days. Why should I have been surprised?

"Your Momma is losing her marbles, Furb," I whispered, stroking his silken fur with my shaky hand.

I glanced out the picture window, settling my gaze on the tangled canopy of trees that seemed lit from within. The forest throbbed with pulsating light as the crimson-colored mist slowly spread over the entire mountainside. Somehow, I knew that they were out there, waiting for me in the woods. My first instinct was to call the police, but I nixed that thought as soon as it popped up. What would I say?

"Hi, this is Karmen Moncrille. Yes, that Karmen Moncrille. I need an entire SWAT team to go out into the woods and stop my mother and my uncle from bringing about the end of the world. It shouldn't be hard to find them. Just follow the fiery-red lights over on Bailey Mountain and look for a glowing stone altar. Thanks!" That call would simply become local fodder, and I would be lucky if the dispatcher didn't hang up on me. No, whatever was going on, whatever evil lurked outside, I would have to handle on my own.

I just acknowledged the presence of evil. That's it, I just became Grand Poobah of Insanity Island.

I glanced at my watch, a smile of relief passed across my lips at the time—it was only eleven o'clock in the evening, not three a.m. Yet another difference and one that filled me with more strength. I needed to refocus my energies on figuring out what to do instead of waiting for doomsday.

I lifted Furby up off my lap and set him beside me on the couch. It was time to get rid of stalker-dude so I could start formulating a plan. I paused at the screen door, ready to tell my unwanted guest to hit the road.

"Mr. Abshire?"

He didn't flinch. His back was ramrod straight, his head still pointed toward the glowing woods. His voice was quiet, his words barely audible. "Yes, Ms. Moncrille?"

Although I couldn't put my finger on the reason, something in his voice made me pause. Pain, sorrow, strength and vulnerability emerged all at the same time from him. He looked lost and forlorn yet determined. I opened my mouth to ask to him leave, but no words came out.

A cool breeze wafted through the door and ruffled my hair. Furby's dainty meow caught my ear just as he brushed past me and pushed his head against the screen door until it opened. He waltzed out with his tail high in the air and headed straight to Mr. Abshire's side. My mouth hung open from shock. Never had he gone to a stranger. He was acting like he and the man were old friends as he nuzzled and rubbed up against him.

Over the bristling of the wind and Furby's purring, I felt inside my mind more than I heard with my ears:

Listen to him, Karmen.

The second the word tickled my ears, the forest went pitch blank, like someone had just turned off the overhead light. Dumbstruck from the sudden feeling of calmness, I let my eyes settle back on my intruder. I should be hysterical at the moment. Mom, Mitchell and Emily were gone and I knew they weren't out for an evening stroll.

On the other hand, perhaps I was still dreaming, and the previous nightmare just segued into a different storyline. At least I wasn't a mind-controlled zombie that just stabbed the man she loves. Whatever was going on, I decided to follow my gut instincts.

I felt a stirring inside of me. This man was here to help me, yet I had no clue *how* I knew that.

"Mr. Abshire, whatever you have to say to me, I think I'm ready to listen now. Please, come inside. And bring my cat. He isn't supposed to be outside."

I didn't know if it was an odd twist of fate, divine intervention or simply blind luck that he was here, and I didn't care. However he came to be sitting on my porch didn't nullify the fact that he was the only source of help I had at the moment.

"HERE YOU GO." I handed Mr. Abshire a glass of water. He was seated on the chair across from the couch with Furby curled up on his lap. I shook my head slightly at the sight of my temperamental feline in a complete stranger's lap. That certainly knocked out blind luck as an answer to his presence.

"Thank you. Well," he took the drink from my hand, "I think it's safe to say I've made a new friend." The skin around the edges of his eyes crinkled as he grinned slightly.

"Honestly, his strange behavior toward you was one of the defining reasons I decided to hear you out. That and the fact that the weird glow in the woods stopped the *minute* he made a beeline for you and *something* whispered in my ear at the same time."

I expected a response that conveyed shock, but all I got was a set of somber eyes that stared back at me. He took a sip of water, his gaze never leaving mine.

"Yes, I know. I heard it too. It was a sweet, tinkling voice that told you to listen to me. I heard the same voice when I woke up this morning. Told me it was time."

"You heard the voice, too? Glad I'm not the only one losing their mind."

"Believe me, I feel the same way. Until today, I thought I was nuts for having the same recurring dream about a faceless woman running through the woods. And for thinking that somehow I was supposed to save her. But after today, I have no doubt that it is true."

Although I tried to control my nerves, I couldn't stop my legs from twitching. I wanted to jump up and run out into the forest. The pull, the urge, was so strong that I was having difficulty sitting still. Beads of nervous sweat dripped down my face and back as I battled to sit and listen.

"Apparently, my insanity is so contagious that it has spread to a complete stranger." I winced at my sarcastic tone. "This is going to sound rude, but I just don't have the time to pussyfoot around the subject, Mr. Abshire. People I love are missing and I need to find them, so make it quick. Tell me, what makes you so sure I'm the person God sent you to save?" I sat on the side of the couch closest to the screen door. My feet were firmly planted on the floor in case I needed to bolt quickly if I didn't like his answer. The voice I heard earlier didn't say how *long* I had to listen.

Mr. Abshire's face softened and his voice turned strong and steady. He set his glass down and leaned forward, his eyes warm eyes glistening with tears

"Twenty-three years ago, I was involved in a car accident about two miles from here. My wife and six-year old daughter died at the scene. We were driving here from Florida so I could start my new job as pastor at Highland Heights. It was my fault we wrecked that night. For just a split second, I took my eyes off the road to look at the map in my wife's lap. Sarah, my daughter, saw the deer in the road before I did and, bless her heart, she tried to warn me. But it was too late. I overreacted and jerked the wheel too hard, and we smashed into the divider wall."

I'm…I'm so sorry," I whispered but I doubted he heard me. Even though he was looking at me, his glossy stare bored right through me. He was obviously reliving the night.

"I suffered some injuries, but the worst one was to my heart. I can't say that I abandoned my faith in the Lord, but I did question His reasoning behind taking my family from me in such a violent way. But those internal struggles I kept to myself. It was my personal thorn in my side, just as the Apostle Paul says we each have, and over time and after many moral slip ups, I learned to cope with the enormous loss. The church members were very supportive and helped me through the hardest time in my life.

"But there was one more thing that kept me going, and that was the dream. The first few times I experienced it, I thought I was dreaming about a grown-up version of my daughter. You see, she had the same red hair that you do. I would see her in the dream, running through the woods in terror and I thought it was the Devil's way of torturing me."

"What do you mean?" I asked, intrigued. As his words poured out of him, I felt the pull from the forest lessen. The chills that had dotted my body began to disappear as a gentle sensation of warmth settled over me.

"I felt such enormous guilt for their deaths. Satan goes after our weaknesses and exploits them. It was terribly painful knowing I wouldn't get to grow old with my wife, but knowing that I would never see the kind of woman that my daughter would have turned into almost destroyed me. I didn't even pray to the Lord for strength to fight the Devil or ask Him to comfort me. I had resigned myself to believe that this was my burden to bear. But, the fourth time I had the dream, I couldn't take it anymore. I fell down and cried out to God. He heard and answered my petition."

"How?"

"The same voice that we both heard earlier spoke to me for the first time that morning on my bedroom floor. It simply whispered that it wasn't Sarah and that I was to protect the woman in the woods. The burden was lifted at that precise moment and the wound to my soul lightened enough to learn to live again and not just *exist*.

"After that blessed morning, the dream would happen sporadically throughout the next twenty years. Like I said earlier, until two days ago, I never saw the face of the woman running. But when I did, it turned out to be you. Believe me, I was shocked when I recognized your face from the book covers I have on my shelves at home."

His voice was scratchy so he paused to take a sip of water. Mesmerized by his story, I remained silent and let him speak.

"My secretary had mentioned earlier in the week that you were in town at your family's cabin. I was already packed and ready to leave town like I always do each year at this time. It's sort of my spiritual retreat, my commune if you will, with the

Lord on the anniversary of their passing. But this morning, my plan changed."

"What happened to that plan?"

"Well, I guess the best answer to that question is that was *my* plan and not the Lord's."

Confused, I asked, "What does that mean?"

Mr. Abshire cleared his throat. "Everything that I attempted today seemed to go wrong. I forgot the flowers I wanted to place at the roadside marker on the kitchen table. On my way home to get them, I had a flat tire—and no spare. Had to walk two miles to the nearest gas station and wait for the lone attendant to give me a ride into Preston to buy a new tire. By the time I made it back and changed the flat, it was after five in the afternoon. I'll tell you, I was beginning to wonder if I was delusional.

"While I was changing the flat, I was overcome with the urge to visit the cemetery next, which would have normally been my next stop during my weekend sabbatical anyway, but I had planned on coming here. When I climbed back in my truck, I decided that I wouldn't go visit the gravesite because I thought that was a personal, selfish distraction from what I was *supposed* to be doing. When I tried starting the engine, it wouldn't turn over. Anger hit me and I thought all the obstacles and distractions were roadblocks thrown at me by the Devil himself."

A few beads of sweat ran down the side of Mr. Abshire's face as he talked, some stuck inside the deep folds of his wrinkled cheeks, others trickling down and off his chin. He was still sitting in the chair, but on the edge of it now, his hands clasped tightly together. I could see that he was struggling to maintain his composure. Furby must have sensed his distress because he had hopped up on the armrest and had both front paws pressed against Mr. Abshire's side, his furry feet patting his lower back. I could hear his rhythmic purring all the way across the room as he pumped and pawed, doing what I had always called happy feet.

"I'm guessing that something happened next to change your stance on the reasons for your... delays?"

"Oh yes. As I said, I was angry and I shouted *'Get thee behind me, Satan!'* as loud as I could. Then, as surely as you hear me now, I heard a voice inside the cab say *'Deborah. Sarah. Karmen.'* and I immediately knew that was the order of the day. Peace settled over me and I tried the truck one more time. It started right up, no problem. I followed my heart and went to their graves, intending on staying for just a few minutes in prayer before heading this direction. Six hours later, I woke up to darkness and the same sweet, angelic voice whispered in my ears—*'It's time.'* I drove straight here after that and found you asleep on the porch."

"Do you remember anything while you were asleep, Mr. Abshire?" I said, sensing there was something he wasn't telling me. I knew I was right when his brow furrowed and a look of anguish crossed his face before he responded.

"Yes, but it was very confusing and really made no sense. You know how dreams are—sometimes they play a full-length movie that is easily understandable. Like my recurring dream about you. It never wavered, never changed. It was like a movie clip replaying the same scene over and over. Others, like the one I had while asleep in my truck, are just disjointed blurbs that form an erratic, nonsensical story from bits and pieces of stored memories. I mean," Mr. Abshire stopped and took another sip of water, "you are a famous writer and so were all the other one's I saw."

My pulse quickened. I forced my voice to remain at an acceptable octave. *"What did you see?"* Shocked by my reaction, Mr. Abshire blanched, his eyes widened in response to my outburst. Through gritted teeth, I said, *"Tell...me...what... you...saw."*

He blinked in confusion as his words haltingly exited his mouth. "First, the faces of Shakespeare, Dante, Dumas, Hemingway sort of popped up, floating around like bodiless balloons. I saw you sitting at a kitchen table, trying to type on a computer, but your fingers weren't moving. You looked so sad, so—I don't know— lost. Then, a ghostly looking figure appeared in your kitchen, you screamed, threw something at it, then the place went up in a ball of flames. That's all I remember."

No soul knew about that except Emily. His words knocked the breath out of me, and I nearly fell off the armrest of the couch. The fragile bubble of sanity I had been sitting on top of my entire adult life had just burst. Everything from the last six years, up to and including my horrific nightmare less than an hour ago, finally melded into a clear, frightening vision. Full clarity of what I was supposed to do, to whom, and why shook me to my innermost core. I knew, without a shadow of doubt that the stranger in front of me with the haunting eyes and tortured soul was sent to help me. I knew it as surely as I knew my name.

Just as I knew that the dream I had earlier was not a dream at all. It was a visual premonition of what was to come. Either that or my break with reality that I had feared so much the last several years just happened and I was forever trapped inside my shattered brain.

Straight jacket, here I come.

I swallowed several times before I found the words to respond. "Let me tell you my story and what I *think* I'm supposed to. Then maybe we can figure out how to stop it from happening."

Early Saturday Morning

"IT ALL MAKES SENSE NOW. THE PIECES ALL FIT together in perfect unity. My dreams and your visions. My decision to stay in Kentucky and my obsession with studying the end times. Your proclivity as a writer, one that's name and face are so well-known and loved that anything you write is immediately absorbed into our culture. And, it explains why the rapture-ready boards I frequent were all abuzz the last few days about the murmurings of a peace treaty in the final stages. I must say, though, that in all my studies, I have never run into any hint that someone would actually pen the lie that the Antichrist tells to enslave the world under his wicked control. Truly, the powers that surround us work in mysterious ways. I mean, I always *believed* the end times would come, but I never considered that I would be at the front lines when they arrived."

Mr. Abshire let out a long, deep sigh and ran his shaking fingers through his hair several times. He was trying to hide his shock and nervousness, but he wasn't doing a very good job of it. Small beads of sweat glistened on his forehead as the enormity of our combined stories hit him. Of course, noticing that was like the pot calling the kettle black because my legs were twitching so badly that I gave up trying to stop them and just let them quake.

He tried to produce a confident smile but it came out more like an odd twisted grin. "It's after midnight, which means you are officially twenty-three," Mr. Abshire said, glancing down at his watch. "My guess, from what you just shared with me, is that they hope the beginning of the seven-year reign of terror will start once the sacrifice is made."

For the last hour, I had regaled Mr. Abshire with every sordid detail from beginning to end. I left nothing out. There was no doubt in my mind that Mr. Abshire had been sent here by some guiding force to help me. As much as my analytical mind wanted to reject that thought, my soul and heart could not deny the strange truth. His dreams of me and his intimate knowledge of the cause of the fire at my apartment were more than mere coincidence. It was statistically improbable without some sort of divine intervention.

Mr. Abshire had asked only a few questions while I told my tale of woe, most to elicit more detail or further clarification of the events I was describing. He absorbed every detail, every word. A few times, his head bobbed in agreement—a nod of understanding—while my story unfolded. I was emotionally drained and physically exhausted after rehashing, yet again, the twisted nightmare that had become my life. I rubbed my tired eyes and decided to head to the kitchen and fix another pot of coffee because I knew that sleep wasn't going to happen anytime soon.

Apparently, we had to figure out a way to stop the father of all evil from taking control of the earth, which meant I needed to be on my A-game.

Wow, my sarcasm knew no bounds.

"Mr. Abshire, before we start discussing a subject matter I have absolutely no understanding about, I'm going to need some liquid courage."

"Ms. Moncrille? You are going to need all your wits about you, so perhaps an alcoholic beverage is not the best choice to quench your thirst."

Had we not been discussing the ramifications of my role that was to bring about the end, I would have laughed at the worried look on his face. "I'm making *coffee*, Mr. Abshire. Would you like a cup?" I rose from the couch and stretched. "I believe a jolt of caffeine is in order. At least for me it is. Never face demons without it—that's my new mantra. Perhaps I will get that tattooed on my back once this is all over."

Mr. Abshire managed a feeble smile at my pathetic attempt at humor. The poor man looked as tired as I felt. He seemed to have aged twenty years in the last hour, which seemed only fair, since I had as well. His facial expression was a weird mix of deep sorrow and strange elation, and I dared not think what mine looked like. He had paced around the living room through most of my story but had finally stopped, his face resting against the window frame as he stared out into the dark night.

"That would be lovely, Ms. Moncrille. And please, call me Jacob. Mr. Abshire was my father," he said as he pulled out his truck keys from his jacket pocket. "If you don't mind, I'm going to grab my bag from the truck. I have something I want to show you."

"Agreed, but only if you call me Karmen. Ms. Moncrille is my mother, and I guess I don't need to explain now why *that* would bother me," I retorted. I turned and walked toward the kitchen, then paused when I remembered that the only cups I had were still outside. "Oh, while you're out there, would you mind grabbing the mugs? Unless you want to drink straight from the pot."

"Yes ma'am," he replied, his voice distant, tired. I walked in to the kitchen and heard him exit the front door and clamor down the front steps while I prepared the coffee. In less than sixty seconds, he was back inside, one hand carrying the coffee mugs and the other holding an enormous bag. He set it down with a thud and reached inside.

"Here," he said, handing me a magazine, "turn to page twenty-four and tell me if you recognize the man there. I'll rinse these out."

He began dumping the remaining cold coffee down the sink while I flipped through *Time* to the page he suggested. Chills ran through me when I looked at the smiling image that stared back. My vision blurred and the events that had been blocked from my memory the night I fell in the bathroom broke free and flooded my mind. The man on the page was the same one that appeared from the white mist that had flowed out from the bathroom wall.

Revulsion hit me and I flung the glossy rag across the expanse of the kitchen. It landed on the floor next to the window with a soft *thump*. Seeing the terrifying face from my nightmare that actually belonged to the President of the European Council, Kiroly Adamik, rather than a figment of my warped imagination, left no room for even a modicum of doubt over my mental state anymore.

"I take that as a yes?" Jacob said, a look of dread spreading across his face as he watched my response.

I wrapped my arms around my trembling body, unable to respond except with a quick nod of my head. The magnitude of seeing his face had left me petrified.

"Thought so. Kiroly Adamik has been at the top of my list for the last year as the most likely candidate for the Antichrist. He fits all the criteria from lineage to his exemplary speaking skills, plus he has been adamant that a peace treaty in the Middle East be signed. And, he has very close ties to Prince Al Fashawan in Dubai, who has been vocal about securing peace in the Holy Land. I listened to a few of Kiroly's speeches that he delivered in Europe and they gave me the willies. A lot of the online end times watch groups that I am a member of feel the same way. Oh child, you're quaking! Here," he said as he reached for the fresh pot of coffee beside him and filled my mug, "this might help some. Sorry, guess that was insensitive of me, rambling like that. I can't imagine how seeing his face must have shocked you."

I grabbed the steaming cup eagerly and clasped my hands around the hot ceramic. I could have jumped inside a pool of hot lava and still not have been able to get warm. The weight of this new reality crushed my spirit to smithereens. Listening to Jacob sound so rational, so *sure* about things that up until an hour ago, I didn't believe in had made me nauseous and doubting my touch with reality.

He poured another cup for himself and motioned toward the kitchen table for us to sit down at. When he raised his cup to his lips to take a sip, he sniffed loudly a few times.

"Wait!" he yelled, snatching my drink from my hands, "Don't drink that!"

"What? Why not?" I said, wiping the hot liquid that had splashed on my hands on my pants.

"Because this isn't just coffee," he said, setting the cups on the counter. "I believe, though I'm not one-hundred percent positive, that it's laced with something else. From the odor, I would say Jimsonweed."

"What the *hell* is that?" I bellowed, my nerves so raw that damn near any sound made me jumpy. Jacob's yelling almost sent me through the roof. I understood how Furby felt when humans made loud noises. It was no wonder that cats were neurotic.

"That's what it's called 'round these parts. Guess it's probably better known as *belladonna*. It's a strong hallucinogenic drug that's been used, among other things, in various pagan religious ceremonies for centuries."

I was dumbfounded. "How do you know that's what it is?"

He dumped the contents of the mugs and the pot down the sink. "I've been studying the end times a very long time,

Karmen. Part of my studies included the practices and beliefs of numerous religions, even pagan ones. You'd be surprised at how many of them use mind-altering drugs in their ceremonies. Some think they expand the mind, open it up to new possibilities and avenues to connect to the universe with. Others use it as a form of mind control, more specifically, to induce fear into the minds of their members. Makes controlling the masses easier, I guess. Plus, I know the smell. The stuff grows wild around here."

"That explains why I passed out on the porch. Oh Jesus, my mother fixed the other pot of coffee! Holy crap, she drugged all of us." I said, fury rising to the surface once more. "That *bitch!*"

I turned on my heels and strode down the hallway to my bedroom without uttering another sound. Never in my life had I even considered invading my mother's privacy, but that misplaced loyalty seemed rather humorous now. My hands were quaking with fury as I heaved her travel bag off the floor onto the bed. It took me a few seconds to toy with the latch and fling it open, and when I finally succeeded, my heart nearly stopped. I had braced myself to find the belladonna, but not what greeted my eyes.

Blinking back my stinging tears, I simply gaped at the contents of my mother's bag. Stacks of neatly wrapped bundles of crisp, one thousand dollar bills filled every conceivable spot inside. The smell of the newly printed cash immediately filled the bedroom and made my stomach flip-flop. No, it wasn't the smell of the money—it was the stench of betrayal.

I had no idea how much sat crammed inside the bag, but it had to have been hundreds of thousands of dollars. I gulped down the nausea that threatened to overtake me and reached my unsteady hand out and slowly pulled open the side pocket. I hoped I found some explanation for the origins of the money rather than where my pounding heart knew it came from.

Please, let her have robbed a bank. Won the lottery. Publisher's Clearing House winnings. Anything else but...

I found two slips of paper inside. One was a withdrawal slip from the joint bank account we shared. A receipt for one million dollars dated Thursday afternoon. It had probably been her last stop before her trip here, judging by the time stamp. I forced my eyes to contain my tears as I let the thin paper float silently to the floor, turning my focus to the other one.

The second one hit me like a freight train and quashed all my hope. I gasped for breath as the words seared themselves into my heart. My knees buckled and a wave of dizziness swept over me. I staggered backward and collapsed onto the chair by the door. Dazed, I didn't have the physical or mental control to acknowledge Jacob's presence in the doorway.

"Karmen, are you…oh my."

Holy camolee is more like it, Pastor.

While I was aware of the fact that Jacob was asking me questions after he bent down and retrieved the nails that just slammed the coffin on my relationship with my mother shut, I couldn't answer him. I couldn't concentrate on anything except the words scrawled in her flowing handwriting that comprised the makeshift press release.

"My brother and I thank each and every one of you for your prayers and thoughts during this incredibly difficult time for our family. The loss of our beloved Karmen has been made all the more heartbreaking by the knowledge that she took her own life, and we missed her cries for help. We take comfort, and we hope that her fans will as well, that she will forever be a part of us through her incredible works. We ask that any donations or memoriam be sent to the Suicide Prevention Center headquarters at…"

With all my intestinal fortitude, I tried to hang on to my anger. I knew if I didn't, the tears of betrayal and sorrow would overtake me and I might never stop crying. Jacob was still talking when I suddenly jumped up from the chair and ran into the living room. My connection with sanity was broken beyond repair. I unleashed my emotions inside the four walls of the small space.

"You sick, twisted bastards! It's all true, isn't it? None of this is some screwed up dream or weakness in my head. You both played me, using me as some pathetic pawn in this game of world domination! Can you hear me? Are you two watching me now through your evil, demented eyes while prancing around naked in the dark waiting for me to come do your bidding?" I roared and grabbed the lamp to my right and flung it against the wall. The dark brown ceramic bottom shattered into hundreds of sharp shards that sprayed across the living room, the cream shade crushed.

"Me, poor little sheltered Karmen that had *no clue* what lay ahead, what demonic path you two were leading me through. You both led me to believe that none of this was real, that those who believed in an afterlife or deity-driven belief system were fools. Dolts. Simpletons that couldn't think for themselves and just blindly followed the sheep in front of them! *How could you!* Uncle Cy! Can you hear me?" I screamed as I spun around and kicked the edge of the couch with such force that the wooden leg broke in half. I picked up a cushion and flung it against the other wall, sending the wall decorations to their shattered death on the floor.

"You're so pious! Spouting out that bullshit about a utopian society where killing is no more. Where humanity can live together in peace because there would be no religion, no poverty, no worries because we all could live as one cohesive society. Well, your little secret is out now! You stood by and watched my *mother* kill my *father* because you wanted to bring about Armageddon! Not only that, but it seems the plan ended by killing me and then faking my suicide! Did you plan on being the right-hand go-to-guy for Satan, Uncle Cy? And what about you Mom?" I yelled, kicking over the end table.

"What are you getting out of this deal...this *pact*...with the Devil? It must be a pretty damn fine reward since you gave up your husband *and* your child for it! Were you hoping to be the Mistress of Satan or something? Oh...my...*God!* I can't believe this! This is the *epitome* of hypocrisy. You've known all this time—stood by and silently watched while my mind was manipulated by the forces you worship—and didn't say a word. You two raised me not to believe in this make-believe stuff, but you both are right in the middle of it! *And apparently on the wrong side!*

I felt my world collapse around me. The firm ground that I had stood upon since I was old enough to walk—the mortar and cement provided by Mom's and Uncle Cy's love and values—morphed into quicksand, and I just sank to the bottom, the remaining rubble of my sanity crashing down on top of me.

The uncontrollable wrath had ripped through me and in the space of seconds, I had destroyed the entire living room. Not one picture, knickknack or lamp remained intact. Just like my life, everything lay in a rumpled heap, broken and shattered beyond repair. The bookcase that used to sit in the corner with a copy of all my books had been smashed to pieces. I reached down and grabbed the book closest to me and began tearing the pages out in handfuls, throwing the creamy pages over my head.

"And this? This is the *greatest* lie of all! These aren't even my words. Implanted ideas and thoughts that some demonic *thing* unleashed inside me. *Entities that you knew about!*"

My breath came in heaving raps, followed by wrenching sobs. I collapsed on the floor and let them pour out of me.

Time seemed to stop, trapping me inside a living nightmare. None of this made sense. It couldn't be real. I had feared before that I was going insane and had hoped that wasn't the case. Now that I knew the truth, I wished for insanity. The existence of Heaven, Hell, God, Satan, powers that created and controlled mankind had always been silly, foreign concepts to me. Yes, I had read volumes and volumes of work written by authors that believed in such things, but I had lumped it all into the category of myths and legends. I viewed them the same way I had mythology—all part of made up tales created by the imaginations of the authors that penned them to teach life lessons through the use of deities to control the minds of the masses.

But now, my entire belief system had shifted. I had been forced to confront the fact that, just as Mitchell had said two days ago, my doubts didn't make the subject any less relevant or real. Obviously, my mother and my uncle believed wholeheartedly and had killed for it, and wanted me to do the same. Whether their actions, or my own, would actually bring about the apocalypse by putting a demonic entity in control of the world, I honestly had no idea. What I did know was that this whole thing was truly happening and that I played a pivotal role in the entire deceitful drama.

A warm hand touched my shoulder, and I heard Jacob kneel down next to me on the floor. His strong arms pulled me into his chest and he held me close. I melted into his embrace and wept like a small child as he held me tight, clinging to his presence like we were the last two people on earth. He never said a word during my emotional breakdown.

Unsure how long we stayed that way on the cold floor of my childhood sanctuary, I finally realized the tears had dried up. The man that I loved and my best friend were out there in the woods, probably just as terrified as I was. Not only did they need me, but apparently, so did the entire human race.

"How do we stop this?" I said into Jacob's chest, my voice muffled.

"I've been praying about that during these last few minutes," he replied. His voice soft, warm and confident. "And I believe I have the answer."

I raised my head from his wet, tear-stained chest and looked up at him. His face was a sea of calm, almost ethereal. I felt strength and serenity flow from him into me and clung to it like it was a lifeline.

"And that is?"

"In your vision, you said that you were to make a sacrifice of the one you loved the most, then say the words *Let the truth be known* correct?"

"Yes, that's right," I whispered. A chill of fear streaked across my heart at the horrific memory.

He swallowed hard, his warm eyes never leaving mine. "If the sacrifice of the one you love the most will give the lie you wrote meaning, then…"

His response was cut short as the ground beneath us began to quake and the loud chanting began once again. We both covered our ears from the deafening sounds while the floor and walls groaned in protest. Suddenly, the front window blew out and the entire living room was bathed in a red, eerie glow that streamed through the gaping hole. Jacob tried to shield me from the peppering shards of glass, but it was no use. The shattered window sprayed the tiny daggers into the air, littering the floor and the exposed areas of our bodies with crystal clear debris.

Scrambling to my feet, I ran out the front door and out into the yard, stumbling to retain my footing on the moving terra firma. I came to a halt in the middle of the yard and stared at the throbbing haze that danced across the expanse of Bailey Mountain.

"Karmen! Come hither, child. It is time. Come, we await."

The ground finally became still, the chanting subsiding just as quickly as it had started. Jacob stood right behind me, his breathing labored from running to catch up with me. Cold anger swept over me again, obliterating my fear and filling my veins with ice. Jacob slid his warm hand inside my own and squeezed.

"As I was saying before we were so rudely interrupted, I have a plan."

I noticed his bag was slung over his shoulder. He patted it with his other hand as a smile crossed his lips. A faint tinge of pink dotted his cheeks as a fleeting look of shame appeared.

"I didn't tell you the *rest* of my dreams, Karmen. The last scene I recall started with the two of us standing right where we are now. So, here's what we're going to do…"

As I listened to his own vision on how the events played out in his dream, a twinge of hope started in my chest, then soon spread throughout my body, melting the frozen crimson in my veins with the warmth of courage.

JUST LIKE THE dream earlier, the orangey light that I knew originated from the altar in the glen served as my guide. The mountainside was quiet. No sounds of birds, bugs or animals greeted me as I walked. Unlike my dream, however, this time, my steps were slow and steady through the dense underbrush. My halting pace was necessary to buy extra time for Jacob to circle back around the crazed devil worshippers and emerge on the other side of the forest. When I had balked at his idea earlier, worried that his presence might be sensed through some form of otherworldly vision, he simply smiled and replied that we had God on our side and not to worry.

Easier said than done.

"Karmen, do not fear. They think they have the upper hand. You were drugged in hopes of showing you their vision of what was to come for you. Under the influence of a hallucinogen, molding your will to theirs would be much easier. As scary as that was for you to witness, it was a blessing in disguise. We have the tools to fight against them with us now. We are going to use their trickery to our advantage. Besides, they didn't count on me."

When Jacob whispered those words in my ear earlier, they had comforted my thumping heart. But the minute he veered from behind me on the dark path, and padded off in the opposite direction and disappeared into the blackness, my panic started to rise. I stopped mid-stride and closed my eyes for a brief second, trying to recall the words that Jacob had prayed over us both before we entered the woods.

Yea though I walk through the valley of the shadow of death, I will fear no evil, for You are with me. Your rod and Your staff, they comfort me.

I recited the words over and over in my head even though I didn't understand the context they had originally been written for. They became my mantra and what I planned on focusing my thoughts on when I confronted my mother and Uncle Cy. Jacob had warned me that there was a high probability that what I experienced in my earlier dream would play out the exact same way tonight. Since Uncle Cy had somehow swayed me to his side and convinced me to kill, I would have to be prepared to battle the same thing again.

"Listen, Karmen. I realize that I am throwing a lot at you, spiritually speaking. All I can offer in testimony is what I believe and why. You are living out the passage in the Bible that the Apostle Paul spoke of when warning fellow believers to be diligent and watch out for seducing spirits. He said that it is not flesh and blood that we struggle with each day, but the unseen spirits and principalities that are at war for every soul—every minute of each day. What you once thought was an issue that only *you* struggled against, you now know is real and affects us all. Your family and friends have experienced the evil phenomenon. You aren't crazy, or sick, or dreaming. This is real life, happening right at this moment, just as we both envisioned.

"You cannot do this without faith. You have seen the side of evil, so it stands to reason that if evil exists the opposite must as well. Yin and Yang. Black and white. God and Satan. And you are about to walk into the midst of a group of people that have not only devoted their lives to serving the Devil but have killed for him. He is the Father of Lies, and those who follow him are just as adept at twisting the truth. You may not believe in salvation through Jesus Christ, but I do, and if you remain strong in your faith in saving your friends, together we can stop them."

I shook the conversation from my head and tried to focus on my steps. The ground began to vibrate under my feet, the same magnetic pull I experienced in the dream pulsed and tingled up my legs and into my chest. Doubt crawled around in my head like a coiled snake, and I began to tremble. I dropped to the damp ground and did something I had never done in my entire life.

I prayed.

I don't doubt Your existence now, although I still don't understand how You work or what I'm supposed to do to feel You or have some sort of relationship with You. All I know for sure is that You sent Jacob here to help. I feel that. I sense his warmth, his compassion and his sincerity. I also know that the love of my life and my best friend are out there and need our help. And, according to both sides down here, I'm some sort of key to the end of the world. If what Jacob says is true about the Earth being Satan's playground yet You control the universe, then please, please help me. I don't want to be responsible for this. I didn't ask for it nor do I want this curse. I loved my mother and Uncle Cy, but I was duped into that love. If I truly am about to face people that worship Your enemy, then I ask You to give me strength to defeat them, and to forgive me for what I'm about to do.

Just as I started to stand, the wind picked up and began swirling around me. The chanting, which had only been a low rumble before, grew to a fevered pitch, matched only in intensity by the collage of colors in the sky. The leafless trees in front of me looked like they were on fire. The sky had turned blood-red, along with the moon, and now the entire area looked like a volcano had just erupted. The chanting stopped abruptly and then the garbled voice of Mitchell rang out, followed in quick succession by Emily and Mom.

"Karmen!"

"Help us!"

"Hurry, Karmen!"

I looked at my watch. Jacob and I had agreed on a ten minute window for him to get situated, and the eleventh minute just passed. I forced the bile back down my throat and took a deep breath.

"Mother! Emily! Mitchell! Where are you?"

I crouched low and began to jog toward the edge of the tree line that led to the glen. I stopped before I emerged and peered around a large oak. A surge of fear skittered over me when I saw the exact same scene as I had in my nightmare. I pulled my eyes away from the hooded figures and the terrified faces of Mitchell and Emily, and quickly scanned the remaining tree line.

Please, God, let Jacob be in place and ready.

I sucked in a huge lungful of air and let out an ear-splitting scream into the night. I stumbled and rolled onto the ground.

"Ow!"

From my position, my location was safely hidden by mounds of the soft kudzu. I saw the hooded figures all look in the direction of my scream. Uncle Cy and my mother exchanged surprised glances. Uncle Cy nodded curtly at her. Mom immediately motioned to the remaining worshipers that surrounded the altar to follow her as she left the circle. Each started walking in the general direction toward my position in the underbrush.

I will fear no evil. I will fear no evil. Please, God, I will fear no evil.

"Karmen? Oh Karmen, thank *God!* Where are you? Please hurry, come help us!"

My mother's pitiful plea reverberated throughout the expansive field as the rob-clad figures strode closer, the stride and posture full of anger.

Wow, what an act she had down…but so did I. After all, I am my mother's daughter. The plan was working! Even Uncle Cy had moved from the inner circle, his attention no longer on the pulsating altar, leaving Mitchell and Emily unobserved. Hurry Jacob!

"Mom? Are you all right?"

"Karmen, why aren't you coming? I'm okay, but Mitchell and Emily are hurt. I need your help. Where are you?" she said, the fake concern in her voice sent shockwaves of anger through me.

"Oh, thank God you are okay! I can't move. I stepped in a hole and my foot is stuck," I whined from my position. It took every ounce of mental strength I could muster to stay put and not run from the imposing figures that were less than twenty feet away from me.

"Not to worry, darling. Keep talking so I can find you."

"I can't believe what a klutz I am. So much for helping you guys. Of course, I wouldn't be out traipsing around in these eerie woods if you all didn't decide to take a walk in them. In the dark. I mean, seriously Mom? What are you all doing out here? And why did you leave me alone back at the cabin? Do you have any idea how worried I was when I woke up, not to mention scared? Come help me, please. And where are Mitchell and Emily?"

The swirling wind ceased. I could hear the light footfalls of everyone approaching from all different directions. Suddenly, Mom was less than five feet from me. I cut my eyes over to the center of the glen and forced my elation to remain inside. *Jacob made it! He had cut Emily and Mitchell loose and they were running toward the safety of the woods. Hurry, run!*

"Well, my dear. You are in a tight spot, aren't you? That's my Karmen—a loveable oddity," my mother said, her voice hard and cold. She bent over and brought her face within inches of my own. The eyes that had reflected a deep, abiding love toward me my entire life were gone, replaced by wicked pools of sheer madness. "Good thing I brought help to extract you from yet another debacle you've found yourself in."

She raised her arm and snapped her fingers, her dark robe floating around her like a death shroud. The red haze glinted off the tips of her long nails, which made it look like flames were shooting from them. Instantly, we were encircled by the hooded figures. The breath I had been holding left me in a giant *whoosh*, my body rendered motionless. I was paralyzed by fear as several pairs of arms reached out and grabbed me.

"Let go of me!" I screamed. My voice was the only weapon I could muster against them.

My mother's cold fingers reached out and stroked my quaking cheek. I wanted to recoil from her evil touch, but the tight grip of the faceless worshipers held me firmly in place. I glowered at her, my anger expelled through my eyes.

"Now Karmen, is that anyway to greet your mother? After all I have sacrificed for you? My entire existence has been devoted to you from the moment I discovered I was with child. And, as you know from your vision earlier, your father and I gave up our lives together to endow you with the gift. By the way," she purred as she latched onto the back of my neck and pulled my face closer, her hot breath washed over my chin as she whispered in my ear, "how *did* you enjoy your coffee earlier? Quite the rush, wouldn't you agree?"

My heart broke at her cold, vicious words. *This can't be happening. Please, let me still be dreaming.*

"How could you, *Mother*?" I choked out, my voice trembling from the tears of anguish I held at bay.

She let go of my head and pulled her face away, her eyes boring a hole through my own. With a gentle swoop of her hands, she removed the hood that covered her head, releasing her blonde curls. They cascaded down her back and looked almost as red as my own hair in the crimson haze that surrounded us. The look of disgust behind her stare as she watched me like I was some sort of crawling pest on her arm crushed any hope I had left of reaching through to the old her. The person that I knew as my mother was no longer there. Her life-force had been sucked bone dry and replaced with the blackness of evil. She cut her stare away from me back to the circle, which cued my captors to begin moving me in that direction. The strong arms holding me lifted me up enough so that my feet no longer touched the ground as we made our way over to the altar.

As we neared the center of the glen, the glow from the stone slab intensified as it bathed the entire area blood-red. My heart pounded with glee when I noticed that Emily, Mitchell and Jacob were gone and that none of the demon-loving freaks were aware that they were missing.

Please, God, let them escape safely.

"Hello, my dear. So nice of you to join us at our little gathering," Uncle Cy murmured as we stopped in front of him at the edge of the circle. "We were beginning to worry about you. I thought perhaps your mother had given you too high of a dosage of belladonna, but I see now that I can put that worry to rest."

The voice that had calmed me and gave me a sense of balance and strength my entire life was the same, but the new effect it had on me was completely different. It was as if for the first time I truly heard the evil depths that his words sprang from. I locked my gaze with his and saw the same dark madness that I had seen in my mother's eyes. It was like looking into an endless cave.

Or a glimpse into the bowels of Hell itself.

While I stared into the abyss that once held the loving eyes of my uncle, my terror immediately fled, chased away from the murky corners of my mind as acceptance of what my new reality had become. My life had been a delusional farce. A cosmic joke played on me by those that I loved and that I thought loved me. I had been born to a mother that didn't want a child, but rather, a vessel to fill her own demented ideals with. Molded and shaped by the virtual hands of the Devil himself, every move watched and every interaction with me calculated, plotted. The short twenty-three years of life I had lived boiled down to one final act. The choice they wanted me to make was simply impossible to do. To be forced to take the life of another was awful, but insisting that I chose between two people that I loved so much was absolutely monstrous.

Emily or Mitchell. Opt to end the existence of my closest friend that had been a part of my life since I was a small child. Our relationship throughout the years had blossomed beyond the bonds of friendship and over into sisterhood. The only other person that my heart held as much love for was Mitchell. My one and only lover, the boy that had captured my soul the minute I looked into his eyes so many years ago. It seemed like a lifetime had already passed since that day at McMann's General Store when I spotted him stocking shelves. Memories of our first kiss, the first time we proclaimed our love for each other, the first time our bodies rocked in heated harmony together flashed by. The heartbreak I felt the day he enlisted. The terror when he boarded the flight that took him thousands of miles away from me. The joy I felt when I saw him standing in the kitchen less than forty-eight hours ago, more thankful that he survived the ravages of war and came back home.

Ending the life of either of them was not an option, for I loved them both with equal intensity. How could I possibly choose to sacrifice one to save the other? I would never be able to live with the remorse and regret no matter which one I picked. Add on top of that the fate of the world, at least according to Jacob and obviously my demented family, hinged upon me. The monumental choice loomed before me as I stood trembling in front of the other two people that I *had* loved with equal zeal.

The hands of the remaining robed figures let go as they moved in quick unison to stand in their previous places around the circle, except the two who still remained on each side of me.

My heart leapt into my throat when the one on my right nodded in silence toward the altar. Immediately, Uncle Cy and my mother turned and noticed their captives had been freed. While their attention was focused away from me, I reached my hand around to my back and extracted the butcher knife I took from the kitchen and had hidden in my waistband earlier.

When Jacob had explained his plan to sneak in and free Emily and Mitchell, then cause a distraction to allow me to escape, I knew it would only be a temporary reprieve. If all of this were true and really happening—not some horrendous dream—then my fate had been sealed already. The Lie had already been written. My mother had taken it and the only logical conclusion was that the words were in the hands of a man that fancied himself as the Antichrist. If the final act to bring him into power hinged upon me, then even if we all slipped away tonight, it wouldn't matter. I would be hunted down like prey until they found me and forced me to complete this unholy ritual. I had come to the conclusion that there was only one way to truly end it all.

The silvery blade sparkled in the reddish glow as I clasped the handle in my trembling hands. The heavy weight of dread that had been my constant companion for the last few days melted away as a warm sensation of peace enveloped me. I resigned myself to the decision I had made earlier to stop the madness once and for all. I was the last of the Moncrille line. Uncle Cy and his wife of forty years, Eleanor, never bore any children. If the sick words my mother had spoken to me in the vision were true, then the bloodline ended with me, which meant no one would be left in our lineage.

I would not be responsible for ushering in the age of evil.

I raised the knife, closed my eyes and prayed silently. *Let the truth be known.*

"Karmen, Karmen, Karmen. Do you really believe that you can stop us?"

Before I could open my eyes, I felt the blade yanked from my sweaty hands. My eyes flew open to see Uncle Cy standing directly in front of me, his eyes alit with twisted amusement. In one swift motion, he tossed the knife across the expanse of the glen. I held my ground and glared back at him.

"I won't be your pawn any longer. One way or another, I will end my life so this atrocity you long for will never happen."

I steadied myself for the explosion of anger I assumed would be next. Instead, Uncle Cy tossed his head back and laughed. His deep baritone rang throughout the open area, bouncing off the rocks and trees. I cut my eyes over to my mother. The devilish grin on her face made my head spin with terror. In a flash, the entire troupe shed their clothes, their robes all landing silently at their feet.

"You didn't think that little trick would work, did you?" Uncle Cy said, his face inches from my own.

Dumbfounded, I stuttered, "You can't stop me from trying again."

"Oh, that is true, little one. You always were a spitfire. So headstrong. So sure of yourself. I must say, I am proud of your decision, your *loyalty* to those you love. You were willing to sacrifice your life to save theirs—how very noble of you."

Anger overrode my sense of wellbeing as I retorted, "You make me sick. Both of you. *All of you!*" I screamed. "I will finish what I started. You won't win."

My mother's long arm shot out and grabbed a handful of my knotted hair. She wrenched my body away from Uncle Cy's and turned her face to mine. Her lips curled into an evil grin. "Oh, but we already have, darling. You really are naïve if you think that we showed *all* of your hand to you, aren't you?"

The peace I felt before was vanquished by her terrifying stare. "What are you saying…" I mumbled.

"She's saying that you are off the hook, Karmen. Your part has already been completed. You penned the lie. Nothing more is required of you now that you brought us the perfect sacrifice. Oh, and don't worry, you won't be required to shed the blood. I will."

My world shattered when I recognized the sultry voice. I pulled my eyes away from my mother's to the direction of the sound.

It was Mitchell.

Emily and Mitchell stood at the edge of the circle, their bodies no longer clothed. I blinked and tried to fathom what was happening in my fractured mind. In between them they held Jacob's limp body. Blood cascaded down his face from the open gash on his temple. I gasped, but no sound crossed my lips. Frozen in horror, I watched helplessly as Emily and Mitchell maneuvered Jacob toward the altar.

"Mitchell? Emily?" I whispered, my voice cracked with pain.

"Surprised to see me, doll baby?" Mitchell replied. His tone was ominous, unrecognizable from the one I associated with the man I loved.

Tears of sorrow raced down my face as I watched them move in perfect unison. The wind left my lungs in a giant *whoosh*. Abject fear rendered me speechless.

"There, moral dilemma solved, my dear. You see, we only showed you what we *needed* you to see, to ensure that you would come—and bring the appropriate sacrificial lamb. What better way to ring in the new world than with the death of one of *His* believers—wouldn't you agree?"

Uncle Cy's words ripped through me like a hot dagger, shredding my being into an unrecognizable pile of mush.

"It's all been a lie…and each of you used me," I whispered to no one in particular.

"Oh Karmen. Your mom is right—you are so naïve. Did you really believe that this hunk of gorgeous manhood was in love with *you*? I mean, seriously, look at you. The boring, crazy recluse that stews away her time fretting over stupid, silly things, that's what you are. Now, look at me—I'm the complete opposite. I embrace who I am and don't deny indulging myself in all the delicious appetites the world has to offer. But, I grew tired of the religious nut-jobs like my parents that tried to curtail my activities by telling me that the lifestyle I wanted to live was sinful. The guilt trip they wanted me to ride on didn't sit well with me, so I began looking for something new, something different. Something more, shall we say, *accepting*. Thankfully, your mother saw my struggles and showed me a new line of thinking."

"Oh Emily," I said through my sobs of heartache.

"Please, save your whining for someone who cares, Karmen. You had the world by the *balls* and you didn't even know it! Do you know how many times I wanted to slap the living daylights out of you?" Emily spat. Each word sliced deeper into my heart as she began mimicking me, "'I feel so guilty about all this money, Emily. I think it's wrong for one person to have so much…I'll give half to charity' or 'I love Mitchell but I don't want to be his wife for goodness sake! I'm too young' and on and on, *for years!* I listened to you bitch and moan about things that you should have been *ecstatic* over."

Emily's mocking tone screeched through my ears, destroying the last vestiges of sanity that I desperately clang to.

"Enough theatrics, Emily," Mitchell said, his voice deep and sinister. "We have business to attend to. The past generations have waited for this day, and I am not going to prolong it any longer. My destiny, as the only remaining heir to my family's place in this circle, is about to come to fruition."

Mitchell and Emily hoisted Jacob's body onto the altar. The enormous rock pulsed and vibrated with intensity the second Jacob's skin touched it. Uncle Cy left my side and glided over to Emily, who stood at the front of the altar over Jacob's head. Mitchell bowed his head as Uncle Cy approached, his bare arms outstretched toward him.

"Brother, do you make this offering of your own free will and enter into this blood pact with open eyes?"

"Yes, Elios, I do," Mitchell replied in an eerie, somber voice. The minute the words were spoken, Uncle Cy bent down and retrieved the elongated, ornate dagger that had been resting at the edge of the altar and handed it over to Mitchell.

Yea, though I walk through the valley of the shadow of death, I shall fear no evil.

In the space of the amount of time it took for me to blink, everything became crystal clear. I realized every single thing Jacob had told me before was true. There was a God in Heaven, a Creator of all life. The Jesus that walked the earth, who I previously only viewed as a man that taught valuable moral lessons, was truly God's son. He had come here to save the world from their evilness as the ultimate sacrifice. A being did exist that once had been the arch angel Lucifer that became the Devil when removed from Heaven. And that humanity was heading straight into the apocalypse when he came into power if Mitchell succeeded in killing Jacob.

The fire of truth raced through me, giving strength and power to my limbs. The chanting started up again but barely registered in my head. The naked bodies of the twelve in the outer perimeter of the circle swayed in harmony, their eyes closed and heads skyward. The remaining four people that once were my world were each lost in their own euphoria as Mitchell raised the knife high in the air. My life, my purpose, my existence boiled down to this very moment.

Thy rod and thy staff, they comfort me.

My legs propelled me in two long strides over to the vibrating altar. In one giant leap, just as Mitchell brought the blade down toward Jacob's chest, I used my collision with Emily's body to launch myself on top of Jacob. For an instant, time seemed to stand still as Jacob awoke and locked his eyes with mine. I smiled, then yelled, *"Let the truth be known!"* as the hot dagger sliced through my back.

First Light Saturday Morning

HEYLEL FINISHED DRYING OFF THE BODY THAT once belonged to Kiroly Adamik inside the airplane's enormous master bathroom. It had taken him a full thirty minutes to wash off all the blood and gore left over from his previous romp in the bedroom. As he shook the water from the heavy blond hair on his head, Heylel marveled at the sensations he had just indulged in. He had forgotten how glorious the feel of causing pain was when felt through the confines of flesh, or how the screams of agony seemed so much sweeter when reverberating through an eardrum.

When Heylel opened the door to the bathroom and surveyed his handiwork, his face broke out into an evil sneer as the fresh memories of shredding the bodies down to mere piles of jumbled, unrecognizable gunk danced in front of his vision. The mess was incredible, but as it had always done in the past, money would wipe away the atrocity and silence those who cleaned it up. Heylel made his way to the closet, picking his steps carefully as he sidestepped the stinking mess. He retrieved his fresh set of clothes and shoes, and shut the door behind him without another glance.

Heylel sauntered into the main cabin and back to his spot by the window. Once dressed, he reached over and gently caressed the cold steel case that held the signed treaty. The new body that he called home tingled with his excitement. He had been close several times over the years to achieving his rightful place on earth only to be trumped by some pathetic act of love or sacrifice by some sniveling infidel. But Heylel knew the chances of someone offering such a selfless act in the current state of self-indulgent behavior that humanity was embarked in was almost certainly zero. Heylel had been busy the last three hundred years bounding from one end of the earth to another, ensuring that very fact.

He glanced at the clock on the wall and noted that in less than an hour, the flight would arrive in New York. In just under thirty-six hours, he would bring humanity to its knees and establish his throne in Jerusalem. The weak, spineless masses would be astounded by his powers, beseech him for every morsel they hungered for, and be his devoted followers.

Those that dared to question his authority would pay. *Dearly.*

Underneath the attaché sat his laptop. He reached down and retrieved it and pushed the "on" button to bring it to life. He was eager to read what Elios had sent him. He wanted to watch the words morph into life when the sacrifice was made, which he knew would occur at any moment.

After a few clicks of the mouse, Heylel opened the email from the person the world knew as Cy McMann but he knew as Elios, and his words appeared on the screen. Heylel's trusted servant had yet to fail him in any way. Of course, centuries of grooming the McMann family to do his bidding didn't hurt, either. Heylel recalled the day that he watched from his ethereal plane when Cy McMann recognized the signs and contacted Kiroly Adamik. Cy's insistence to meet with Kiroly worked, and after just one brief visit in Cypress, Kiroly Adamik finally understood and accepted his role in life, just as Cy McMann had.

Cy McMann: Heylel's false prophet that would stop at nothing in his insatiable quest for power and wealth. When Heylel heard Cy's prayers offered up from the jungles of Vietnam so many years ago to him, begging for his life to be spared in exchange for his unyielding devotion to the deity his family worshipped, Heylel listened. Once Cy had escaped the clutches of the enemy that day, he never wavered from his promise to serve Heylel. And when Heylel witnessed the sacrifice made twenty-three years ago, from the hands of Cy's sister no less, Heylel knew the time was nigh.

The printer spat out the pages in quick succession, and Heylel walked over to the other side of the cabin and retrieved them. Although the handwriting was atrocious, the words he needed to speak to rule the world were staring back at him. He recognized the symbols and numerous languages that it was written in and caught himself saying the words out loud. Had Heylel been capable of the emotion, he would have laughed at the sound of his voice as he spoke in gibberish.

The anticipation, the wait, was more than Heylel could stand. Although he knew it would weaken him and put his new physical body in jeopardy, he settled back into the soft folds of the leather couch and closed his eyes. He reached out through his mind, past the confines of space and time, and sought out the glen in the hills of Kentucky where his reign would officially begin.

He wanted to watch.

As Kiroly Adamik's body fell into a deep, hypnotic trance, Heylel's spirit moved across the ocean, following the pull of the sacred stone that migrant worshippers had placed there thousands of years ago. Just as he caught a glimpse of the valley shrouded in red, it was gone.

"Mr. Adamik? *Mr. Adamik?* Are you all right?"

Heylel found himself back inside the sickening boundaries of flesh again. The body jerked out of the trance as Heylel's essence slammed back inside. When he opened his eyes, the frightened stare of one of the pilots glared back at him.

"What can I do for you, Mr. Nazir?" Heylel replied, controlling the annoyance he felt.

"Sir, I'm sorry to bother you, but this is urgent. Please tell me you haven't eaten anything since you boarded?"

Intrigued, Heylel replied, "No, I have not, Mr. Nazir. The only item I indulged with since arriving is a glass of champagne so graciously provided by your benefactor. Why do you ask?"

Mr. Nazir, clearly relieved by the answer, cleared his throat. "We just received word that the chef is an imposter. An infiltrator sent to kill you before you arrived in New York, sir. I balked at the notion when I first heard it, since he surely looked like no assassin I've ever seen before. But then it hit me—he would use food. There is no finer food in the world than Middle Eastern cuisine, but the spices and flavors would mask any poison in it, should someone chose to use that route."

"That certainly was an insightful idea on your part, Mr. Nazir. I am grateful that you came to warn me before I decided to satiate my hunger."

"Sir, if I may?" Mr. Nazier inquired, lowering his voice. "Please, come with me…"

Mr. Nazir's words were cut off in mid-sentence by a low rumble that resonated throughout the cabin. Heylel felt the tremble and realized it emanated from him. He looked down and saw the papers he still clutched vibrating, the words alive and writhing on the pages. The edges suddenly burst into flames and the words swirled in circles, like a vortex was pulling them to the center of the page. In a flash of smoke, the pages evaporated.

Uncontrollable rage erupted out of Heylel. Something had gone terribly wrong, he felt it. He leapt off the couch, knocking the stunned pilot on his rump. He roared with anger, his piercing voice so loud that the entire plane shook.

"Nooo!"

The cabin filled with bright, intense light. Then a voice that Heylel hadn't heard in ages boomed. "It is not your time yet, Lucifer," Michael shouted.

Heylel couldn't stop his being from bursting out of the shell that housed him. The body that was once Kiroly Adamik's exploded, coating the entire cabin with his dripping remains. The force of his expulsion from the earthly realm back into the ethereal one caused the windows to blow out of the Airbus. Frigid air rushed in then right back out, the pull so strong that an enormous hole was ripped open in the fuselage and it extracted the body of the screaming Mr. Nazir out, along with several rows of seats.

As the emergency lights flashed throughout the plane and the panicked pilots squawked over the radio for help, the massive Airbus took a sharp nosedive and like a bullet, raced to its final resting place at the bottom of the Atlantic Ocean.

BURNING PAIN TORE at me as the sharp steel sliced through my back and into my chest. My ears were bombarded with screams of anger all around me. Mitchell, who had been unable to stop the trajectory of his thrust, immediately yanked the blade out, and then I felt nothing. My entire body had gone numb. He grabbed the back of my neck and twisted me around to face him.

"Nice try, bitch," he grumbled, then spit in my face. He tossed my body aside and stepped back over to Jacob, who was fully awake and on his feet.

I couldn't move. My voice was locked along with my torso, my spinal cord shredded. In a crumpled heap next to the altar, my vision blurring, my body struggling for oxygen, I knew it was over.

"Jesus, help us!" I heard Jacob scream. His voice boomed across the glen, the cry so loud that it made my ears ring.

Slap!

"Shut up, old man! This is our time, not his! He had his time on earth, now it is Heylel's!" Mitchell screamed, his voice just as loud as Jacob's had been.

Suddenly, the earth shook so violently that the ground underneath us began to split apart. Uncle Cy must have lost his balance because he fell down right next to me, his wicked face smashed into the dirt by my ear. In the distance, I heard trees snap and crash to the forest floor.

"Mitchell, *move!*" I heard Emily yell from my left.

"Not until it's finished!" Mitchell screamed back.

A clap of thunder, louder than I had ever heard before, crackled above us, followed by a brilliant bolt of lightning that skittered across the blood-red sky, turning it a vibrant light pink.

"The time has not yet come!"

The second the words were spoken from the stratosphere, the red that had permeated every inch of the open glen disappeared, replaced with a white, intense light that burned through my eyelids. A flash of heat raced through me, and I felt a presence surround my head. I began to sob when I realized I could feel something cover my entire body, enveloping me in a loving embrace.

"Do not fear, Karmen."

An explosion ripped through the field. As the ground quaked beneath me, I heard the screams of panic from the souls that had been chanting earlier. Just as quickly as they started, they were snuffed out one-by-one. Deadly silence overtook the glen and the earth moved no more.

The warmth that had covered me shifted to my back, the concentration of heat immense, yet I felt no pain. My gurgling breath stopped and I realized I could feel my limbs once more. I sucked in a huge gulp of air as my eyes flew open.

What I saw in front of me was utter devastation.

The altar was gone. No, not gone, *obliterated*. A huge, round crater was all that was left of the huge slab, a gaping crevice that stretched from one end of the field to the other running through it. The valley was no longer glowing red for the source of the evil hue had been blown to kingdom come. All the pieces that remained were no bigger than the size of small pebbles. Puffs of hazy smoke dotted the landscape, as if someone had started several small campfires then put them out.

The acrid smell from the smoke hit me, and to my disgust, I realized that the source of it was flesh.

I rolled over and pulled myself onto all fours, waiting for the stabbing pain in my back to hit me once more. It never came. My legs seemed to work again so I stood up slowly and scanned the destroyed area for any signs of life. That's when I saw a figure limping toward me from the other side of the glen. It took me a moment to realize it was Jacob.

"Jacob!" I yelled, running to him.

His face was covered in soot, his clothes just as dirty. His hair had turned snow white, his face shining so bright that it looked almost like he was holding a flashlight to it. Then it hit me—it was pitch black, which meant he *was* glowing.

I threw my arms around him and hugged him tight, sobbing into his shoulder. "Oh God, Jacob. I thought Mitchell killed you. I tried…I tried to save you. What…what happened? Where are they? And why…what happened to your hair and face?" I sputtered through choked sobs.

Jacob's strong hand stroked the back of my hair. "Shhh, it's all over now, Karmen. It's over. That is all that's left of them," Jacob said, nudging me to follow his gaze. "He destroyed them with his words."

Confused, I replied, "Who destroyed them, Jacob?"

"I'm not sure, but my guess would be Michael."

"As in the angel, Michael?" I whispered. "All of them?"

"Yes. Didn't you see him?" Jacob replied, the awe and reverence in his voice unmistakable.

"No, all I saw was a bright light. I couldn't move—something was covering me."

"Not something, Karmen. An angel. I watched him take you into his wings before another one whisked me away over there," Jacob pointed to the edge of the glen that he had walked from.

I didn't ask any more questions. My mind was overloaded with information as it was. My entire core of loved ones, everything and everyone I had ever known and believed in, had been rendered down to several piles of smoldering ashes. Death came on swift wings and slew them all, leaving me alone in the world. Alone and full of so many unanswered questions that I doubted I would ever fully understand the answers even if explained to me.

Jacob released his grip and pulled back, his eyes focused on something behind me. "Stay put, Karmen. There is one more thing that needs to be disposed of."

"What?" I said as I watched him limp over toward the crater.

"This," he said, and bent over and picked up the dagger that had ripped a hole through me earlier. He flung it into the crevice and the second it left his hand, the ground began to sway again. Jacob was at my side in a split second. He grabbed my hand and pulled me to the ground, then covered my body with his as the entire area shook. I closed my eyes and refused to look, terrified of seeing any more. In seconds, it was over. Jacob slowly released his grip on me and stood up. I only opened my eyes when I heard his low whistle.

"Well, don't that beat all?"

My mouth hung open in shock. It looked like we had been transported somewhere else because the destruction from before was gone. No, not just gone, *it was as if it never existed.* There was not one scattered pebble, pile of smoldering ashes or even footsteps left. Thick, tall grass covered every inch of the glen. There was not one telltale sign of the circle, the altar or any of the evil participants who had been vaporized—there was nothing left.

"I…" was all I could get out. I reached around to feel the wound it had made in my back. To my surprise, the only thing I felt was the hole in my shirt.

"Jacob! It's gone." I squealed with delight.

"Not gone, Karmen. Healed. There is a big difference," Jacob said as he walked back toward me, his shining face leading the way. That's when I noticed that the huge gash that Jacob had on his head earlier was gone. The only sign it had ever been there was the blood stains on his shirt.

"I must have found favor with God or something. You too—not only did he heal your wound, but it seems he decided to make you a human candle. Complete with a white wick on top!" I laughed, tears of joy running down my face.

Jacob reached out his hand, and I gladly embraced it. He was all I had left and somehow, I knew that would be enough.

"I wouldn't laugh too hard there, missy. You are no longer a carrot top."

"I'm not?" I pulled a strand of hair in front of me. "Oh wow, I'm not! It's pure white, just like yours. Please tell me my face hasn't become a flashlight like yours too?" I said, shocked by my new appearance.

Jacob laughed. "Nope, only me. I guess since I was in the middle of a struggle for the knife from Mitchell when the cavalry arrived and looked up, the light infused me with this Heavenly glow. Now I know how Moses felt. Hope it goes away before next Sunday's sermon. Not exactly sure how I would explain it to the flock."

"What do you mean?" I asked as we slowly made our way through the new, fresh grass back toward the cabin.

"I have a lot to teach you, don't I?" Jacob teased. "When Moses came down from Mount Sinai with the Ten Commandments…"

As we gently picked our way through the glen, I was shocked when I realized I was smiling at the sound of Jacob's voice as he spoke, my grin becoming bigger when I heard another sound that had been absent before.

The sound of the creatures of the forest was like music to my ears. I stopped and turned around and took one last look. The sun streaked across the sky amidst the fluffy white clouds, the rays streaming through them and caressing the green grass.

"Beautiful, isn't it?" Jacob said from behind me.

"Yes. And very strange. After all that happened, I feel…I don't know…tranquil? How can that be?" I muttered in response. I should be a blubbering fool at best, catatonic at worst. After all, my life had just undergone not only a one-eighty, but my entire belief system had just violently been shoved in another direction after being stabbed and then miraculously healed. I had witnessed—sort of—an epic battle between good and evil, ending with the destruction of the four most important people in my world.

Jacob moved beside me, his warm hand gently touched my shoulder.

"Peace that surpasses all understanding, dear. Consider it a gift from above."

I nodded in silence and turned to face him. It was a gift all right.

A divine one.

IT TOOK US over an hour to make our way through the woods. Both of us were physically exhausted but neither of us could rest until we knew that it was truly over. In only a few hours, Kiroly Adamik was due to give his speech to the United Nations.

The minute we walked into the living room, I sighed. "We won't be watching anything on that," I said, pointing to the demolished television set. "I forget I broke it, and there isn't another one here."

"Grab a bag and let's head over to my place. We can catch the morning news there. Once we are certain things are okay, we can decide what to do about...the disappearances."

I sighed. I hadn't even let my mind wander over into *that* territory yet, and I wasn't going to enter that area now. We had much bigger concerns on our plate at the moment.

"Only on one condition—I have to bring Furby," I said as I grabbed his carrier from next to the demolished couch. I looked up when I heard Jacob laugh.

"Oh, not a problem at all. As I said earlier, I believe I have a new friend."

Sure enough, Furby was perched on Jacob's shoulder like a parrot, his furry face buried in Jacob's neck.

"How did he...? Oh, never mind. You watch him and I'll go grab a few things."

When I walked into my bedroom, I was confronted with the open bag, the blood money still neatly packed inside. My first instinct was to grab my own bag and then set the whole damned place on fire, obliterating every trace of Mom, Cy, Mitchell and Emily in a fiery inferno. A fitting sendoff, considering what happened to them in the glen earlier. Maybe the burning flames would incinerate each of them entirely from my memory.

While I packed my suitcase, I took one last look at the money. Before I could change my mind, I called out to Jacob.

"Jacob? Will you please come carry this?"

I stood by the edge of the bed when he walked in, finger pointing to the now closed suitcase. I slung my bag over my shoulder and waited while his eyes darted between me and the bag of money. For a minute, I thought he was going to say something, maybe balk at the idea. He reached down and grabbed the two pieces of paper that we left behind earlier, shoved them in his front pants pocket and hefted the bag off the bed. We walked in silence out to his truck, my heart thumping in my chest as I took in the last glimpse of my ol' Kentucky home.

Ten minutes later, as the morning sun reached its full height over the top of Bailey Mountain, we were on the main road. Furby had refused to be put inside his carrier and now sat on Jacob's lap, curled up into a tight ball. We hadn't said anything during our short drive. Both of us were lost inside a myriad of thoughts. I started to comment about Furby to break the ice, but something on the radio caught my attention.

It was the annoying wail of the Emergency Broadcast System.

"*Repeating...The flight carrying European Council leader, Kiroly Adamik, went down over the Atlantic at around 3:54 a.m. At this time, it is still unclear as to the reason for the crash, although several credible sources are reporting that numerous terror groups are claiming responsibility. Reports are flooding in from witnesses who claim to have seen the plane explode in mid-air before impact. At this time, it is feared that all on board perished. Until all claims are fully investigated and the wreckage found, all flight travel in the United States has been grounded...Repeating...*"

The floodgates opened inside me and the tears gushed out faster and heavier than a raging river. I couldn't form a clear thought in my head. Sadness. Heartache. Betrayal. Loneliness. Fear. Joy. Every emotion possible spun through me as I finally wept for it all. I felt like an empty shell, a withered husk of my former self. The Karmen Moncrille I had always known had a mother and uncle who adored her, a best friend whom she could count on for *anything* and was loved by a man whose heart she adored as well. That woman didn't exist anymore. Coming to grips with that reality shredded all my ties to my former life. My entire life was based upon one enormous lie just so others could use me for their evil ambitions.

It felt like I cried for hours in the small front seat of Jacob's truck. The tears simply wouldn't stop, but they did begin to slow down enough for me to hear Jacob's.

While I wept like a baby, Jacob must have pulled over because I realized that we had parked on the shoulder of the road. Jacob's face was buried in his hands, resting on the steering wheel. His chest heaved with each mournful sob.

As I watched him suffer, I felt a stirring inside of me. It rose from deep within and quickly spread up to my heart, then engulfed my mind. True, pure love filled every crevice in me. My former life was over, burned away just like those that had betrayed me, but that didn't seem to matter anymore. I was sitting next to the most honest, stoic, truthful and heroic person I had ever met—and yet I had only known of his existence for less than forty-eight hours. A man who lived what he believed and risked everything, including his life, to help me. I had been a total stranger—a figure who haunted his dreams.

Gently, I reached over and touched Jacob's shoulder. "Please, Jacob. Don't cry. I can't stand to see a grown man sob. Besides, you didn't give me time to finish my meltdown before you started yours."

He pulled one hand away from his face and reached up and covered my own. After a few sniffles and one good wipe of his face on his shirtsleeve, he turned his wet face toward mine. His snow white hair was sticking out in every direction.

"Karmen, I...I don't know if I possess the words to properly thank you."

I blinked in shock. "Thank me? For what? Seems like all I did was invade your dreams for years, drag you out into the dead of night to confront a coven of devil worshipers and then almost get you killed. Yeah, which part of that are you thanking me for?"

I smiled warmly at him, hoping my inappropriate humor would lighten the heavy situation. Unfortunately, it didn't work.

"You are a pistol, Karmen. I'll give you that. Spunk and strength still shining through even in the midst of enormous emotional upheaval. I'm sorry I'm bawling like a starving kitten, but I just can't believe that you risked your life to save mine. I feel…so…I don't know, unworthy. And extremely blessed."

I sniffed back my tears and released humor instead.

"Well, our original plan didn't work out the way we'd hoped, so I improvised."

"Actually, it did," he responded, his voice quiet, reflective.

Confused, I replied, "Run that by me one more time?"

"I left out a few details of the vision I had. I saw that you were going to kill yourself to end all of this. I couldn't let that happen, so I asked God to let them kill me instead. My life in exchange for yours—the wrong sacrifice would be made, thus nullifying the words you wrote and saving us all."

"Wait…what? You…me…so was that it? It was our willingness to sacrifice ourselves for the other that stopped it?" I sputtered.

"Could be. But I believe the real reason is just as the angel said. The Devil will have his shot at ruling for seven years, but the time wasn't right today. I knew, no—*I felt*—that. The Holy Spirit—I still felt His presence inside of me—comforting me. According to scripture, the deceiver will not be able to reveal himself to the world until the Holy Spirit is removed from the earth. At least that is how I always read *2 Thessalonians 2:7*.

Oh boy, I have a lot to learn.

"You really were going to lay down your life for mine and the world," I whispered, the full magnitude of what happened less than three hours ago settling in. The words I had read countless times in numerous books finally hit home:

Greater love hath no man than this: that a man lay down his life for a friend.

My façade broke and I felt the tears pour out of me again. I leaned over and hugged him, and we sat in the bright morning sun on the side of Highway 27 and wept like lost, orphaned siblings that had just been reunited. I broke away from the embrace first.

"You know, Jacob, you really need to stop reading my mind, because it's getting kind of freaky. Let's just call this day even—I saved you, you saved me—and together, we managed to save the entire human population. I would say that's a successful day, wouldn't you?" I said, wiping my tears with my shaking hands.

Jacob did the same then started the truck back up. As he pulled onto the highway and headed toward his house, he smiled. The enormity of his grin was only matched by the glow of his newly illuminated face. I suspected his guest bedroom was going to be where I ended up permanently, since I really had no place to go and felt like I had a lot to learn from him, not only as a mentor, but as a pastor and friend.

"Don't get too cocky there, missy. One win in a skirmish does not mean victory over the entire war. The battle still rages, as it has since Lucifer was ousted from Heaven. Today wasn't his time, but one day, it will be. The Bible is very clear on that premise. No one knows when that day will be except the Lord God. All we are commanded to do as His followers are to watch the signs and pray, and seek out His wisdom as the time grows shorter. When the final soul on this earth who will hear His words and accept the truth believes, then there won't be a thing anyone can do to stop the Antichrist from his short-lived reign."

I let out a slow, heavy sigh. "You don't think that…"

"No, Karmen. I don't. You made the conscious choice to reject the lies and held onto the truth. You won't be the one that is used next time. Believe me when I say that your family and friends are simply droplets of water in a vast ocean of followers of the Evil One. He will seek out and find another venue to gain entry through—and it won't be you. I'm sure of it. Feel it right here," he said, pointing to his heart.

I swallowed hard. *Please, God, let him be right.*

"If my former destiny was to write the lie…I wonder what will happen if I decide to tell the truth?"

"If you write for the glory of God, my dear, the truth will always set you free."

Jacob pulled up in front of a quaint house that sat next to a small, white church about two hundred yards away. The graceful steeple was topped with a simple yet delicate cross glittered in the morning light. I stared at the symbol that had never meant anything to me before, but now, meant everything.

"I just thought of something, Jacob. What are we going to tell people is the reason for me being here? I mean, I don't know a lot about rules of the church and all, but somehow, I think your members might bristle at having a young woman visiting overnight with you. I doubt they are going to believe that our relationship is strictly platonic."

Jacob shut the engine off and gathered Furby under one arm and then reached over into the bed of the truck to retrieve the suitcase with the other.

"Way ahead of you, my dear niece."

"Niece? Oh come on, Jacob. People are going to ask you why you never told them that you were Karmen Moncrille's uncle, don't you think?"

Jacob paused in mid-stride and turned back to me, the look of amusement on his face apparent.

"You seem to forget that you don't *look* like Karmen Moncrille anymore. Perhaps a good once-over in the mirror when we get inside will ease your worries. No one will bat an eye, I promise."

I laughed at his candor. Yeah, with a head full of white hair and probably the wrinkles from all the stress to match, I definitely wouldn't resemble the woman I once was. Like the explosion that destroyed the altar, she was completely gone.

"So, *Uncle Jacob*, what's my name?" I said when we crossed the threshold of the front door. Inside the living room the first thing I saw was an old picture of a beautiful little girl on top of the mantle. I knew instantly that it was a picture of his daughter, Sarah.

My gosh, but we did look alike.

Jacob set Furby down to let him explore his new surroundings. Furby never glanced back at either of us. He curled his fluffy tail over his back and began to wander around the living room, his padded feet never made a sound as he followed his nose. Jacob walked up behind me and said, "That choice, my dear, is entirely up to you."

I stared at the picture of the young girl who I resembled so much and contemplated the name Sarah, but something niggled in my mind that wasn't right. Finally, it hit me.

"Eva. Eva Abshire."

Tears welled up in Jacob's eyes. He held them at bay and smiled, pulling me into a bear hug. Relief and gratitude fell from us both in the form of our salty tears as we clung tight to each other in his small, welcoming living room. Over his shoulder, I could see the rise of Bailey Mountain.

"I had the unmistakable feeling that I was meant to live here at the base of the mountain, so here I am. I didn't realize I would be on the other side of it, though," I muttered into Jacob's chest.

"This time, my dear, you are on the *right* side," Jacob replied as he released me from his bear hug.

"Yes, because the truth set me free," I said, moving over to the enormous stack of books on Jacob's shelf. "Looks like I have a lot of studying to do."

"First things first, *Eva*. We have some rather urgent issues to take care of now that we know the world is safe, at least temporarily."

I sighed. The tasks that loomed before us would be arduous. After the day I'd just experienced, tying up the loose ends of the disappearance of five people, myself included, should be a piece of proverbial cake.

Not.

Jacob sensed my apprehension and smiled. Our familial bonds already solidified, he held out his warm hand, which I clasped with my shaky one. Furby purred at his feet so he bent down and picked him up, then handed his furry body over to me and grabbed my bag.

"This won't be easy, but I don't believe it will be as difficult as you are imaging. Think about it—all those who knew you were in Kentucky are gone—nothing was left in that glen, not even a trace of DNA. An investigation into the disappearances of all of you will ensue and turn up diddly-squat. After all, the only remaining evidence that any of you were ever in Kentucky are three vehicles at your cabin, none of which belong to you. The place is trashed and your fingerprints are all over the shattered items. I would think the conclusion would be that you put up one heckuva fight."

The sting of Mitchell's and Emily's betrayal bit into my heart and took a prominent spot next to the treachery of my mother and uncle. I wondered how many years, if ever, it would take for me not to have nightmares about all of them, as well as the supernatural events that happened in the glen earlier. I pushed the vile memories out and buried my face in Furby's silky fur and pondered Jacob's words. An idea was forming.

"True, and since they had been seeing each other behind my back, I imagine that entailed communication between the two of them in various forms that can easily be uncovered during an investigation." I paused and silently continued with that line of thinking, my creative mind working overtime.

"If I had to guess, the probable conclusion will be that Mitchell and Emily had something to do with the mysterious disappearance of you, your mom and your uncle. Perhaps the authorities will conclude it was for monetary reasons. I mean, look at the evidence they will inevitably find. The relationship between Mitchell and Emily; Emily secretly leaving school and whisking you away to a remote location; your mother with-drawing the money from the account. It will look like Emily and Mitchell might have been holding you for ransom or some-thing. But in any event, Karmen Moncrille and the rest of the missing group will eventually be declared dead. The missing million dollars from your bank account the catalyst that started the ball rolling, so to speak."

I looked up at Jacob in astonishment.

"Gee, *Uncle Jacob*, I didn't realize your thoughts could be so—demented."

Jacob's crooked grin and knowing wink made me laugh, which was something I had wondered if I would ever do again and really feel the humor. "Hey, just working with the mess in front of us," he said as he led me down the hall. "The circum-stances are such that they don't leave room for any happy out-comes for the police to conjure up."

We stopped at the first door. He opened it and deposited the bag that held the cash next to the small bed. The room was sparsely decorated and would require a feminine touch but that was a good thing. Redecorating would give me something to occupy my brain while I settled in and kept myself hidden from the prying eyes of the world.

We headed back toward the kitchen in silence. As we passed the bathroom, I contemplated excusing myself but refrained. I wasn't quite ready to see the new me. Jacob motioned for me to sit at the dining room table. "I don't know about you, but I'm starving. I'm not much of a cook, but I can heat up a mean bowl of soup."

Furby began to squirm so I set him down. He immediately trotted over to Jacob and began rubbing his legs. Traitor.

"I didn't realize how hungry I was until you mentioned food. Now, my stomach won't stop grumbling, so I guess soup it is." I turned my gaze back out the picture window to the beautiful mountainside. "Jacob, do you really believe that people around here will buy this whole uncle and niece thing? When the news hits that I am missing…" my voice trailed off.

"Recall that this town has kept secrets for generations. Big ones—so don't fret. Besides," he said quietly as he walked over and sat down across from me, "the Lord will watch over us."

"You're going to have to cut me some slack here on this whole faith thing. I'm kind of a newbie."

He patted my leg as he stood and went back to the pan of soup on the stove. "As I told you before, I have plenty of faith, and I'm willing to loan you some until you acquire your own stash. Let's get some food in our bellies so we can think straight, okay?" He poured the steaming liquid into two small bowls.

"Sorry, can't shut the wheels down. I mean, Eva Abshire only exists in our minds. She has no social security number, no way to ever work… what do I do with her when you get tired of having me here as a guest? Resurrect Karmen?"

Jacob bristled. "A guest? Tired of you? I promise you, dear, that will never happen. I've been given a second chance at being a parental figure—do you really think I am going to tire of that?"

I felt a lump form in my throat as I watched him prepare our breakfast, such as it was.

"Do you…do you really think we can get away with it? What if people start asking questions? What if the police discover…?"

"Oh ye of little faith. Recall what we witnessed today. If the Lord can handle His adversaries, how could He not handle ours? Seems to me that one million reasons you will never have to be Karmen Moncrille again are sitting in your room."

I wrinkled my nose is disgust. "That's blood money."

Jacob rummaged through the cabinets and produced some napkins, then set the bowls on a tray. He reached into his pocket and extracted the crumpled pieces of paper. He rolled them around in between his hands. "I can understand why you would feel that way. But maybe you should try looking at it from a different angle. It is, after all, your money. Regardless of how it came to be in your possession or the original intent for its use by others, it serves now to open a door for you—one that leads to a new life."

I remained silent, ingesting his words. Could it really be that simple? Could I truly just disappear?

Jacob smiled an impish grin. He held the small ball of paper over the sink. In one swift motion, he dropped the paper into the disposal then flicked the switch on the wall. The grinding metal shredded the remaining evidence down the drain.

"There now. One door closed, another opened. Easy-peasey."

My mouth dropped open. "Did you just...dispose of evidence? Isn't that against the rules of the priesthood or something?"

Jacob threw his head back and laughed. "I am a pastor, not a priest. And it may have been against the rules of man to do so, but that was trumped by my newly rediscovered parental instincts to protect my loved one. Now, what would you like to drink? I have pop, tea, water or coffee."

The warmth of our bond washed over me. He was right: I needed more faith. As crazy as it seemed, as improbable as it sounded, this could work. No, this *would* work.

"No coffee," I shot back, then we both burst out laughing. Jacob set our sustenance on the table then plopped down next to me, his eyes dancing with happiness.

"Welcome home, Eva. Welcome home."

epilogue

Two Days Later

NIKO CAPINSKI SAT ON HIS FRONT STOOP AND watched the hordes of people crowd the narrow cobblestone street in front of his house. Men, women and children wept openly as they pushed and shoved their way toward the center of the city, which had become a makeshift memorial to Kiroly Adamik. Two days had passed since the death of their hometown hero in such a violent fashion, and the shock had brought Niko's small town of Dunaua to a halt. The entire village literally shut down as every heartbroken Hungarian who could walk converged into one throbbing mass of mourners.

Even though the wailing and gnashing of teeth pained his ears, it was better than watching the pathetic drivel on the television inside the cramped house. When his mother left to join the teeming throng, she was unable to convince Niko to join her or pull him away from the television. Niko hung on every report, every new lead, every little detail uncovered.

It had made him almost physically ill when all the major stations cut into the reports of the plane crash and investigation with reports of the disappearance and possible death of some American writer. Niko narrowed his eyes, bristling at the memory of seeing her face splashed across the screen. The news coverage of his beloved Kiroly's tragic, untimely death was soon overshadowed by some woman whose only contribution to the world was that she wrote books! The reporters all spoke with hushed, professional tones when they spoke about Kiroly, but they almost seemed emotionally involved, saddened, when they spoke about that stupid, young girl. Who cares? She was just another rich, spoiled American brat who had no redeeming value. When the last reporter actually choked up, Niko exploded and kicked the small television off the stand, shattering the screen, and made his way out to the front stoop to cool off.

The pitiful sounds of women wailing and beseeching God for comfort over the loss of such a remarkable man made Niko's ears ring. Not to be outdone, the men that intermingled in the mass of bodies raised their fists in anger, vowing revenge for Kiroly's murder even though it still was not clear which terrorist group was truly responsible for his assassination. Niko watched them all with fierce intensity, forcing his fourteen year old eyes to remain dry. He would not cry or show any emotion to the outside world for the loss of his idol. No, Niko would never display such weakness because that would demean the memory of the noble Kiroly.

Niko sat erect, stoic, refusing to act like the crazed, impotent men who shouted for justice yet wouldn't lift a finger to obtain any. They were strutting around like angry roosters, clucking and making all sorts of annoying racket, but eventually they would return to their homes and resume their pathetic lives.

Kiroly Adamik's untimely death would only be remembered at yearly memorial services held in his honor around the gaudy bronze statue that had been erected several years ago when he became the leader of the European Council. Kiroly's vision for humanity would be a fleeting memory to the useless fools who cried their crocodile tears, his contributions to the world would evaporate just as quickly as the tears on the faces of his countrymen.

But Niko would never forget. He wasn't like them and never had been. He recalled the first day he had watched Kiroly Adamik give a speech at the library when he was less than five years old. Kiroly's words, his fierce presence, his strength of character and commanding voice had drawn Niko in, and ever since that day, Niko felt a deep connection to him. He followed his every move, listened to every speech and read every newspaper article about the man who Niko sensed would conquer the world. Niko swallowed hard and forced the hot lump back down. In its place, he let his seething anger free to control his thoughts.

It didn't matter to Niko which side ordered the death of his beloved Kiroly. The truth was that both sides argued over the soil in Jerusalem for countless centuries. In Niko's mind, the groups were scourges on the world. Hatred for each ethnic group raged inside him, burning the last vestiges of compassion for the Jews or the Muslims from his mind. Niko closed his eyes and envisioned the destruction of that slender stretch of dusty land that had been the source, the breeding ground, for every despicable war and atrocity that mankind had endured since the dawn of time.

Niko felt a surge of power, an influx of white-hot energy flow through his veins. He let the hatred take control, determined to wipe out the enemies that placed the center of their religions upon the small tract of land in Jerusalem. As Niko's intensity level on his vision rose, he realized he didn't hear the sounds from the crowd anymore. His hands clenched at his sides as fury coursed through him, his blood boiling. Just when Niko thought his heart would burst from the rage, he heard a voice whisper inside his mind.

"Come, Niko. Follow me. I will show you the way and guide you. Let not your heart be troubled, for together, we can make the enemies of Kiroly pay. The world shall cower at your feet, my boy."

Niko nodded his head in silent agreement to the deliciously tempting baritone. The eloquently spoken words were like a drug that dulled his sorrow.

And fed his rage.

Please note the following previews are unedited, early versions from the upcoming novels, *Fine As Frog Hair* and *Empty Shell*. In their final versions, the material will be fully edited and the content may slightly change.

Fine As Frog Hair

Sneak Peek

Coming Soon

fine as frog hair

Chapter One

I CLIMBED UP THE SPRAWLING CONCRETE STEPS AS the smell of gardenias and jasmine clung to the humidity-laden air, settling their natural perfume on my damp shirt. My thick Montana skin was never going to come to an amicable agreement with the heavy, tropical atmosphere, and the sweat was sprinting down my back and face in protest to the torture I was submitting it to.

Stopping at the final step to catch my breath and wipe my sticky forehead, I removed my soaked bangs from my eyes in one quick swoop. I glanced around and was greeted by the brick inlaid sign that proudly proclaimed the name of the place, "Rolling Brooks Estates." The faux-gold, trimmed lettering was overly ostentatious, like it was announcing the entrance to the Royal Palace or something.

All I cared about right was that the place housed a large air conditioning unit, and I wondered how people survived the earthly version of Hell without some form of arctic air blasting them constantly. It was days like today that I questioned my sanity in accepting the academic scholarship offered to me and moving "down South." What was I thinking? Yes, Montana summers were hot, but it was a *dry* heat. The minute I dared venture from the cool confines of a building, I was accosted by the perpetual steam bath experience. I made a mental note to step up my research on transferring my scholarship to a location where the word "humidity" was foreign.

When I looked past the long walkway ahead of me, I wanted to gasp at the beauty of the building and grounds, which took my mind off the heat for a moment. From the red brick exterior to the six enormous, white columns gracing the porch that encircled the entire place, to the well-manicured yard dotted with weeping willows dancing in the hot breeze, it looked more like a scene from *Gone With the Wind* than a retirement home.

I took out my camera from my bag and snapped a few pictures that would accompany my story, smiling while I thought, *Yep, if this is what retirement is like, sign me up!* Then the stinging burn of my sweat waylaid my eyes, so I hurried up to the colossal front door and took in a huge gulp of cold air that greeted my drenched body with an almost tangible force.

"Welcome to Rolling Brooks Estates. May I help you?"

The sweet young nurse behind the desk, whose nametag read Nurse Langston, spoke in an accent that matched up perfectly with the surroundings, her hair and makeup a little overdone for my taste, but pretty nonetheless.

"Yes, I'm Roger Fox, and I have an appointment with Mr. Marvin Hermech at three," I replied absently while my eyes swept across the expanse of the entryway and living area. It was just as grand as the outside in terms of décor but with one minor difference: it reeked. Even those meticulously cared for grounds couldn't hide the fact that indeed, the beautiful surroundings were in fact a place that people came to die. The smell of bleach, plastic, stale food, and death overtook the fragrant aroma of the gardenias and jasmine from earlier, filling my nostrils with their stench and making my eyes burn again.

"Oh, you mean Mr. Hermesch! You're here for the story, right?" Nurse Langston replied. I nodded in agreement as I reached for a tissue off the granite counter and dabbed my leaking eyes. "You're doin' the article for the paper, right?"

"Well, school newspaper, yes," I said, holding back a sneeze.

"Mr. Hermesch…oh, by the way, you pronounced his name wrong…it's *Her-mesh*. He's a quiet man, but if you call him by the wrong name, he can get nasty. Respect, ya know?"

I snorted, which sounded rather disgusting given the fact that my nose was thoroughly clogged. *Exactly how nasty can an eighty-five year old man get? Would he fling his bedpan at me? Spit a cough drop in my face? Hurl his gelatinous food on the floor at my feet?* The imagined possibilities were endless and extremely comical, no doubt showing up on my face.

Nurse Langston came around to my side and handed me the ID badge with my name written in flowing cursive and continued to chatter away while she led me through the intricate twists and turns of the place. We ended up on the west side of the building in front of two massive French doors. Nurse Langston paused for a moment before opening them, turning to face me, pointing her long, slender finger in my face.

"Now, you listen here, Mr. Fox. I can tell right away that you don't really want to be here and plan on just *'la-de-dahing'* for a few minutes with Mr. Hermesch to get your story, maybe plannin' on fillin' in the blanks with your own imagination so you can hurry up and leave. I am here to tell you: that would be a mistake. Mr. Hermesch will take a bit to warm up to you, but once he does, and if he chooses to bless you by sharing the incredible life he's led, you'll walk out of here with that smart-ass chip off your shoulder, and perhaps some respect for your elders." Her irises were barely a blue blurb behind her narrowed eyelids, her irritation radiating some intense heat in my direction.

"Wow, what did I do to deserve that little outburst?" I said, shocked by her abrupt change in attitude. I thought I was making headway with her toward a date on our walk over.

"Because I see through that mask you're wearin.' You're here because you have to be, not because you *want* to be. I have been takin' care of Mr. Hermesch for the last three years and have grown quite fond of him, and I won't have some smart-mouthed punk wastin' his day away," Nurse Langston replied, her Southern drawl becoming more pronounced as her ire grew. "You are the first non-staffer to speak with him in over four years, and I aim for it to be a *pleasant* experience for him, understand?" Her perfectly proportioned chest bounced pleasantly as her hands settled hard on her slender hips.

"Nurse Langston, I'm sorry if I came across that way. It's the heat. I've only been here for a year, and I'm just not used to it yet. Makes me a little rough around the edges, you know? We Northerners just aren't as adaptable to it as you natives are." I cleared my throat and continued, watching her eye me with disdain, hands still clenching her hipbone. Any second now, I just knew the foot tap was coming.

"Let me assure you, I take my education and my assignment quite seriously. Not only is my article going to be published in our school paper for my Journalism class, but it will be part of my thesis on World War II for my major, American History," I replied, forcing my voice to portray my true intentions. *Gees, Roger, great first impression!*

Nurse Langston's hackles recessed, and she graced me with her beautiful smile again, her fingers released her hips and moved silently to rest by her sides.

"As long as we understand each other, Mr. Fox. Now," she said turning her head toward the door, "let me tell you a few things 'bout Mr. Hermesch before you begin."

Producing my best smile, I nodded in silence and awaited her instructions, motioning for her to wait while I removed my notepad from my backpack. Pen at the ready, I nodded once more. My attention to detail seemed to relax her a bit more, so she began.

"For patient confidentiality reasons, I can't tell you what's wrong with him. I can tell you that Mr. Hermesch is from a generation that demands politeness from others and don't tolerate no 'sass' from anyone. In case you *Montanians* aren't familiar, 'sass' means 'smart ass back talk' in Yankee speak. You may feel the need to get fired up time you need to repeat questions to him, but don't. He will shut down like a steel trap and not answer anymore if you do."

I continued to nod while I scribbled, hoping I could read my scratch later. Trying to keep my pen moving as fast as her words was difficult, plus the language barrier wasn't helping. A year under my belt and I still had so much to learn about the local linguistics. I made an entry, noting he was hard of hearing and to speak loudly.

"Now, Mr. Fox, you aren't listenin' to me, are you?" Nurse Langston said, her voice rising at least one octave. "Don't you go writin' stuff that ain't true! I never said Mr. Hermesch was *hard of hearing*, I said you may need to repeat questions to him."

My cheeks felt the heat racing to them at her irritation with me. *Strike two, Roger.*

"I'm sorry, *ma'am*," I said quietly. "I realize you are bound by ethics and limited on what you can say, so how about we approach this from another angle? I will tell you what I do know about Mr. Hermesch, and if I am wrong, will you stop me?"

Nurse Langston rolled that idea around for a moment before she replied, "That sounds easy enough. No harm, no foul, right?"

"Right. Ok, so in my research, I discovered that Mr. Hermesch was born in 1926 in Sheridan, Arkansas, to sharecroppers that worked the cotton fields, and lived in the rural community until the age of sixteen. He joined the Navy during World War II and was a gunner on the U.S.S. Langley for two tours, then received an honorable discharge. Married, two children, all of whom he has outlived."

Pausing momentarily, I glanced up from my earlier notes from my research on the Internet, looking to see if Nurse Langston had come to terms yet with the fact that I was, indeed, serious. She tried her best to hide her surprise, but those big, blue eyes told another story. Maybe there was hope for a dinner date yet! I smiled a bit and continued.

"I made the mistake earlier, as you pointed out, that Mr. Hermesch is deaf and/or hard of hearing. I would like to recant my previous statement and rephrase my answer. I believe the correct one is that he suffers from some type of short term memory loss and needs to be reminded about what he is talking about, yet has full recall of memories from his past? In other words, he suffers from Alzheimer's?"

Nurse Langston smiled, her white Chicklet teeth almost blinding me. *Score one for Roger!*

I made a few more observations about the man sitting on the other side of the French doors to the eager ears of Nurse Langston, impressing even myself with my accuracy. Each new revelation was rewarded with an even bigger smile, along with a faint hint of curiosity behind her eyes. My odds of scoring dinner were now hovering around the fifty-fifty range, and if I kept this up, maybe dessert at her place.

Her hand was warm and soft when she looped it around my wrist, holding my arm still before I could turn the handle to meet with my interviewee. Her voice was low and husky, her cinnamon-flavored breath caressed my cheek as she said, "Please, Mr. Fox, treat him with dignity and kindness. This may be the last sunset he ever sees."

She let go and retreated, her rubbery nurse shoes making a funny noise as they whisked her away, her round ass swaying nicely behind her. Now *that* was a reason to withstand the volcanic heat! I remembered now my main reason for opting to move: Southern women were unlike any other women on the planet.

I forced my mind (and my eyes) off her ass and back to the task at hand. Her sweet whisperings were not about what I wanted her to murmur to me, but they did carry just as much emotional impact: Mr. Hermesch was dying, fast.

Thoughts of old age and death weren't part of the normal repertoire of a twenty-four-year-old college student, and I was no different. My life consisted of studying, deadlines, research, work, and occasionally, a romp with a cute little coed now and again (or a hot nurse). Even though history was my major, it never really dawned on me that all those facts, all the observations, all the artifacts dug up and on display at the museums I loved to frequent actually stemmed from *someone's* life—a real, live human being that was full of energy at one point, just like I was now.

And I was about to meet one, right before he departed our world.

My tie straight and my nose and eyes no longer exuding bodily fluid, I opened the door and stepped out onto the small sun porch, closing the entrance behind me. I announced my presence with a small clearing of my throat, stepping around the black, wrought-iron table where Mr. Hermesch sat. The first thing I noticed about him was the snow-white head of hair, still full of gentle waves that curled slightly upward at the ends. When I stood in front of him and held out my hand to introduce myself, I was astonished by the intensity of his light blue eyes that were surrounded by his crinkly, tissue paper thin flesh.

"Good afternoon, sir…um, Mr. Hermesch. I'm Roger Fox. It's a pleasure to meet you, sir," I said, shocked by the formality of my words. It wasn't just Nurse Langston's warning about respect and politeness that caused me to stand up a bit straighter—there was something in the aura surrounding Mr. Hermesch that I was responding to.

His eyes bored into mine while he gave me a good once over before he removed his gnarled hand from his lap and clasped mine. Although the skin was nearly transparent and mottled with enlarged blue veins, his grip was firm and forceful. An awkward smile crossed my face while he pumped my arm.

"Mr. Fox, mighty fine to meet you. Please, have a seat. Tea?" he gestured to the tall, plastic pitcher sitting in front of him.

Dots of sweat were already forming just about everywhere on me, so I accepted his offer. "Yes, sir, that would be fantastic."

While he poured a glass for us both, I set out my note-pad, pen, and digital recorder, ready to begin, and snuck a quick glance at him while he busied himself with the drinks. I guessed that he was about six feet tall when he stood, perhaps a bit taller in his youth before gravity took its heavy toll on his body. Not much was left of him now due to aging and muscle atrophy, but at one point, I bet he was a muscled-up firecracker.

A tattoo decorated his right forearm. It was difficult to make out the exact design since the bluish black ink was faded, but it looked like a skull and crossbones with some words that I couldn't make out etched above and below. His thick, silver wedding ring still held its place of honor on his left hand, and I smiled, recalling that his wife had been dead for over ten years.

It was hard to believe that he was on the verge of dying at any moment. Maybe Nurse Langston's assessment of his physical state was skewed by her emotional attachment to him? While my eyes etched mental snapshots of him into my memory, I couldn't help but think that when I reached his age, I hoped I looked as good.

"Done eye-ballin' me yet, boy?" he said while handing me my glass of tea, a hint of amusement creasing the corners of his mouth. His voice was raspy and deep, his drawl slow and melodic.

"I'm sorry, sir, I…well…um…it's just a habit. I like to learn everything about the subject I write about, including my own interpretation of the surroundings I see." I replied feeling a bit like the time when I was ten and got caught with a girlie maga-zine in my bedroom.

"Son, I'm just joshin' ya. You Nawthern boys never did learn how to relax, did ya?" he said, laughing at his own joke, which caused an immediate coughing spell. The horrid sounds that spewed out from his chest and the gun metal gray his skin turned made me rethink my previous assess-ment of his health.

"I…I…well, I just want to show respect and all—Nurse Langston told me…"

He raised his hand up to stop me. "Now, you never mind what that ol' gal said to you. I ain't goin' nowheres until the good Lord decides to call me home. I am fine as frog hair, I tell ya! Could be today; could be tomorra; could be next year. I 'magine though, He ain't takin' me until I at least get to finish this here tea and tell you the story of my life…if ya'll are ready with all them fancy gadgets."

With that, he raised his glass in a fake salute in the direction of the items on the table and I followed in suit, lifting my cold glass to meet his. He smiled, leaned back in his chair and began, his blue eyes sparkling as he visited distant memories.

"The first thing I can recall is my Meemaw whoopin' my ass for accidently smotherin' some baby chicks while she was cookin' breakfast. You see, I was three and the rest of the family was a workin' in the cotton fields that day, 'cept me and Meemaw. She had sent me to fetch some fresh eggs from the pen, and the chirpin' of the chicks caught my 'tention. The lil' fellers were so soft and cute, and all I was doin' was huggin' them, but then when one would quit fidgitin', I'd grab me another. It was 1931…."

EMPTY SHELL

EXCLUSIVE PREVIEW

COMING SPRING 2014

empty shell

Prologue: Monday Morning

"TURN THAT DAMNED THING OFF!"

"I'm trying, but it's stuck or something."

Jack jerked the bathroom door open and stormed into the bedroom. In three quick strides and he crossed the floor, his face beet red from the hot water in the shower. With a sheepish grin, I held out the noisy thing to him. He didn't even try to hide his irritation. His body language was enough to read his thoughts about my inability to perform such a simple task. He yanked the screeching clock from my fumbling hands.

Angry hands that used to touch me with gentle caresses. God, how I missed them.

I shrugged in silence at his nasty attitude and walked back over to my side of the bed. I searched under the pillow for my glasses. Without them, I couldn't see anything that wasn't within eight inches of my face. No wonder I couldn't find the off switch on the alarm.

With my back to my annoyed husband, I let a small grin of triumph niggle at the corners of my mouth. Listening to him struggle to silence the little plastic piece of hell was rather entertaining. At least I wasn't the only one finding it difficult to shut off.

The noisy clock was another irritating purchase that Jack had made online while watching one of those brain-numbing reality shows that he loved so much. Served him right that he now held a worthless pile of junk. What a waste of the forty bucks. We now owned an alarm clock that was supposed to wake us up to sounds of nature but sounded more like a screaming, rabid howler monkey. One that had its tail caught in a trap—and it seemed to be stuck in the permanent "on" position.

My grin became a full smile when I found my glasses so I could fully watch him attempt to find the off switch. It disappeared in a flash though when I turned around to ask Jack if he was ready for a cup of coffee. When I realized what he was about to do, I forced myself not to flinch at yet another outburst of anger from him. With one final grunt, Jack launched the clock against the wall in utter frustration. It disintegrated into a pile of broken plastic—and left a fist-sized dent in the newly painted sheetrock.

The only good thing from my loving husband's tirade was that it finally killed the incessant buzzing. Jack's damp, dark brown hair flopped forward, releasing his thinning bangs over his eyes without a sound. The way his hair tumbled almost made it look like it was taking a bow for successfully saving our ears.

"Guess you just answered my question about coffee. Obviously, you haven't had any yet."

Jack didn't acknowledge my veiled verbal dig. Instead, he simply used his hooded, deeply set brown eyes to shoot daggers of rage at me. As he moved past me, he didn't even speak. I couldn't help but jump a fraction when he slammed the bathroom door behind him.

Since when did I become cloaked in invisibility?

I let my own irritation out with a small sigh. Briefly, I stared at the two-inch thick wood that separated us, wishing that was the only barrier that life had erected between us. At least the door was a blockade I could see—and knock down if I really wanted to.

Problem was, did I?

I looked over at the mess Jack left on the floor. I started to bend down and gather the broken remnants, but stopped short as my fingers hovered over the rubble. No. Not today. Not again. I opted to leave the twisted wreckage right where it was and let Jack pick up after himself for a change—a small test to see how long it would take for him to do so.

Any maybe to let him know how fed up I am with his mood swings. Whoever said that men don't suffer from hormonal influxes was obviously in a serious state of denial. Maybe I would start spiking Jack's coffee with my hormone pills. He needed something to take the edge off and make him less bitchy. They always worked for me...

The smile I sported earlier came back in the form of a sly grin. My knees popped as I stood back up and made my way down the quiet hallway toward the kitchen. Bright, early morning rays of vibrant yellow danced across the freshly remodeled countertops and floors and reflected off the polished steel of the new appliances. I thought about the hole in the bedroom wall. After months of dealing with hordes of crack-showing, tobacco-spitting and stinky construction workers, they finally finished and left us in peace two weeks ago. Now I would have to call the owner back and make arrangements to have him send a worker back to patch and repaint the bedroom wall.

No, not me. Jack. His temper tantrum—his dilemma to solve. Not mine.

I pushed out the images from seconds ago and followed my nose to the intoxicating smell of freshly brewed coffee. I had enough on my "to-do list" and I wouldn't allow any more to weight me down. I was barely able to breathe as it was.

Ahhh, another fun morning in the Dickinson household...thank goodness for an automatic coffee maker...Monday, Monday...da da la de da...

Minutes later with coffee fixed and eyes finally focusing correctly, I decided to offer a flag of truce. No sense in starting the week out on a sour note. I carried two steaming mugs back down the hall toward the bedroom. Jack's with two sugars and mine black as coal.

Thoughts of my mother's wedding day advice on marriage years ago made a quick lump form in my throat. While she had pretended to be having trouble with the clasp on my dress, she spoke about the various duties of a wife and how a couple could weather numerous ups and downs over the years. "The key to a long lasting marriage, darling Melody, is communication. You can never stop the sharing of yourselves with each other. Communication is the water that nourishes the seed of love."

I had responded with some gushy, naïve comeback about how there was no *way* that Jack and I would *ever* stop talking and sharing with each other. After all, we were in love. There was no subject that we hadn't broached in our three year courtship. Our tastes for life were very similar. We both adored classic rock, Italian food, fast cars, dogs and hours spent watching reruns of *Star Trek*. But our biggest two connectors, which were what brought us together in the first place, was a strong affinity for history and deep Christian faith. That first *World Civilizations* course in college threw us together as study partners, later leading to our first date. The moment Jack held my hand in his during a walk across campus, I was hooked. The connection that travelled between the two of us was more than electric—it was cosmic.

Back then—*oh my god it was almost twenty years ago*—I couldn't breathe without Jack. My existence hung upon his every movement, every touch and every caress. His deep voice would lull me into a state of bliss at night while we would lie awake and plan our life out after college. What career paths we would take. The fact that we both wanted two children—a boy and a girl—named Jacqueline and Jordan. The type of house we would live in, the vehicles we would drive. The various places we would visit and make love in before parenthood arrived.

Jack's eyes would mesmerize me with their liquid stare, pulling me inside his soul and leaving me breathless. When I looked at him, I became lost in a sea of warming tranquility. His muscular arms embraced me in a cocoon of warmth and provided quiet shelter from the world. Back then, we couldn't get enough of each other.

My, how times have changed.

Somewhere, as we meandered down the path of marriage together, we got separated. Our loving grip yanked apart by unseen forces. The fork in the road appeared when, after ten years of trying and thousands of dollars spent on fertility treatments, we realized that I would never be able to carry a child. We both dealt with our grief alone, trying to hide the pain from the other instead of working together to overcome our mutual sadness.

Big mistake. Huge.

I went flying in one direction and Jack practically ran to the other. Our late night cuddling and cooing sessions began to stretch out to twice a week, then once a month, then maybe every six months. Now, I couldn't even remember the last time we had held each other close and let the world around us disappear. Two, three months? We were like that old, raunchy joke about how elderly couples engaged in sex by passing each other in the hall and yelling "screw you" to each other.

I approached the bedroom door and snorted at my mother's words that still resounded in my head and sniffed back the tears that tinkled in the corner of my eyes.

Well, communication may be the key, but what does one do when the signals are hopelessly crossed and nothing remains but dead air? The magical sparks are gone. Quick, someone get the paddles out and crank us back to life! Clear!

Jack was still in the bathroom so I set his mug by the door and walked back into the kitchen. I didn't have time to coddle him. I had to get ready for work and stop mulling over things I couldn't change—at least not with a simple cup of coffee. It was the end of the month which meant I would be swamped while preparing the billing for over three hundred clients. Oh, and to experience the joy of fixing numerous data entry mistakes just as

I had been forced to do the last nine months. I knew they would be there, input by the newest assistant at my office.

Serena, the young blonde with racehorse legs who wore skirts so short that what she ate for breakfast was damn near discernible to anyone within twenty feet of her. It made my stomach churn at the way the male attorneys at the office ogled her—like she was the last meal before the executioner's noose or something. Since the girl was the daughter of one of the firm's biggest clients, none of the drooling males had the balls to chase Serena around her desk physically, but oh the mental gyrations they threw her direction!

The entire female population at work instantly hated Serena the minute her long, shapely limbs walked through the front door. Nothing like having cellulite on your ass, arms that jiggled and a not-so-flat stomach changes your perception of youth. No woman, including me, wanted to be confronted on a daily basis with the fact that—*gasp*—her youthful tight rear and abs had mysteriously been replaced by gelatinous goo. It irritated me even more because I couldn't even blame motherhood for the changes to my body.

It was simply due to age, stress and countless hours spent glued to my chair at work, which made it even worse because it was *my* fault.

Unfortunately, watching Serena prance around like a prized show horse in her not-on-any-plant-would-this-ever-be-appropriate office attire every day was like someone constantly screeching in our ears: hey, you're OLD!

Lost in thought about how I could cajole my boss Roger to fire her for her mountainous mistakes, I padded over on auto-pilot to the cabinet to grab a cupful of kibble to feed Simba, my surrogate child. She was my adorable six year old mongrel someone dumped in our backyard five years ago. Poor thing was so starved she couldn't even whimper. Patches of her fur had been missing, almost like it had been torn out in chunks. Jack had chastised me for trying to rescue her, saying that she didn't stand a chance and the most humane thing I could do for her was have her put down.

Like hell. The look I gave him that sunny morning outside silenced his mutterings as I scooped the dying pile of flesh and sporadic fur up off the soft grass. It took three weeks of constant nursing and two very expensive trips to the veterinarian before Simba roared back to life. Her loving spirit, clumsy nature and enormous tail that never stopped wagging filled the longing for a child that had been churning inside of me. The bond between dog and master was set in stone. I saved her, she saved me. We were even.

I noticed a slight tremble in my hands when I scooped up Simba's breakfast. Guess my nerves were more frazzled than I thought. I wasn't doing myself any favors by getting all riled up about Ms. Serena Short-Skirt this early in the morning. I had other things to tend to.

Yeah, that's it Melody. Unleash all your inner angst from your crumbling marriage and sagging ass out in the form of the green-eyed monster, rather than confronting the problems with Jack head-on. Serena isn't the issue. Your relationship with Jack, or rather, the lack of one, is the problem.

I shook my head and willed myself to not think about my disintegrating marriage until after work. Maybe I would leave early and come home and fix Jack's favorite dinner, light a few candles and serve the food in front of the fireplace. The finishing touches would be relaxing music, fine wine and chocolate covered strawberries for dessert. Set the mood and maybe open up the channels to start talking again, once our minds were plied with food and alcohol.

Wow, how cliché Melody. Yep, life's troubles can be solved over a yummy dinner and some booze. Right. When did your life become a commercial?

Simba's breakfast retrieved, I was in full stress mode about upcoming hectic day and what salve I could use to soothe my irritated husband. At first, I didn't notice Simba wasn't in the kitchen. Normally, she performed a morning ritual of circles and jumps in eager anticipation for her breakfast.

"Simba...her girl. Come eat."

I felt a twinge of worry in my gut when no response came.

I started down the stairs to the lower level of the house, thinking that maybe she had accidently shut the door to the laundry room again. Silly girl had done it twice before and what a mess it had been to clean after a night with a bursting bladder! As my foot made contact with the second to last step, Simba's hairy body bolted around the corner and collided with mine. Somehow, I was able to stay on my feet but Simba's bowl of food tumbled down the remaining stairs. The small round bites shot out in every direction.

"Well, good morning to you too! Looks like you will get a bit of exercise while you eat, chasing all your food around."

Simba's black tail thumped the hardwood in response, then she dropped something from her mouth and began to chomp on the kibble.

"Whatcha got there, girl?"

I bent down to pick up what I thought was a pair of my underwear. Simba developed a taste for underwear, socks and t-shirts in her youth. I groaned, realizing that Jack must have left the clothes hamper on the floor of the laundry room again, which meant I was about to stumble upon a shredded mess of clothing.

I walked over to the laundry room door and eased my hand inside, grazing the wall until I felt the light switch. I was surprised when I was greeted by a clean and tidy room, which is exactly how I'd left it last night. The clothes basket sat on top of the dryer and was full of only the clean blue jeans I had folded last night.

Huh, wonder where Simba found my underwear? It's not like I dropped them for Jack during a heated session of lovemaking.

I flicked off the light and shut the door. I would figure out when I got home later where Simba confiscated my undies from before she ingested more. That would end up costing...

Wait…these are silk…

Upon closer inspection, my heart skipped a beat when I realized they weren't cotton. I caught a whiff of a familiar scent of perfume but couldn't quite place it. Chanel? Obsession? I walked over and held them in front of the window, examining them under the morning light. They weren't even *close* to what I would consider wearing. Perhaps they weren't really called panties, because the miniscule swatch of sheer material was barely enough to cover about three inches of skin and maybe four pubic hairs at best.

Confused, I stared at Simba while she happily crunched on the remaining nuggets of her breakfast. She'd been inside all night, so where did she get these from?

"Hey girl. Good girl. Here, you want these back?" I cooed, squatting down to her level and dangling the chewed up panties in front of her. "Come on, come here. Show Mommy where you found these, huh?"

Simba ignored me and continued to scurry after the bits of food. I stood up and glanced around the room Jack and I called the media room, which really was nothing more than a couch and a big screen television. The downstairs only consisted of the laundry room, media room and the small room next to the stairs that Jack used as his office. My heart pounded faster as I scanned the area for any signs of other clothing and found none. The knot in my stomach formed as the sensation of something wrong began to take control. Hard, tight and pounding, the pressure pushed a wicked thought up to my brain: that I would find the answer in Jack's office.

I spun around and darted down the hallway and stopped. Jack was a stickler to keep his door shut because he didn't want Simba (or me) messing up his workspace, or nosing around the neatly stacked piles of papers that he graded or the lesson plans he worked on for his honors history class.

I winced when I noticed the door was slightly ajar. When I pushed the door open completely and saw the mess inside, blood whooshed in my ears at the thought of Jack's reaction. He was going to flip when he saw the after-effects of Simba's night of fun. Oh well, he should have made sure the door was locked before he came to bed last night.

With minimal effort, I pushed the door all the way open and briefly scanned the room. My eyes settled on the brief-case amongst the shredded papers, useless pillows and one leg that Simba had nearly chewed off of Jack's computer chair. The edges of the black leather case were full of teeth marks and it sat opened in the middle of the floor. Work papers were covered in dried slobber and teeth marks. I almost laughed—until I spotted another pair of panties on the floor next to it.

I bent down and picked up the silken material and unearthed a small scrap of paper. It looked like a receipt from a hotel. My hands shook when I brought it up closer to my face. The five-hundred dollar receipt for a one night stay in room 510 was from The Duchess, an overpriced hotel downtown that I had never stayed in, nor had Jack, at least to my knowledge.

A receipt dated for last Friday night when he was supposedly at an all-day conference for work. But the thing that really caught my attention was the faint smell of a familiar, feminine perfume.

The scent was stronger now. I recognized it. Chanel. The fragrance that Serena wore. And Friday? Serena called in sick…could it be? No way…

A small vibration caused me to nearly jump out of my skin. I realized it was the buzz of a cell phone on silent. This made no sense because Jack's was upstairs on the charger right next to mine. He had another one? I felt around in the zippered pocket and sure enough, there it was. One of those disposable phones that were cheap and paid for in cash. I flipped it open and read the first, unviewed text that had a picture attached from *"SR"* from Sunday morning:

> *"Do me again, baby. I want you now. Fri & Sat rocked!*
> *Meet me @ lunch Mon? Ur wife will be busy…got some*
> *new panties since u ripped my other ones."*

Then, the crotch shot of a very beautiful woman popped up. A woman with long, tan legs wearing hot pink underwear that looked exactly like the ones I found in Jack's briefcase. I pushed the back button and felt my stomach churn when I recognized the number that the text was from. I had seen it numerous times because she would call at least twice a week with some inane excuse for being late.

I pushed my glasses up and brought the receipt closer. I almost fainted when I saw the name.

Serena Rowland.

It took a full minute for me to regain control of my faculties. Sorrow and anger fought for control of my mind. A wave of dizziness threatened to knock me off my feet, so I braced myself against the doorframe for support. After all these years, all the love we shared, how could Jack betray me like this? Worse yet—the betrayal sealed with a boney-assed dingy blonde who worked at my office? A flashback to last year's Christmas party clouded my vision. I recalled the look on Jack's face as he tried to keep his mouth from dropping when a tipsy Serena sauntered over and introduced herself in her skintight blue dress. I remembered the pang of jealousy that poked in my gut, but had dismissed it as nothing. Hell, all men looked at her like at, so why wouldn't my all-American, red-blooded husband be any different?

Because he was my husband.

Memories of our nights together, holding tightly on to each other for comfort at yet another disappointing attempt to conceive almost made me cry. My heart was shattered—visions of Jack in the arms of another woman made me clutch my chest in physical pain. Was Serena the first? Oh God, what if she wasn't? I glanced back down at the phone in my hands. Her text seemed to magically remove the blinders I didn't realize I had been wearing from my eyes. The last seven months of Jack's explosive temper, his moodiness and complete and utter lack of interest in me sexually finally made sense.

Guess he doesn't need any hormone pills after all.

No, I wouldn't succumb to the tears that threatened to burst out of me. Not today. Later, I knew they would come, the deluge would be enough to cause a raging river to flow out of me. I stuffed them deep inside and let my anger take full control of my mind.

Decision made as to which emotion would win at the moment, I found my voice. I stepped out of Jack's office and walked over to the edge of the stairs. Simba had just finished her last morsel and waited patiently by the back door to go outside and do her business.

I ignored her. Hopefully, if the urge to relieve her bowels hit she would do so on the briefcase. Maybe throw up her kibble, too. That would be a nice touch since it was what I wanted to do.

"Oh honey, could you come down here? Seems Simba made a bit of a mess in your office last night. Looks like you'll need a new briefcase, too, unless you want to keep one that is covered in teeth marks."

I heard Jack grumble, his footsteps heavy above my head as he moved quickly down the hall. An evil grin pulled my lips tight as I wondered if he felt even the briefest sense of panic, knowing I was in his office. Was his mind frantically recalling if he locked his briefcase? Were the wheels spinning off their tracks, wondering if his little secret was exposed?

The doorframe was strong, the wood smooth against my skin. I leaned against it and waited for the war of words.

Communication was about to commence. Oh yes, *lots* of communication. One-sided communication. I didn't plan on giving Jack a chance to say much.

My fingers were wound so tightly round the little piece of black plastic that my knuckles were bone white. The minute I showed the undeniable, incriminating evidence to Jack, I planned on doing the exact same thing to it as he did to the alarm clock this morning.

Well, with one minor difference.

I didn't plan on throwing it at the wall.

ABOUT THE AUTHOR

Award-winning and international bestselling author Ashley Fontainne is an avid reader of mostly the classics. Ashley became a fan of the written word in her youth, starting with the Nancy Drew mystery series. Stories that immerse the reader deep into the human psyche and the monsters that lurk within us are her favorite reads.

Her muse for penning the *Eviscerating the Snake* series was *The Count of Monte Cristo* by Alexandre Dumas. Ashley's love for this book is what sparked her desire to write her debut novel, *Accountable to None*, the first book in the trilogy. With a modern setting to the tale, Ashley delves into just what lengths a person is willing to go when they seek personal justice for heinous acts perpetrated upon them. The second novel in the series, *Zero Balance*, focuses on the cost and reciprocal cycle that obtaining revenge has on the seeker. For once the cycle starts, where does it end? How far will the tendrils of revenge expand? *Adjusting Journal Entries* answered that question: far and wide.

Her short thriller, *Number Seventy-Five*, touches upon the sometimes dangerous world of online dating. *Number Seventy-Five* took home the bronze medal in fiction/suspense at the 2013 Readers' Favorite International Book Awards contest.